ACKNOWLEDGEMENTS

Acknowledgements are dangerous things. More so for the things you forget, as opposed to the things you remember. If your name doesn't appear here, please know that each and every contribution, big and small, was noticed. Thank you.

Every tale has a journey of its own; the winding road that takes it from a muddle inside my head, to the pages before you today. It's no easy thing, that journey. So I'd like to acknowledge a few of my guardian angels. Those wonderful people who showed me the way.

To Chris Casey, the man who believed. You saw something and you took a chance. I will never forget that.

To Vicki Marsdon, my agent at Wordlink; you picked up that chance and, through great bouts of perseverance, you turned it into a dream come true. What more can I say.

To Megan Duff and the amazing team at Black & White Publishing; you heard Eddy's voice between the pages and decided the world needed to hear it too. Thank you for your patience, your tireless coaching and your dedication. I have learned so much and I will be forever grateful.

You are the points of my compass, leading me on a fantastic adventure. Certainly one I could never have imagined without you.

And to you, dear reader; thank you for giving Eddy a chance too. I hope you enjoy the ride.

T is for Tree is dedicated to all my friends and family who always believed in me more than I believed in myself. Thank you for your kind words of encouragement, they meant an awful lot. And to my wife, Fiona, the wonderful woman who not only caught me when I was falling, but lifted me to new heights. I can never thank you enough. But I'll keep trying anyway.

Hailey knew she was still bleeding but it was now or never.

Nobody told her it would be like this. Wasn't that the doctor's job – to tell her that something had gone drastically, horribly wrong and how to make it all just go away? Maybe she should stick around in case they were going to tell her they could make it all better. That this could all be fixed.

But her instinct to escape was stronger. She couldn't bear the thought of a lifetime of disapproving glances. All of those 'I told you so's, the first of which would cruise out of her mother's mouth with a smugness she couldn't bear to witness.

The nurse, who was pretty nice, all things considered, had wandered out a couple of minutes ago and the doctor was probably off checking his bank balance somewhere. The only other obstacle would be her mother and she was bound to be back at any moment. No, Hailey knew she had to get out and keep going until there was nobody left to find her.

Climbing gingerly out of the bed, she folded the cover back over the red splotch on her sheets. She'd grab some paracetamol or something at a pharmacy on the way out of town.

As she slipped her jeans up her legs, leaving them unzipped because it hurt too much to do them up, the object in the corner made a noise. It was just a simple noise, the sound of a living thing and for a fleeting moment Hailey felt compelled to go over to the clear plastic crib. To go over there would be wrong though. It was a trap.

Taking a purposefully wide berth, turning her head away from the wriggling arms and legs, Hailey paused in the doorway.

No ... I have to go. I can't love this thing. I don't even know how to.

But, unable to help herself and despite the certainty this would ruin it all, she strode back to the place where her newborn son kicked and punched at the strange world around him. Did part of her feel something for this needful thing, this thing that had no control over the way it was made? Yes. Probably. Maybe.

Reaching in, she felt the baby's tiny hand clench hold of her little finger as his grip tightened momentarily around her heart. This, she recognised, this very moment was a massive fork in the road of her life and whatever she did now, it had to be decisive.

'I'm so sorry,' she whispered and surprised herself

in the process as she wiped a tear from her eye. 'Be a good little boy.'

Then pulling her hand away, pretending not to notice how strong the boy's grip really was, she retreated back to the doorway. No more looking back now … this was all about moving forward. Never mind the leaden lump in her throat.

Checking left, then right, Hailey counted to three inside her head and stepped out into the corridor as though she had every reason to be there.

Assuming her first real obstacle would be the nurses' station out by the entrance to the maternity ward, Hailey suffered a sudden pang of horror when she turned a corner and found her mother walking towards her. In the half-second it took for her to duck into the closest room, a thin sheen of sweat broke out on her brow and for a moment she thought she might actually need to sit down before she passed out altogether.

Had her mother seen her? They certainly hadn't made eye contact but that didn't mean anything when it came to Daisy Sullivan. That woman had keener eyes than an eagle.

Hailey could hear her mother's footsteps now. She could recognise them anywhere.

Slipping away from the door, Hailey faced into the room and discovered a whole new set of problems. Staring back at her, with some confusion and a growing curiosity, was a postnatal mother, new babe in her arms, and a nurse, who had obviously been in the midst of some piece of advice or another.

'Can I help you?' asked the nurse.

Shaking her head soundlessly, Hailey felt, more than heard, her mother's sturdy stride now. She was right outside the door.

'Are you lost?'

Listening intently and feeling about as inconspicuous as fireworks in March, Hailey ignored the question and focused on the doorway beside her. If her mother walked in now, all hell would break loose.

'I'm going to have to ask you to leave please,' the nurse said, growing obviously irritated.

Afraid she would be heard, Hailey clenched her teeth and prepared to leave the room, straining her ears for movement outside. Where were those footfalls now? Her mother hadn't pounced through the door.

'Sorry. Wrong room.' Cautiously slipping back out into the hallway, Hailey found her mother nowhere in sight.

'You're the girl from 413, aren't you?' the nurse called from behind her.

It wasn't worth answering.

Ignoring the pain, Hailey hit the corridor at nearly a jog. The sliding door that promised to be her escape was only a few seconds away now.

'Where are you going?' The nurse was in the corridor now. Hailey didn't look back; to do so would only advertise her guilt. 'Ruth!'

A head poked out from the nurses' station just as Hailey rushed past.

'She's doing a—'

Hailey guessed the last word was probably 'runner' but she didn't stick around to find out.

She piled through the sliding doors and along the next corridor before bursting out into the brightly lit foyer. Unashamedly limping now and clutching her screaming belly, she straight-lined it for the main entrance. Mercifully the security guard looked like he was a day away from retirement and paid her no heed. After all, she was just a kid.

Jumping into the first taxi in the rank, Hailey patted the bank card in her pocket for reassurance.

'The nearest train station please,' she instructed. 'And please hurry.'

As they pulled away toward the maze of mid-town traffic, Hailey swivelled around and checked through the back window. With one last reflection, Hailey looked to where she figured her room was. Or where her room had been. It wasn't hard to find either. It was the one with her mother staring out of the open window. Had she seen her leave?

Perhaps she was just getting some fresh air, Hailey told herself. She was surprised to find herself feeling an entirely unexpected emotion. It wasn't guilt, even though that would be understandable. It was sadness. In that hospital room were both ends of her life. A life as it had every right to be. A mother who, in spite of her shortcomings, had loved her in her own way, and a baby ... a strange little baby that she didn't know how to love.

Turning to face forward, Hailey watched as the meter churned away what little cash she had and cried silent tears.

TWELVE YEARS LATER

1

Shower Time

'Eddy. Get yourself ready, it's shower day.'

Grandma Daisy punctuated her authority with a short, sharp rap on Eddy's bedroom door.

Eddy obediently got out of his chair, the one by the old wooden desk, and proceeded to undress. He knew the routine. T-shirt, trousers, undies, socks. Always socks last. Always.

Within two minutes of Grandma Daisy's knock he was standing on his side of the closed bedroom door, old clothes in his arms ready for washing, and as naked as he'd been that fateful day his mother had snuck out of the hospital, never to be seen again.

The bedroom door flung open and Grandma Daisy seemed almost to touch both sides and the top of the doorjamb. Eddy knew well enough to stand back because that was the way she always opened his door.

'Good,' she said. 'Now go get under the water. I want half that soap gone by the time I come to get you out.' Grandma Daisy reached down and took the old clothes out of Eddy's hands. There'd be a new set waiting on his bed when he got back. There always was and there always would be. 'Now get going before you miss the warm water.'

Shower days were all right as far as Eddy was concerned. It gave him a chance to see new stuff. Had Grandma Daisy changed one of the pictures in the hall? If one of the other doors was open, he could get a glimpse of another room, a whole different room than his own. He also got to walk past the top of the stairs, and if he walked slow enough and craned his neck just right, he could actually see the front door. The white front door with windows in it. Windows that showed the big, wide world on the outside.

But there were no doors open today. Grandma Daisy had changed no pictures and she chose today to tail him all the way to the bathroom. There was no dawdling at the top of the stairs. That was okay though. He still liked shower day.

As per usual, the shower was already running by the time he stepped into the small upstairs bathroom. Eddy pulled the shower curtain aside, stepped under the lukewarm water and felt the wetness cover his body like a new idea. He knew Grandma Daisy was off doing her own thing by now and she wouldn't be back until well after the water had turned ice cold, cold enough so that he had to squeeze into the back corner of the shower cubicle where only the odd drip could reach him.

'Make hay while the sun shines.' That's what

Grandma Daisy would say. 'Make hay while the sun shines.'

So he grabbed hold of the slippery soap from the little shelf beside him and began rubbing it all over before the water turned nasty. You had to do it quick because it wasn't just a matter of getting it on, you had to get it off as well. Grandma Daisy didn't like it at all if he still had soap in his hair when she came to dry him off. Not only that. She always did a load of washing at the same time as his shower and that made it like Russian roulette. He never quite knew when that rush of cold water would come with each new washing cycle downstairs.

What Grandma Daisy didn't know, however, was that while she was downstairs doing her thing, Eddy played a trick on her. Yes, he washed himself good and well, but he'd learned to do that real quick. When he'd finished though, he'd pull the shower curtain ever so slightly aside, hop up on to the little step that divided the shower cubicle from the bathroom floor and look at himself in the mirror on the opposite wall. He'd have to be careful though. Good thing that Grandma Daisy's stairs were creaky. Two of them always creaked and most times three or even four.

But the mirror, well, that was magical.

He could actually see himself looking back at him.

Eddy had always known he was different. Grandma Daisy was forever reminding him of that in one way or another. But what he didn't understand until he was tall enough to see in the mirror was what exactly 'different' was.

And she was right. He was different. He wasn't like Grandma Daisy or the lady that came to visit him sometimes (he could never remember her name for more than half a day after each visit). He was different too from the people in the photos on the hallway table. The ones he'd never make the mistake of asking about again. And last but not least, he was different from all the other people he watched going about their lives from his bedroom window.

His eyes were different. That was the easy part to see. But the rest of his face was different too. He couldn't exactly explain what was different about it but it definitely wasn't the same as all the others. When he'd asked Grandma Daisy she'd told him that was simply what 'dumb' looked like. So maybe that's just what it was. Dumb people were given different faces just like the runners in his *Guinness Book of World Records* book were given long legs.

So for as long as his courage held out, Eddy stood on tippy-toes and made faces at the dumb boy in the mirror. And when he smiled, somebody smiled right back at him and that was the most marvellous thing in the world.

2

BENT NAILS

It was a Saturday. Eddy knew that because of the way the street played out in the morning. On weekdays the street went into an hour's worth of frenzy as people dragged themselves off to work and kids trudged to the school somewhere around the corner. In fact, the school was close enough so that, on a still day, Eddy could make out the chorus of children's voices yelling and screaming as they tangled themselves around the playground during breaktime and lunch. It was a good sound; he knew that because it made him smile and it made him want to walk in circles around his room. But at the same time it was a sad sound.

Eddy saw pretty much everything that went on in his street. His upstairs bedroom had a grand view. It had two windows, one which poked out the front of the house and one at the side. The one at the front was quite big. It was actually three windows, side by side. One, two, three. The one in the middle wasn't supposed to move but the two on either side of it were made to open up. Grandma had fixed the brackets, though, so they hardly opened at all. When they were as wide as they could get, he could fit his hand and part way up his arm out but there was no way he could squeeze his head through that narrow gap. Eddy could literally spend hours with his face pushed up against that precious hole into the real world. He would fill his lungs with the fresh breeze and listen to the sounds of people living their lives. If he lodged himself up against the right-hand window, at just the right angle, he could see all the way down to the corner where another mysterious street headed off in both directions towards a whole imaginationful of adventure. If he did the same thing up against the left-hand window, he could see where his street ended in a cul-de-sac, and on weekends and summer evenings he would watch the other kids use the place as a three-ring circus, packed full of bike and skate-board tricks.

The window on the side of the house was good too, but for a very different reason. The view was nowhere near as good. All it did was point across to the same sort of window, in the same sort of bedroom, in the same sort of house. What made this ordinary window so wonderful was what lay between the twin houses – a tree. A big tree. It must have been there for an awful long time, Eddy reckoned, because it had grown too big for the space the houses had left for it. The window-stopper on the window had given way years ago, so it opened wide enough for Eddy to fit through. Not that he'd ever dared. Muscled branches had first grown up against each house and then, refusing to give way, they had toiled up the side of the weatherboard planking like a climbing vine on steroids. Even better was the fact that one knuckled and barky elbow had lodged itself so steadfastly against the sill of his window that the window itself could no longer close all the way shut. It was one of those windows with a latch at the bottom and you lifted the whole frame up to open it. Now, with a knobby and determined tree in the way, when you closed it as low as the branch would allow, you were left with a good two or three inches of wide open window.

Grandma Daisy had threatened to have the tree seriously trimmed. It was ruining her house, she kept saying. She called it 'that damned tree'. And she had meant it too. She was going to have the whole thing chopped down if she could. One, two, three with an axe.

What Grandma Daisy says, goes. Eddy knew that as a time-honoured tradition. If she said – and she did – that the world was the Devil's playground and that God had given up on His creation years ago, then she was undoubtedly right. If she promised him a 'whooping' if he ever so much as stepped a foot outside his door without her permission, then a whooping was what he would get. Grandma Daisy wasn't like the tree. If she ran up against a house, she'd just crash right through it.

So it surprised even Eddy himself when he'd put

up a fuss about her having the tree, *his* tree, cut away. He'd sobbed and he'd pleaded. 'Peese, peese, peese,' he must've cried a thousand times, ignoring the very real potential of Grandma Daisy's backhand. Even more to his amazement was her eventual surrender. To this day the tree had not so much as sniffed a blade and, if anything, had further entrenched its hold on the house.

Grandma Daisy wasn't going to leave it without at least some points on the board though. No, that wasn't her style. Instead, she nailed the window frame to the jamb so that six or seven inches was all that he was ever going to get. At least that's what she thought anyway.

For the first few months Eddy refused to take this small mercy for granted and he didn't dare fiddle with the nail. But as the weeks and months passed by something strange happened. Well, at least he had a suspicion that something strange had happened.

When he wasn't sleeping or looking through one of the many secondhand books that Grandma had scooped from the library's throw-out rack, Eddy was invariably glued to one of the windows. The fact that there was a big, wide world out there absolutely fascinated him. His favourite books had pictures, pictures that showed things not just beyond his window but beyond his street, his town, his country and even his planet. He was never going to see all these things through the narrow focus of his bedroom windows but, unlike the pictures, what he saw out on the street changed each and every day. Starting with the first neighbourly ruffles in the morning, every day carried with it the potential to deliver something entirely new. And that was the key. For Eddy, and he most certainly couldn't encapsulate it in this way, this was his connection to the human race. If he could see it in action, he could believe he was a part of it.

While the front window was the one that delivered all the 'action', he would often find himself folded up against the side window, forehead nudged up against the glass so long that it left an impression on his head for over an hour afterwards. When Grandma Daisy saw the red mark on his brow, she'd call it his 'nosy head' and shake her own head to herself. It was the sort of shake that said more than it did. It said Eddy was indeed dumb and dumb people simply did dumb things.

But that tree, that special, stubborn tree, was a very real connection to life beyond this house. Unlike the tunnel vision afforded by the front window, he could actually touch it. Smell it. He'd just lean up against the cold glass, reach through the gap in the window and pat the rough bark like it was a loving and loyal dog. It was relaxing, almost hypnotic, and Eddy quite often found himself drifting away on a magic carpet of daydreams, or even talking quietly to himself about anything from dinner to dinosaurs.

Day in and day out, he followed this routine. It wasn't as though there was much else to do. And so it was, as with many things that live around us every day, Eddy didn't really notice the incremental growth of the branch as it continued its dogged search for the sun. As the weeks turned into months, the single nail holding the window frame in place was beginning to strain. As the tree exerted itself against the house it literally began reaching into the gap, one eternally slow millimetre at a time, and there was no way that a few taps from Grandma Daisy's old hammer were ever going to restrain it. By the time Eddy noticed something strange was going on, the nail had all but surrendered.

When Eddy saw what was happening it astonished him. It was like the tree was coming to visit. But it was also a worry. What if Grandma Daisy saw this too? She couldn't necessarily blame him, even though she'd do her very best to, but this would undoubtedly give her the excuse she needed to rip the whole thing out, roots and all. And that would be bad. Dreadfully bad.

So Eddy did the only thing he could. He left the nail to fight a losing battle and crossed his fingers fifty times a day in a hope against hope that Grandma Daisy would keep looking right on past it like nothing was happening.

3

STICKS AND STONES

Saturday mornings were always exciting for Eddy. The routine was always the same inside, but outside on the street, you never knew what was coming next. Especially in the summer when the sun came up early and kids had energy to burn.

Eddy would always eat his cereal with hearty anticipation and as soon as Grandma Daisy had collected the plate and left him to his own devices he'd be up to the front window, watching for signs of movement like a soldier on patrol. On the basis that Grandma Daisy was an early riser, so was he, and that meant that it could be a good hour or so before the first murmurs of childhood activity resonated along the cul-de-sac. This particular Saturday was no exception.

While he waited, he did what he always did and grabbed one of his tattered books, lodged it up against the windowsill and exchanged about a hundred glances a minute between the pictures in the pages and the world outside. Somebody had to go outside soon. If he could, he'd be outside every waking moment of the day. These kids just didn't know how lucky they were.

This Saturday, Eddy's book was about volcanoes. There were lots of pictures showing what they looked like inside and how all the hot stuff exploded out the top. He didn't know if there were any volcanoes nearby but it would be an amazing thing to see. All that smoke and fire. Sometimes when he read this book he would think hard inside his head, picturing that there was indeed a volcano just down the road, and that one day soon it would explode. That way there'd be danger and the policemen would make Grandma Daisy take him away from the house, take him outside and along the road and around the corner to where everything would be wide open and new. Yep, Eddy liked volcanoes.

The words were tough though. If any of his books had a page full of words he'd just flick through to the next picture. All those squiggly little shapes annoyed him. He knew they had a story to tell all by themselves, and that they were simply shapes for the words that came out of your mouth, but he just couldn't get it. How could shapes be sounds?

Grandma Daisy had tried to teach him a couple of times. No matter how hard Eddy had tried to concentrate, it just wouldn't fit in his head right. She'd ended up throwing the book across the room and screaming at him about how even kids half his age could at least read a few words. That was the same day she'd said to him that if he ever wanted to jump out the window and kill himself that was just fine by her. Maybe that was why she had left the side window partly open. It sure was a long way down. On those long weekday afternoons, when he could hear the children laughing over at the school, he'd look down from the side window to the hard ground below, with all its knotted and gnarled tree roots sticking out here and there, and think about what it would be like to break his body against them. Would it hurt or would he just die before he could feel it?

Or would the tree catch you, Eddy? Would the tree catch you and lift you right back into your bedroom?

Somewhere a door slammed shut. Not a car door, a front door. All thoughts of volcanoes and trees disappeared and Eddy scanned the street with eagle eyes. At last someone was out and about.

Straining against the right-hand window, Eddy looked up the street towards the intersection. The noise had come from somewhere up there. For an immense minute or two there was nothing else, just expectation as thick as treacle and a *chug-a-chug* heartbeat.

And then there they were. Bert and Ernie. Eddy didn't actually know their names. What he did know was that one of them was tall and thin and the other quite short and a bit tubby. That alone was enough to classify them on the basis of his *Sesame Street* expertise, all thanks to another one of his tired old picture books.

21

They were brothers who lived about five doors up the road from him but on his side of the street so he'd never actually seen their house. He could imagine it, though. He was very good at imagining.

One thing for sure, it would be messy. The sort of messy where the neighbours wished Bert and Ernie and their parents would move. The lawns would be scraggy and there'd be old toys and stuff almost lost in the weeds. The paint on the house would be peeling and no one ever seemed to pull the curtains open, no matter how bright and sunny it was outside. Even worse than that, if you ever got through the front door, the whole place would reek of rotting leftovers and unwashed dishes.

On the other hand, Bert and Ernie were free to wander to their hearts' content. It seemed almost everything in this world had a catch.

The boys were walking along the footpath in his direction. Bert had a football tucked under his arm and they both had that Saturday morning eagerness about them.

Eddy knew exactly what they were going to do. There was an empty section at the end of the cul-de-sac and until somebody bothered to build on it, it had become the local hang-out. One of the dads down that end of the street even mowed it on a regular basis and someone had drawn pretend football goal posts on each of the neighbouring fences. On a good day, it seemed half the town's kids were down there with one shaped ball or another and when Eddy squashed up against the left-hand front window he was able to see almost all of the action. Sometimes he thought about how much he'd love to be down there with them, laughing and throwing and kicking, but mostly he simply enjoyed watching it. He'd accepted the fact that he was never going to be one of those kids and, other than the odd pang of envy, he'd learned to reap his own version of fun from the enjoyment of others. It was like he would feed on the sights and sounds, the pure emotions of joy and exuberance, and translate them as his own. Invariably, five minutes into looking down at a neighbourhood football match, he'd have a grin stretched across his face that wouldn't leave until well after the street's mums had called their sons and daughters home.

Bert and Ernie were now sauntering past Eddy's place, lost in some conversation or other. Eddy couldn't quite make it out so he shifted against the windowsill, trying to get his ear closest to the thin opening between the frame and the jamb. It was this movement which caught Bert and Ernie's attention and they both looked up to see their spectator.

'Hey, Freak,' called out Bert. 'What ya lookin' at?'

Both boys stopped in their tracks, now on the footpath right in front of Eddy's window.

'Yeah, Freak,' echoed Ernie. 'Why don't ya just take a photo. It'll last longer.'

'H-h-hi,' Eddy stammered. These kids were actually talking to him. Saturdays were definitely his favourite day. 'I'm Eddy. One, two, three.'

Bert bent over and whispered something into Ernie's ear. It must've been good because they both broke out into a Cheshire grin.

'Hey, Freak—,' continued Bert.

'No, um, I'm Eddy. E, A, B, C…Eddy.'

Eddy figured he must've said something good because both boys laughed. Eddy laughed too.

'Your name's Freak,' corrected Bert. 'E, A, B, C … Freak.' Ernie obviously agreed because he was looking up at Eddy and nodding. 'You got that?'

'What?' Eddy was confused. He was sure his name was Eddy. He didn't know much but that's what he was called. That's what Grandma Daisy called him.

'How dumb are you?' asked Ernie. 'Cos I heard you're dumber than a really dumb thing.'

Bert let the football drop from under his arm and trapped it with his foot.

'Y-you-you're good,' praised Eddy as he nodded down at the ball.

'Just answer the question, Freak,' insisted Ernie. 'How dumb are you?'

'Um …' Eddy closed his eyes for a second and rocked back and forth as if it would shake his answer free. 'Um … Grandma Daisy, she says that I'm as dumb as dumb can get.' Eddy self-examined his answer and nodded again. 'Yeah. One, two, three. As dumb as dumb can get.'

He was on a roll here because Bert and Ernie thought that was hilarious. Making friends was so easy. Saturday friends. Brand new Saturday friends.

'Hey, Freak,' called Bert. 'Do you wanna be part of our club?'

'What – what's a "club"?'

'You're kidding me, right?' Bert and Ernie were

now looking at him with that same expression Grandma Daisy sometimes gave him, the one that usually ended up with her throwing her hands in the air and walking out of his bedroom, door slamming behind her.

'Yep, yep,' blurted Eddy before it could all go wrong. 'I wanna. Sorry, I was dumb.'

'Okay then.' Bert appeared to be thinking real hard. Eddy liked Bert. He was real smart. 'This is a very special club…and it's secret. You got that?'

'Secret means I don't tell. One, two, three, just you and me.' Eddy was real proud of himself. He knew that one. 'One, two, three, just you and me'. That was the song he and Grandma Daisy had made up. The one they sang over and over before the lady came to visit every month.

'Man, you are a freak,' chimed in Ernie.

'Eddy, E, A, B, C. Eddy,' corrected Eddy.

'Well your club name is Freak,' continued Bert, 'and if you want to be in the club you have to keep it a secret. You're not allowed to tell anyone, you got that?'

'Yep.'

''Cause if you do tell, you'll die.'

'Die? Die like Grandpa Nevil?'

'Die, like a vampire bat will fly into your room and suck all your blood out until your eyes fall into your head.'

Eddy most definitely didn't like the sound of that, whatever a vampire bat was. He opened his eyes wide and tried to imagine what it would be like to have his eyes fall inside his head. It wasn't a nice thought. 'One, two, three, just you and me.'

'Promise?'

'I – I – I promise.'

'You just gotta pass a test to see whether you're good enough to be in our club,' explained Bert.

'Test?'

'Yeah,' agreed Ernie. 'You gotta prove to us that you're our friend, our *secret* friend.'

'Eddy's your friend,' spurted Eddy. 'Eddy's really, really your friend. I p-promise.'

'Okay, here's your test then,' decided Bert. 'I want you to stand up on a chair or something so we can see you properly. Have you got a chair up there?'

Eddy glanced across at his desk on the other side of the bedroom. Tucked in underneath it was the wooden chair he used when he was reading.

'Yep, yep. Eddy has a chair.'

'Cool. Now go and bring it over to the window and stand on it.'

Reining in his nerves, Eddy tiptoed across to the desk and carefully dragged the chair over to the window. He didn't want to give Grandma Daisy the slightest reason to pay a visit. Pushing the chair up against the wall beneath the window he did exactly as he was told and stood up on it, making sure not to lose his balance. Once he was certain he had it all under control he looked back down at the two boys as if to say *See, dumb ain't so bad after all.*

'Now, this next bit makes sure you're part of our club,' Bert instructed. 'You need to wet your pants so we can see it, and then throw your pants and under-wear out the window.'

'I can't do that!'

'Don't be our friend then.' Bert made as if he was bending down to pick up the soccer ball.

'Yeah, don't be our friend then … Freak,' added Ernie.

'But – but, I can't. I'll get into trouble.' And it was true. Eddy knew that all too well. His bed-wetting phase was a memory that would forever haunt him. Grandma Daisy got angry a lot but when it had come to his bed-wetting, she'd been scary, really scary. Once he'd been convinced she was going to kill him. That she was going to send him to where Grandpa Nevil was. He had tried so hard to stop it. He hadn't done it on purpose; it was the dreams. He kept wetting himself in his dreams and when he woke up it had happened for real. Grandma Daisy didn't believe him though. She said he'd done it on purpose and that he was doing it to drive her mad. But that wasn't true. He could vividly remember those early mornings, before the sun had even dared show its face, when he would wake up, feel the wetness in the bed and know that his fate was sealed. Those hopeless hours before Grandma Daisy sprang through his door like a booby trap were some of the most terrifying hours of his twelve-year-old life.

So Eddy stood there on the chair, not knowing what to do. He was jammed between his very first friend-ship and the memories of a wrath that still made him feel sick to his stomach.

Bert and Ernie started walking, Bert with the ball dribbling at his feet.

'Wait,' called Eddy as loud as he dared. 'I want to be friends. One, two, three, just you and me. But … But … I will be in trouble.'

Bert and Ernie stopped and looked back up at the window.

'Hey, we're your friends now, Freak,' Bert explained. 'We wouldn't let a friend get into trouble.' He peeked across at his little brother with a sly grin. 'That's exactly why we asked you to throw the pants and undies out the window.'

'W-w-why?'

'So we can take them straight back to our place and get them clean before you get caught. We just live up there,' Bert pointed back the way they'd come. 'We can get them clean and throw them back up to you like nothing ever happened.'

'Oh.'

'Yeah, we promise … Freak.' Ernie wasn't as nice as Bert, but when they were friends Eddy was sure he would be nice too.

'Will you be my friend forever? Longer than dino-saurs?'

'Of course,' assured Bert. 'Longer than from here to the moon and back.'

Friends for longer than the moon and back. Wasn't that incredible. The moon was an awful long way away. Eddy had seen that in one of his books. And if someone was your friend for that long they surely wouldn't let you get hurt. No way. Friends didn't hurt friends.

Eddy swallowed big. This was a huge decision. A huge and very, very important decision.

'Will you be back quick time?' he asked. 'I need my pants back quick time.'

'Real quick. Not even five minutes.'

Wow, five minutes. That wasn't long and Grandma Daisy hardly ever came up between meals if she didn't have to. Yeah ... friends didn't hurt friends.

'O-okay. I'll do it.'

'It's a secret remember,' checked Bert. 'You can't tell anyone.'

'Yep ... just you and me.'

Eddy stood tall in the chair, both so he could steel himself for the very risky task ahead and so Bert and Ernie could see he was indeed keeping up his end of the bargain. At least the timing was good. Breakfast always came with a large glass of water and it was about this time every morning that his bladder called for relief. Today was no different. While he wasn't busting, he could feel that the reservoir was ready and he wanted to get this 'test' out of the way as quick as he possibly could.

Taking one last look across at the only other door in his bedroom, the one that Grandma Daisy had put in there to attach his room to the toilet next door, Eddy took a deep breath and pushed. At first his bladder refused to give in. It held fast to the discipline which had been hammered home day after day a couple of years ago.

Bert and Ernie were still staring up at him, a mixture

of amusement and expectation written across their faces.

Come on, Eddy. This is for friends.

Eddy relaxed and the rush came. He felt the warm wetness stream down his legs and soak his corduroy trousers to his skin. It wasn't exactly a comfortable feeling and when he looked down to see long dark stains down the inside of each leg, his pulse went into overdrive. He'd actually done it. There was no going back now.

He returned his attention to the two boys outside, making certain they could see exactly what was going on. There was a smile on Eddy's face now. Yes, this was very, very bad but somehow that made it good. He had friends, he had a secret and, for once in his life, he'd gone against Grandma Daisy on purpose. This was exciting, E, A, B, C...exciting.

His spectators on the footpath were wide-eyed in disbelief and that only made Eddy push that much harder, emptying his bladder to the last drop. When there was absolutely nothing left Eddy just stood there with a smirk and waved out to them. He'd passed the test.

'Now take 'em off and slip them out the window,' instructed Bert.

He'd gone this far, the rest was easy. Still standing on the chair but resting one hand at a time against the window frame for balance, he dragged his trousers down each slippery leg. Then, taking a moment to stand on them so they soaked up the puddle on the seat of the chair, he followed up with his underwear.

So there he was, naked from the waist down, standing in the front window on the second storey of his Grandma Daisy's house, his urine-sodden pants in his hands and his two very first friends staring up at him. Had there ever been a Saturday morning more exciting, more wonderful than this?

Bert raised both hands and gestured for Eddy to hurry things up.

Slipping the soiled clothes through the thin gap in the window, Eddy let his forearm go out as far as the space allowed and let go. Signed, sealed and delivered. He watched them somersault down to the short front lawn. His undies made it the whole way but his trousers landed on one of Grandma Daisy's bushes so that the big dark stain sat up tall for all to see.

'See. I did it. See.'

'You're a fucking freak, kid.' Bert said the 'F' word as little more than a whisper, taking extra caution to look up and down the street as he said it.

'Yeah,' echoed Ernie. 'You're a fucking freak, kid.' Not bothering to whisper the naughty word, he earned an elbow in the shoulder and a glare from his big brother.

'But I did it ... see.' Eddy reached back through the window again and pointed down at the evidence with a look of growing consternation on his face. 'Just there.'

'Come on,' stated Bert, directing it at Ernie but not taking his eyes off the dumb kid in the window. 'Let's go play football and leave pissy pants alone.'

'Pissy pants, pissy pants,' taunted the younger boy. 'You gotta be the dumbest kid I've ever seen.'

'But LOOK!' Eddy was now poking his finger manically down at his pants. ''Member, just you an' me, one, two, three. It's a *seepit*.'

'You mean *secret*, pissy pants,' corrected Bert. 'And the only secret going around here is your dick. It's so small I can hardly see it.'

Eddy looked down at himself with a quizzical expression.

Ernie cracked up laughing so hard that Bert figured it was time to make haste. Picking up the football, he grabbed his little brother by the scruff of the shirt and pulled him towards the empty section at the end of the cul-de-sac.

'No, Eddy's your friend!' Eddy scrambled across to the left-hand window, where he could get a better view of the boys as they departed the scene. Neither Bert nor Ernie so much as looked back. 'Please. Please be my friend. Please clean my pants quick. Friends, be good … pleeease.'

Bert brought a hand up behind his back and extended his middle finger as a parting wave. Eddy had no idea what it meant but that was the least of his worries. It all came crashing in on him. His friends weren't going to wash his clothes and he was in a whole mountain of trouble. No, forget mountains … this was a volcano of trouble because Grandma Daisy was surely going to blow her top.

As if on cue, Grandma Daisy flashed open his bedroom door.

'What the heck is all that noi—' She stopped dead in her tracks and stared bewildered at her simple grandson who was standing on a chair in front of the window, naked from the waist down in a room reeking of fresh urine. Eddy had nowhere to run and nowhere to hide. He was a wounded animal in the crosshairs and such was the terror that engulfed him he found his bladder hadn't quite been empty after all.

'You little shit!' Grandma Daisy charged toward him, a sudden fury burning in her eyes.

'Sorry. Sorry, Grandma.' Eddy forgot he was on the chair and all he managed in his effort to retreat was an unceremonious tumble to the floor and a nasty crack to his head. Not that he felt much of either, for he knew the worst was yet to come.

4

NAPPIES & NO FRIENDS

It had been a week since that horrible day and Eddy was sure that when a breeze came through the side window just right, he could still smell a whiff of pee.

When she'd finished taking her anger out on him she'd dragged him into the shower and never even bothered to turn on the hot tap. He didn't deserve hot water, she'd yelled at him. People deserved hot water, not filthy animals. So while she took an age to scrub and disinfect his bedroom he'd curled up in the basin of the shower and cried silently while the frigid water rained down on him. Maybe friends weren't all they were made out to be.

When Grandma Daisy had returned to the shower he was pale and shivering, but he daren't move from under the water. She'd had a floor mop with her and she'd used it to mop him from head to toe in a series of rough sweeps across his body. His skin was red raw by the end of it but he was in no condition to complain.

There'd been no fresh pile of clothes waiting in his room either. Not even underwear. Instead she'd shoved him into his room, closed the door behind him and the next thing Eddy'd heard was the car reversing out the driveway. He hadn't dared check things out the window, instead choosing to tuck himself into bed where it was warm. From there he could at least daydream that she'd be gone for a long, long time.

Upon her return he'd listened intently to every sound. The car door closing, the back door screeching as it rubbed against the kitchen floor, shopping bags being placed on the dining table and, the stuff of nightmares, Grandma Daisy's footfalls as she climbed the stairs.

When the bedroom door opened Eddy had fully expected round two. He'd sat up in his bed wishing that life could be different, or at the very least that today could be different. Instead, to his great relief and startled confusion, she'd tossed a plastic bag on the floor and left with some parting words that he couldn't quite understand as she slammed the door behind her.

That plastic bag had contained a packet of adult diapers and, since that Saturday to this, they'd been all he'd worn. It'd taken him a while just to get the packet open, let alone work out exactly what they were. Not that he went to the toilet in them. Good gracious no. He still used the en suite for that but Grandma Daisy insisted on lecturing him about them each time she delivered his meals. Babies wore nappies, she said, and if he was going to be a baby, then she would treat him like a baby.

A couple of times during the week he'd heard some of the kids outside his window. On at least one occasion he'd been certain it was Bert and Ernie. They'd been calling him names. Names like pissy pants and dumb ass. Those were the ones he could understand anyway. Eddy'd just sat in the far corner of his bed, the furthest he could get from the window, and tried to block them out. Part of him so wanted to get up and go over to the window. He wanted to ask why they'd made him do those things. Maybe he'd misunderstood the test and they might still be his friends. Another part of him insisted that was just him being his dumb old self again. And he didn't want them to see him in a nappy. He'd have to wait until he was allowed to wear clothes again.

The last time the kids outside yelled at him Grandma Daisy had charged out the front door and had really let them have it. They'd all scattered like startled sparrows and Eddy hadn't known whether to be happy or sad.

One good thing had come out of it, though; it seemed that Grandma Daisy was joining some of the dots and from that point on she hadn't been so angry. In fact, he'd even had some sugar on his cereal this morning.

Making friends was really, really, really hard work. Maybe Grandma Daisy was going to be his only friend in the whole wide world. One, two, three, just you and me.

5

A Tree on the Move

By the end of that next Saturday Eddy was proud to be back in real clothes again. He was so happy that he'd given Grandma Daisy a great big hug and a hand-on-heart promise that he'd never so much as drip a drop of pee anywhere but in the toilet again. Grandma Daisy seemed to have liked that because she'd hugged him right back and she wasn't the type to do that very often.

For Eddy, the world was full of roses again. When Grandma Daisy was happy even the sun was brighter.

Dressed properly now, he could also feel comfortable looking out the front window again. So as the evening sun sank towards the horizon of wrinkled hilltops and the shadows spread across the street below, Eddy shoved himself hard against the left-hand window and watched the neighbourhood kids careen around the empty lot. There must've been about twenty of them at least and from somewhere close by came the mouth-watering aroma of meat sizzling on a barbecue. Yes, it was a marvellous summer's night indeed.

Soon enough the parents' calls came echoing through the twilight. It was 'dinner time' here, 'homework time' there, and slowly but surely the herd of children thinned until the last couple of stragglers decided enough was enough and headed home of their own accord. After all, a kid can only stand so much fun.

Bert and Ernie were one of the last to wander by but this time Eddy played things cautiously. He pulled back from the window, just far enough so he was out of the line of sight, and waited for them to pass on by. They didn't shout up to him this time and that brought about a pang. Had they not called out because they hadn't seen him, or maybe they really weren't as mean as Grandma Daisy had told him they were? Was there still a chance to make friends with them? Racing back up to the right-hand window, he watched their backs as they dawdled along the footpath and eventually turned in towards their house. Eddy wanted to call out to them. In fact, more than once he'd felt the words charging up his throat like a runaway train but at the last moment he'd held them back. After a nightmare week, things were finally good with Grandma Daisy again and he didn't want to rock that boat right now.

For another five minutes or so he looked down upon his street. Dogs barked, somewhere kids still scuffled and tussled in a backyard and, one by one, lights turned on and curtains closed.

When Eddy was certain that the day's drama had truly wound down he got up and drew his own curtains, officially closing down the show for another day. Then, standing in the centre of his room, he surveyed his options. He could read some of his books, do a jigsaw or draw some pictures.

Books it was.

He never quite got to the bookcase, though, because something caught his eye. Stepping over to the side window he placed his hand on the unstoppable tree and two things immediately occurred to him. Firstly, a surprising surge of growth had taken place. At the point of the gnarly elbow, where the branch popped in and then turned back out again, the shoot of a fresh new branch was birthing into his bedroom. How he hadn't noticed this earlier Eddy had no idea. It wasn't that big, maybe the width of his middle finger, but it was a good six or seven inches long. Secondly, if he stayed really still, the bark seemed to vibrate beneath his fingers. Not an all out shake or anything but a very fine vibration, like a hum without noise.

Reaching over to pull his chair in close (the same chair which, a week ago, had been the cause of his troubles), he sat down at the window to have a good look at this strange new visitor. How wonderfully weird this was. Eddy let go and touched it again. Sure enough, that same quivering sensation raced through his hand and up his arm. It seemed to sing inside his head.

Now he put both hands on the baby branch, ever so gently so he wouldn't hurt it, and let this funny new energy settle into his bones. It was such a relaxing sensation that Eddy soon found it very hard to keep his eyes open. In the end he simply gave in and rested his heavy head in the crook of his arm. Deeper and deeper he unwound but at no time did he let go of the budding branch.

As Eddy slipped further into a stupor, the darkness behind his eyes began to change. In the void ahead of him came at first a bright light. The kind that happened when he stared at the lamp for too long. After a little while, though, the bright spot began to change from one beautiful shade of colour to another. There were greens folding into blues, blues into purples, purples into pinks and reds, then yellows and back to greens. As these amazing kaleidoscopes changed and shifted in his mind, Eddy became aware that he was experiencing these colours as so much more than visions. Each seemed to have a flavour of its own.

The greens were fresh and vibrant. The blues burst with life. The purples, pinks and reds beat with a living pulse and the yellows breathed with warmth. The colours absolutely mesmerised Eddy. He had seen some cool things from his front window but this, the only thing that had ever come inside, was better than all of it put together.

6

Secrets In &

Eddy awoke the next morning in exactly the same position he'd gone to sleep, crooked up against the side window. Somewhere in the night his hands had fallen from the new branch to his lap. It certainly wasn't the most comfortable place to sleep and Eddy figured he had a right to feel pretty tired and cramped, but to the contrary, he felt entirely rested. In fact, he felt great. He felt like Superman.

Coming to terms with his unusual position, Eddy's next chain of thought linked back to the previous evening. Had it all been a dream?

Colours. Lots and lots of magic colours.

Eddy checked. Yes, the baby branch, as he was coming to know it, was still there. If anything, it was already longer than he remembered from last night. Yep, it definitely was. Maybe by another good couple of inches. And to add to the mystery, there was a

leaf getting ready to unfurl halfway
ngth.
owing inside my room!

Reaching out timidly, Eddy tickled the edge of the fledgling leaf with his finger. It had to be one of the most beautiful things he'd ever seen. Then tracing it back to the baby branch it had sprouted from, he was reassured to feel those wondrous vibrations coursing once more.

This time yanking the chair aside, Eddy poked his upper body out of the gap in the window and reached as far down the broadest branch as he could get. Those vibrations were still there all right. He looked all the way down to where the tree met the ground, to where the roots held on tight for dignity and for life. There wasn't anything he could see that explained the vibrations. It was just grass and dirt, then tree.

'Are you magic, Mr Tree?' he whispered against the solid bark.

No voice came back and for a moment Eddy was actually a little disappointed. What he could hear from out the window, however, was Grandma Daisy pottering around in the kitchen below. She was getting breakfast prepared.

Favouring the tree with one last pat, he ducked back in the window and got himself ready for Grandma Daisy's entrance.

Sunday mornings were good. All Grandma Daisy did was drop his cereal in and then she'd head off for church. He wouldn't see her again until she got back and if she was in a good mood, she'd be loaded

with a plate of leftovers. Sometimes there'd even b̶
chocolate biscuits. Just the prospect would have his
mouth watering for the best part of an hour before
her old car cruised back in the driveway.

Slipping quickly out of his clothes, he folded
them just the way Grandma Daisy had taught him
to and placed them on the desk. Next he threw on
his pyjamas and ruffled his bed sheets in such a way
that it looked as though he'd slept in his bed and
had tried to make it. Eddy was pretty pleased with
himself for thinking of that. The ritual was the same
every morning. Folding clothes was one thing but
making a whole bed was something else altogether.
So when Grandma Daisy paid her morning visit she'd
invariably look at his bed, sigh that heavy sigh, and
straighten out the bedclothes so that you could run a
ruler by it. It was just her way and he saw no sense
throwing more chaos into an already odd day.

In the few minutes it took to get himself organised,
Eddy must have glanced across at the branch a thousand times. If he wasn't in such a rush to get things in
order before Grandma Daisy climbed the stairs, he'd
be over there, checking again to see if it really hadn't
been a dream. Lucky too. He'd only just finished
crumpling the blankets when the door swung open
and she strode in, tray in hand, new set of clothes
tucked under her arm.

'M-morning Grandma Daisy.'

'Good morning, Eddy.' Sticking to the routine, she
placed the tray on the desk, plopped the new clothes
beside it and gave the room a once over. There was

e. If Eddy wasn't using something, it
t away in its rightful place. No excep-

rning was easy. Since sitting down at the
yesterday evening he hadn't used anything.
The big books were on the big bookshelf. The little
books were on the little bookshelf. The pencils and
crayons were all back in their packs, all ranked in
colour-coded order. The jigsaw boxes were stacked
the right way up, biggest box to smallest, and his
fire engine, his one and only toy, sat upon them,
facing into the centre of the room at just the right
angle.

Grandma Daisy pursed her lips and gave that curt
nod of hers, designating a pass mark. She wasn't
finished though. Yep, there it was. That sigh, the
shrug of the shoulders and the martial-arts swipes
that straightened the bed sheets table-top flat.

'Okay, I'm off,' she stated. 'Don't go talking to those
fool kids while I'm away. You hear me?'

'Yes, Grandma Daisy.'

Picking Eddy's old clothes off the desk, she made
to leave the room but stopped mid-stride.

'What's that?' Grandma Daisy gestured over
Eddy's shoulder, towards the side window behind
him. His heart sank immediately. She didn't miss a
beat, not one.

'It's n-nothing, Grandma Daisy. It's just a little tree
come to visit me.' Eddy put on his happy face. 'See.'
He stepped over to the window and proudly cradled
the budding twig in the palm of his hand.

'That damned tree.' Grandma Daisy's frown spoke of nasty thoughts within.

'Please, Grandma Daisy. It's just a friendly tree.' Eddy's entire body twitched with his absolute desire for Grandma Daisy to let him have this one thing. She could take his books, even the jigsaw puzzles but he had to have his tree. 'I p-p-promise.'

'It's ruining the house, Eddy,' she said, standing tall and looking him in the eye. 'I should've had the silly thing cut back months ago.'

'Please, please, pleeeeeease.' Eddy felt salty tears well up in his eyes and wished he could make them go away. Grandma Daisy hated it when he cried. She said it made him pathetic. But they seemed to come up all by themselves, from a place right down deep inside where things really mattered. So when the first wet track slipped down his cheek he was caught in a dilemma. 'Grandma Daisy,' he said, mustering all the inner strength he had just to stare back at her stern face. 'This is m-m-my tree.' He took the hand that wasn't still patting the lively twig and tapped it against his chest. 'It is, and I want to l-look after it.'

Eddy knew his Grandma Daisy even better than he knew himself and so when he saw her expression change from one of single-mindedness to one that meant she was thinking things over, his heart pitter-patted with hope. Whether he liked it or not, it was always Grandma Daisy's way. Just like you had to always find the edge pieces of jigsaws first, it was always going to be Grandma Daisy's way.

'I p-promise, Grandma Daisy. I honestly promise.'

'You're a waste of space sometimes, Eddy. A waste of space.' Then to Eddy's triumphant delight, she turned on her heels and started out the door. 'But I'll tell you one thing,' she continued as she closed the door behind her, 'if that stupid tree annoys me one more time, it gets the axe. No ifs, buts or maybes.'

We did it, Mr Tree! We can be friends!

7

THE LADY WHO VISITS

Eddy nearly jumped out of his skin when Grandma Daisy rapped on his door.

'Eddy,' she said through the wall, 'get yourself ready for a shower.'

'B-but it's not shower day, Grandma Daisy.'

'Don't talk back to me,' she scolded. 'Just do as I say. I'll be back in two minutes.'

A shower and not on shower day. What was going on?

I don't think I've done anything new to be in trouble. No ... I've been a good boy for Grandma Daisy, I have. No messes. Not one.

Just to be sure, once he'd stripped down he scanned the room for anything even slightly out of kilter. He'd had time to quickly straighten a couple of books in his bookshelf when Grandma Daisy came blustering in.

'Okay,' she said, giving him the once over, 'Now get yourself into the shower and be quick about it.'

Something was definitely going on. Eddy could feel it in the air and it made him all jumpy like he knew he was in trouble but couldn't remember why. Grandma Daisy didn't even have to say anything for him to feel that way. When she was moody, she carried it like a great big coat. The sort you put on to keep the cold out. Today that coat was heavy and Eddy felt the temperature drop like a stone. He thought about asking her what was going on but hardly needed to second-guess himself before slipping on past her and into the bathroom. It wasn't even worth slowing to glimpse down the stairs today.

When he got back to his room, he had his first hint waiting for him. On his bed, as per usual, was his change of clothes. But these weren't normal clothes, these were his good clothes. And Grandma Daisy never, ever, ever put out his good clothes unless …

Someone's coming to visit!

Eddy clapped his hands and did a little jig, careful not to take too long but unable to contain his joy. Then he pulled on his clothes. Socks first. Socks always first on. Socks always last off.

As if she could see through walls (and Eddy reckoned she could), Grandma Daisy piled on in with the finishing touch in her hands: his shiny black shoes. He never got to wear them very often and they were beginning to get a little too tight on his growing feet, but he agreed with Grandma when she said they had a lot of wearing in them yet. They were way too cool to throw away. If you looked close enough, you could actually see yourself in them.

Shoe laces were hard so Eddy did as he usually did and sat back on his bed, poking his feet out so Grandma Daisy could slip them on and tie the knots. As she eased herself down on one knee and fiddled the shoes past his cramped heels, she gave him the rules. The same rules he had heard before.

'Mrs Stanton's coming over,' she said matter-of-factly as she pulled the laces tight. 'So what do you have to do?'

'Be nice.'

'And what else?'

'Smile.'

'And what else?'

'Only talk when she asks me a q-q-question.'

'Exactly. And when she asks you about home-school?'

'I say, "I like it and I l-learn lots."'

'Good boy.' Grandma Daisy propped herself back up. 'Now stand up and let me have a look at you.' Eddy got to his feet and felt his toes scrunch up at the front of each shoe. For the first time since Grandma Daisy had brought them home from the shop, he found himself looking forward to taking them off. She grabbed each side of his shirt collar with a big, bony hand and tugged so hard he almost toppled over. 'Stand still, boy, for goodness' sake. Now remember, we have to tell Mrs Stanton what she wants to hear ... or what will happen?'

'Sh-she'll take me away to a mean place.'

'And what happens at the mean place, Eddy?'

'They h-hit you until you bleed ... every day, they

do…that's right, they do. Don't they, Grandma?'

'Yes, they do, and you don't even get a room. They make you sit in a corner and they throw food at you.'

'And we don't w-want that.'

'No, Eddy, we don't want that.'

Grandma Daisy was just about to say something else when the doorbell rang. It was a sound of delight for Eddy but it made her nearly jump out of her comfy slippers. 'Oh bugger, she's early. I swear that woman can't tell time.' She turned tail and sped out of the bedroom, leaving a curt instruction for him to sit and wait at his desk. In just about the time it took for Eddy to get comfortable she was back with an armload of schoolbooks, which she dumped on the desk in front of him. 'Open one,' she demanded as she once again exited the room.

The doorbell rang again and Eddy heard her footsteps on the stairs. 'Coming, coming,' she called out in her specially reserved visitor's voice, and then he heard the door open with the familiar squeal of wood on wood as the door scraped across the floorboards. 'That's summer for you. You can tell the seasons by this door, I swear. Come in, Mrs Stanton. It's lovely to see you. Have you lost weight?'

'Thank you, Mrs Sullivan.' *That's Mrs Stanton, yes it is.* 'I'd like to think I've lost a little but I reckon the scales would make me a liar.'

'Well, you're looking very fit and healthy then, I must say.'

Hard shoes on the floor. She's wearing those funny shoes that make her tall.

'I wish I had a man to tell me that.'

'A man doesn't know his own eyeball from the inside, let alone the outside.' Grandma must've said something good because both ladies let out a little laugh.

'How's Eddy doing?'

'Oh, he's just dandy. Come on upstairs; he's waiting for you. Can I get you a drink or something to eat? I have some wonderful chocolate biscuits.'

Grandma Daisy was certainly a lot friendlier when Mrs Stanton came over, Eddy thought.

'No thanks, I've got three other appointments this morning and God only knows how I'm going to make it.'

'Shall we, then ... ?'

Two sets of footsteps came climbing up the stairs. It was a sound that had Eddy's heart *thump-thump-thumping* and when the door folded in he had a smile on as wide as the space between his ears.

'Hello, Eddy.'

'H-h-hello, M-Mrs Sta-Stanton.' Grandma Daisy knew Eddy stuttered a bit when he was excited but that didn't stop her from frowning and shaking her head when he looked over Mrs Stanton's shoulder.

Come on, me. Be good. I don't want to go to the bad school.

'How are you?'

'Um, I'm real good.'

'That's good to hear. Boy, how do you keep those shoes so clean?'

Eddy felt the warm rush of blood make tracks to

his cheeks. 'Grandma Daisy … she c-cleans them for me.' Grandma Daisy gave him a tiny nod.

I know what secrets are.

'Well, they're very smart.' Mrs Stanton wandered over to where Eddy sat, that big, friendly smile still shining on her face, and checked the cover of the book he had open beside him. Eddy didn't know what it was. 'How're your ABCs, Eddy?'

'Real good. A is for apple and apples are g-good for you.'

'That's good.' Mrs Stanton knelt down now and looked Eddy in the eye. Eddy looked straight back but in the lazy, hazy space at the edges of his eyes he could see Grandma Daisy begin to fidget a bit. He had to get this right because people bled every day if they got it wrong. 'Okay then, what starts with … let me see …' Mrs Stanton surveyed the room, 'T. What starts with the letter T?'

About a million objects went through Eddy's poor mind and for the life of him he didn't know if any of them started with the letter T.

Come on, Eddy.

'Are you sure I can't get you a glass of water or something, Mrs Stanton?' Grandma Daisy was nervous too, yes, she was.

'No, thank you, Mrs Sullivan. Eddy, do you know something that starts with T?'

Please stop looking at me like that, Mrs Stanton. I want everyone to be nice.

'T,' stammered Eddy, feeling like the whole wide world was staring at him, 'B-bed. Bed starts with T.'

No one needed to say anything. Grandma Daisy's shoulders told him all he needed to know and even Mrs Stanton's smile turned upside down. She was thinking real hard, Eddy could tell that too.

'Eddy's been feeling a bit under the weather lately, haven't you, Eddy?' Grandma Daisy came around and placed a hand on his shoulder. Her fingers squeezed in on his bones but he didn't dare wince. He knew a warning when he felt it.

'Y-y-yes, Mrs Stanton.' Eddy lowered his head, no longer wanting to look his visitor in the eye. 'Bad weather. I hate b-bad weather.'

Ouch, Grandma, you're really hurting me!

'Mrs Sullivan, could we speak in the hallway please?' Eddy watched Mrs Stanton's knees straighten as she stood but he wasn't prepared to look up at her. If he did that, she'd see the first tear threatening to tumble over the pained ridge of his bottom eyelid. He was in enough trouble as it was.

As if solely to confirm his fears, when Mrs Stanton led the way out of the room, Grandma Daisy had enough opportunity to bend down by his ear. 'Tree, you idiot. Tree starts with T.' Then, with one almighty squeeze of his shoulder, she turned to let him wallow in his own stupidity. She'd be back, though, and that was the worst part. She always came back and the waiting was excruciating. Eddy could never relax when she was in this sort of mood. Every sound, even the tiniest tinker, would charge his entire body, knowing that she was bound to be back for seconds at any moment.

Why am I so dumb! I wish I was smart like school.
T is for Tree.

As he wiped the evidence of tears away, Eddy realised that he could hear what was being said outside his room. He understood that he probably shouldn't be listening but at the same time he couldn't help it.

'Look, Mrs Sullivan, I'll be honest. I have serious reservations that Eddy's being homeschooled at all.'

'I'll have you know, young lady, that I spend the best hours of my God-given day with that boy. He's a slow learner. *You* were the one that warned me about that.'

'Yes, but even despite his condition I would've expected him to be more advanced by now.'

'So what are you saying?'

'Kids with his condition do struggle academically but in more cases than not their grasp of the basics is delayed, not denied. Eddy's twelve years old and he doesn't even know the alphabet.'

'Okay, so we'll try harder. But he's a simple boy. It just won't stay in his head.'

'Then maybe homeschooling isn't right for him.'

No, not the bleeding place. T is for tree and F is for friends.

'Do you know how hard it is living on benefits these days? It's more like rations, if you ask me. We struggle to put food on the table as it is and you want me to halve his benefit just so he can go and be bullied like a freak of nature all day? No, thank you very much. We get enough of that here.'

'Sorry? Is Eddy being bullied?'

'No, nothing.'

There was a long pause before Mrs Stanton spoke again. 'Mrs Sullivan, there are hundreds of children with his condition living normal lives out in the real world. They make healthy contributions to society every day. Eddy can have that too.'

'Do you think I want him stuck around this house all day? He's not *my* son! I'd like a life too, you know, but God doesn't hand everyone an ace from the pack. No, all I got was a joker, but I'll make do with it because that's His plan for me. Like it or lump it.'

Silence, as thick as mashed potatoes, bounced around Eddy's head. He daren't move though, not even to slip an unforgiving shoe off an already blistering heel. Grandma Daisy not only had eyes in the back of her head but she had ears in the walls. Eddy hadn't seen them yet but he knew they were there all right.

'Okay,' sighed Mrs Stanton, 'how about this then. I'll give you another six weeks to really concentrate on him. I'm not expecting miracles, just a solid improvement. If he shows that, we'll go on as usual. If he doesn't ... then I might have to make a recommendation to the department that he has proper schooling arrangements. That's the best I can do.'

'Six weeks isn't long.'

'It's all I can give, Mrs Sullivan. My neck's on the line too.'

'Well, we'll do our best. That boy's not made for thinking.'

'Six weeks, Mrs Sullivan.'

'I know, I know. I heard you the first time. Now if you don't mind us, we've got a busy day ahead.'

Footsteps in the hallway…heart in the mouth.

Mrs Stanton poked her head around the door and this time she was smiling again. But it wasn't a real smile, even Eddy could see that.

'I'm going to go now, Eddy, but your grandma and I have agreed I'll be back soon. Okay?'

Eddy nodded but still struggled to meet her eye. He wished she could stay…for hours and hours. At least until Grandma Daisy wouldn't be angry any more.

'Your grandma is going to help you, Eddy. She's going to help you read. Wouldn't that be great?'

Another nod.

'Well, you keep well and maybe next time you can read me one of those lovely books you've got on your shelf there. Bye-bye.'

'Say "bye", Eddy,' prompted Grandma Daisy from somewhere out in the hall.

'Bye, Mrs St-Stanton.'

T is for Tree. He wanted to say it but couldn't bring the words to his mouth.

Eddy listened in cold stillness as four feet made their way down the stairs and two feet left the house.

That afternoon wasn't a good afternoon. It was bad. B is for bad.

8

RED VANS & OTHER NEW THINGS

Eddy was sitting at the front window, watching the neighbourhood kids mingle down at the empty section, when the van arrived. It was a real big van with a picture of a chair and a table on the side of it. And it was red; red like a fire engine.

Vans hardly ever came down his street. The road didn't really go anywhere. So any van in his street had to have a reason to be there. Even a stupid boy like Eddy knew that.

The big, red vehicle drove right by Eddy's window and the driver, mostly hidden by shadow, gave him a wave. How wonderful was that! Eddy waved right on back and then was completely enthralled when the van came to a squeaky halt about two doors down.

Beep, beep, beep.

Back it came, the front end swinging out wide,

almost catching the far-side curb, and the back end slowly but surely carving a path toward the driveway next door. Yep, the van was actually going to pull in right beside his house.

Beep, beep, beep.

As the vehicle reversed deeper into the neighbour's driveway, Eddy switched positions and dashed over to the side window where he hoped to get a better view. Nope, that was no good so it was back to the front window again, where he snuggled up, chin pressed against the windowpane, hoping he could see as much as possible.

The beeping suddenly stopped and the engine turned off with a wheezy hiss.

'Did you see that, Mr Tree?' Eddy beamed over at the branch with a look of delight. 'There's a b-big van over there.'

Mr Tree had in fact been a busy tree. Yes, indeed. Instead of a burgeoning baby twig it was now at least a foot long. Not only that but where there had once been a single leaf there was now a collection of half a dozen, all at various stages of unfurling into the universe that was Eddy's bedroom.

Mr Tree was his friend, with a big F.

Eddy fiddled with his fingers and crossed and uncrossed his legs, watching, waiting for events to unfold next door. He didn't have long to wait either. Two more vehicles pulled up outside the neighbouring house. One was a saloon (a 'normal' car in Eddy's world of definitions) and the second was a smaller van, painted the same colour red as the big van and with the same chair and table on the side of it. Out of the van popped four men and they seemed to know exactly what to do straight away. They went to the back of the van and folded the big red doors wide open like the mouth of a whale. Eddy didn't know for certain what was in there but he was beginning to have a pretty good idea. And if he was right, well…today was going to be about the most exciting day since Grandma Daisy won a hundred pounds on a horse race and bought him McDonald's.

Don't say it yet. Don't think it. If you do, it won't come true.

Then both front doors and one of the back doors of the saloon opened up. A grown-up man and a lady got out of the front doors but that barely mattered when Eddy saw who climbed out of the back. It was a girl. And if Eddy had to guess, she was about the same age as he was. Maybe a year or two younger, maybe a little older, but close enough to be called the same from his perspective.

Not yet. Don't say it, Eddy. Don't even think it.

Knowing full well that if Grandma Daisy heard it he'd be in for a world of trouble, but too wound up to stop himself, Eddy knocked hard on the window. Any harder and the glass would've shattered everywhere, any louder and police would've turned up thinking that shots had been fired. For a slow-motion moment Eddy found himself tugged between two ends of an emotional continuum. At one end was the absolute dread that Grandma Daisy was going to come thumping up the stairs and let him have it for trying to ruin her house and, at the other end, dream-like delight as both the lady and the girl peered up in his direction. When the girl's eyes fell upon him, he felt electricity bounce from the tip of his nose to the tip of his toes. She was really, actually looking at him. And she was beautiful. Not just pretty. All girls were pretty. Eddy reckoned she had lots of friends and she was probably smart too.

Then she lifted her hand up, and waved. Barely able to contain himself, Eddy waved back manically.

I can say it now. I have a friend. F is for friend and T is for tree.

Eddy, of course, couldn't see his own smile ... but he could feel it and it almost cramped his cheeks right up as he waved furiously back at this wonderful new adventure in front of him. And, as if Heaven itself had arrived on his front doorstep, she smiled too.

9

WINDOW TO WINDOW

It took a long, long time before Eddy saw that girl again. It must have been at least two or three hours. She'd gone inside the house as soon as her dad had unlocked the front door and since that point it had been non-stop action. The men from the red van had been busy lugging furniture to the house, and Eddy thought they were about the strongest people he'd ever seen. He had a book with Superman in it and Eddy reckoned they looked pretty similar.

Every now and then he'd spy the girl's mum or dad at the front doorstep, looking at some paper and pointing where the men needed to go. The mum smiled a lot. Eddy liked that. He liked that a lot. The whole family looked happy, and he could almost breathe in their joy. Indeed, he tried on more than one occasion that late morning and early afternoon, and when he did he could taste the intoxicating spirit of change and the bountiful evergreen of the newborn leaves unfolding in his bedroom.

As piece after piece of furniture went into the house, Eddy swapped from front window to side window to see which offered the better view at any given moment. He didn't want to miss a single thing. Once in a while the delivery was meant for the room exactly opposite his own, the one with a mirror version of his own side window. It was the deliveries into this room that intrigued him the most. After all, they gave him the best view of what was going on and, by the time it was all over, this would be the room into which he would face every day.

There were boxes and boxes and boxes. Eddy thought every box ever made was being unloaded next door. With everything packed away like that he didn't have a clue what was in them but when two heavy men dragged an even heavier bed into the room opposite he held his breath with bated anticipation.

More boxes. A chair…a white one. Some drawers… they were white too.

'It's rude to be nosy.'

Eddy fairly jumped out of his skin. He'd been so intrigued by all the activity across the way that for once he hadn't heard Grandma Daisy climbing the creaky stairs. There was a glint in her eye that suggested she savoured the thought of bettering his senses, as if it was a reminder to all concerned who was in fact in charge.

'Th-th-there's new people next door, Grandma Daisy.'

'I can see that, thank you very much.' Grandma Daisy stepped over to his side and had a good old peek for herself. 'But like I said, it's rude to stare. Why don't you get back to your reading. You've got a lot of catching up to do, you know.'

'Y-yes, Grandma Daisy.' Eddy dropped his shoulders and trod over to his desk where, since the lady's last visit, his learning books lay open. He didn't like his learning books. They had pictures and things but not like his other books. They weren't exciting pictures and there were way too many words for his liking. Just looking at them made his heart sink. They made him feel sad. They made him wonder if he would ever have a friend and that maybe Bert and Ernie and Grandma Daisy were right, he was just a stupid boy.

After the lady's last visit, Grandma Daisy had told him he had to read the books every day, 'no exceptions' – whatever that meant. At first he'd tried, real hard, but he didn't even know how to start. Every time he so much as opened one of the books up, especially the numbers one, his head went funny. It went hazy and he couldn't think clearly. It'd be so much better if Grandma Daisy would help him. And it'd be even better again if she didn't keep giving him that look when he couldn't answer her surprise tests. Yes, he hated those books all right, and having them piled up right in the middle of his desk like that meant that he couldn't escape them either. Whenever he cast his eyes around the room, they teased him. But still, he did what he was told. Not just today but every day. He didn't want to be stupid. Stupid boys got hurt.

Slumping down in his chair he pulled the top book off the pile and flicked the cover open to where a big picture of an apple jumped out at him. Eddy didn't look up for Grandma Daisy's approval. Even when he did something right, it wasn't her style to give it anyway. But she was watching him. He could feel it against the back of his head.

'That's right,' she said, turning her attention back out to the house next door. 'A is for apple.' With that said, she sighed a deep, tired sigh and strode out of the room, closing the door behind her. She didn't go straight down the stairs though, she was waiting out in the hallway, ready to trap him if he got back up from the desk. After a couple of stalemate minutes, however, Eddy heard her slippered feet make their way down to the lounge. Two of the steps always creaked more than the others. One, two. Two steps.

Giving it another couple of minutes, just in case, Eddy found a compromise. He pulled the chair away from the desk, a good arm's length, so that when he leaned forward he could still look at the learning book and, more importantly, when he leaned back, he could get a half-window glimpse of the action across Mr Tree. Where there's a will, there's a way.

More boxes piled upon more boxes.

And then ... there she was. She sauntered into the room next door with her mum close behind. Her eyes were big and wide and she was about to say something when she disappeared from Eddy's limited view. That was way too much for him to handle with poise and, forgetting the books utterly and completely, he got out of the chair and crept up to the window with all the stealth he could muster. He didn't want to be rude and nosy, because if he was the smiley girl might not like him. Instead he huddled up to the very edge of the windowpane and peeked one eye around, holding on to Mr Tree's arm unconsciously as he did so.

Those, by now familiar, soothing vibrations travelled up his arm and through his body. Green. Yes. The smiley girl was bright green. Not in real life, of course, but this was the colour he sensed when he thought about her.

There she was, pulling some sticky tape off one of the boxes while her mum hung a bunch of clothes up in the wardrobe. He watched, enthralled, as she pulled the flaps of the box apart, nice and wide, reached in and, with more than a little effort, stood up tall with a big plastic house grasped in her hands. It was just like a real house, only much smaller, and it was about the best toy Eddy reckoned he had ever seen in his whole entire life.

'Look, Mum,' Smiley Girl called out, her voice floating on the air like silver dancing with gold. 'I found it.'

'Good girl,' responded her mother, still unloading an endless stream of clothes into the wardrobe. 'You can play, but don't get in the way of the movers, okay?'

'Okay.' Smiley Girl took the toy house and plonked it down on a handy box. Handy for her and handy for Eddy too because it was high enough so he could see just what it was she was doing. When she pulled the front of the house wide open, just like opening a door, he couldn't help but slink out of his hiding spot so he could watch over her shoulder. Inside the house were rooms, lots of little rooms, and if his eyes weren't cheating him there was tiny, baby furniture in there too. That must've cost about a million pounds. Grandma Daisy would never buy him anything like that. The best she ever got him for birthdays and Christmas was toys from the McDonald's store.

And was that a teeny, tiny person in one of the rooms upstairs? Eddy leaned forward, straining to be certain. He was so intent that, when Smiley Girl suddenly turned around, he was caught completely by surprise. It was only pure fear that made him react as fast as he did. For a millisecond their eyes met and then he was gone, diving back around beside the window with his chest pounding so hard it echoed in his ears.

Jeepers, jeepers, jeepers. I think she saw me.

Was that a good thing or a bad thing? Would she tell on him?

Eddy waited for his heart to go from *BOOM, BOOM* to *pitter-patter* again. He didn't know how long that was but it seemed awfully long to him. Surely she'd be back playing with her house by now. He would be if he had a cool toy like that. Inch by anxious inch, he edged back toward the window, his back planted against the wall like it was his only barricade against a charging enemy. When he could safely go no further and his shoulder budged against the pane he found himself caught in a spiralling game of 'now, no, now'. He must've gathered his wits a dozen times and backed down eleven of them before he finally mustered the willpower to peek around the corner, where in all likelihood he expected to find Smiley Girl back at her little house.

But she wasn't.

There she was, standing loud and proud in her window, staring straight back out into his room like a statue.

Another millisecond of eye contact and Eddy literally fell to the floor, half as a means to escape being caught all over again and half because nearly all the strength went out of his legs.

'Hello?'

Eddy heard her all right but he had no idea what to do about it. His cheek pressed firmly against the prickly carpet as he worked hard on controlling his breathing, afraid that she'd hear his flustered panting even from her house.

'Hello?'

'Who is it, sweetie?'

'It's the boy next door. The one who waved to us before.'

Then nothing for an eternity. Not a sound. For Eddy, it was like the whole world was waiting to see what happened next. Surely she couldn't stand there forever.

'I don't bite.'

Okay, maybe she could.

'I promise...and I always keep my promises.'

Eddy was trapped and he felt it acutely. She sounded so nice but so did the other kids in the neighbourhood when they were playing on the street. He was afraid. He wanted so much to be Smiley Girl's friend but if she saw him, actually saw him properly, she'd see how stupid he was and end up calling him names like the others. But if he hid for a while longer, then at least he could still imagine them being best buddies. He was good at imagining and, as he was coming to understand, his imagination could be a great place sometimes. About the best place there was, as a matter of fact. Eddy closed his eyes tight, as if the effort alone would make her voice go away.

Please. Please. Please.

'I know you're there.'

'Leave him alone, hun. He's just a bit shy, that's all.'

No, Eddy's not shy. Eddy's stupid.

'Well, he should still talk to me. It's rude not to say hello back.'

It seemed to Eddy that just about everything was rude. It was rude to be nosy and it was rude not to be nosy. He'd never ever be able to understand all these rules.

'Do you want to play with my house? I'll let you.'

Oh yes, he so wanted to play with that wonderful house. Not that he figured he'd ever be able to. Grandma Daisy would never let that happen. But the very fact that she'd offered was better than all of those McDonald's presents wrapped into one. No one had ever asked him to play before. That was what friends did. Real, true to life, honest to God, friends.

Wrestling against the knowledge that this could only ever end in pain, Eddy raised himself gingerly up to his knees and reached for the window ledge with one hand and his precious tree branch with the other.

It's okay, Eddy. She's green, remember?

Slowly but surely he lifted his head above the ledge and there she was, Smiley Girl, true to her name and about as bright as the sun on a late summer's afternoon. He'd never really seen a girl live and up close like this before. He'd watched them from the street, of course. From his lofty view they didn't seem all that different but now, up close, he couldn't have been more wrong. Smiley Girl was like no person he'd ever seen before. She looked so wonderfully delicate that Eddy felt certain that if he could reach across the tree-filled void between their rooms and touch her, she'd break. She'd shatter into a thousand pieces like the one and only time Grandma Daisy had let him use a real plate.

Her hair was long and dark and her eyes were B for blue. Instantly Eddy decided one day he too would get blue eyes. How could anyone not have a marvellous life with eyes like that?

'Hello,' she said again in her soft girl's voice. 'My name's Reagan.'

Eddy knew the silence that followed was awkward but he felt compelled to let it happen. He just knew, absolutely knew, that he would ruin this whole dream as soon as he opened his mouth. She'd pop like a bubble as soon as he stuttered his stupid stutter. What was it that Grandma Daisy said? 'If you don't have anything good to say, don't say it at all.' How could he ever say something so good as to make this amazing girl like him, to make her want to be his friend? He couldn't. So instead he just stood there, not wanting to look her in the eye but, at the same time, unable to look away.

'What's your name?' she said, still smiling.

'Um. Um. M-m-my name is E-E-E-Eddy.' Eddy tried to smile too but it wasn't like hers. His felt too much on one side of his face to be like hers.

'Hi, Eddy.' She didn't budge. He'd stammered like he did when Grandma Daisy was having an angry day and still she hadn't budged an inch. She didn't even have that look in her eye, the one that said she'd rather be somewhere different all of a sudden.

Yep. She's green all right.

'Guess what?' she continued in an infectiously bright and breezy way. 'I'm your new neighbour. And this,' she added, gesturing behind her, 'is my bedroom.'

'C-c-cool. W-we both have windows.'

'I know. I like the way the tree grows in your window like that. I wonder if it'll grow in mine too.'

'Yep. It's a g-good tree. T is for tree. D-did you know that?'

'Yep. T, R, E, E. That spells tree.'

'Y-you're smart.' In fact 'smart' was at the bottom

of a whole pile of words Eddy would have used to describe Reagan, if only he knew what they were.

'Thanks, Eddy.' Reagan furrowed her brow a little, certainly not enough for Eddy to change the way he felt about her. 'Why do you sort of look funny?'

'M-my Grandma Daisy ... well ... sh-she says it's cause I'm dumb.'

'Well, I don't think you're dumb at all.'

'You don't?'

'Nope.'

Another silence, but this one nowhere near as awkward.

'Why are you crying, Eddy?'

'Um ... I'm just happy. That's all.'

10

No Point in Asking Again

The rest of Saturday and all day Sunday were the best days Eddy could ever remember. Reagan spent a lot of time in her bedroom as it unpacked around her and Eddy watched just about every moment of it. As each new toy unravelled itself from the brown packing paper, she'd bring it over to her window ledge and show it to him. There were dolls with clothes, dolls with cars and even a doll with its own swimming pool. There were pink-and-white ponies with long hair for combing. She even had a thing called an 'iPod', where you could put things in your ear and listen to music. Eddy liked that one the most. Reagan had said that real soon she'd let him have a listen too. How cool was that!

Everything she did, everything she said, he breathed in like a breeze delivering the spice of an untouched wilderness. She was amazing.

By close to dinner time on Sunday, Reagan's

room finally took on the characteristics of a proper bedroom. Eddy couldn't see all of it from his side of things but there was definitely a bed (with a flowery duvet on it), shelves on the wall instead of a book-case, some posters on the wall of people that must be really important but Eddy had no clue who they were, and a huge wooden box with carvings on it. On that box sat the toy house Eddy had spotted so keenly before and in it was the massive collection of other toys Reagan had displayed throughout the weekend.

'Hey, Eddy,' called Reagan from across the way.

'Yep.'

'Do ya wanna come over and listen to some music?'

'I can't.'

'Whaddaya mean you can't?'

'I'm n-not allowed.'

'How do you know you're not allowed? I only just asked you.'

'Grandma Daisy says "no".'

'Why?'

'She says it's d-dangerous for s-someone like me to go out.'

'Oh.' Reagan gave this a bit of thought. 'Does that mean forever?'

'I d-don't know for sure but I th-think so.'

'That's weird. So where do you go when you go out?'

'I don't.'

'You don't go out?' Reagan stopped fiddling with the doll in her hands and committed her entire sense of confusion across at Eddy. 'Not at all?'

'No. I just go to the sh-shower.'

'The shower inside your house?'

'Yep.'

'So you don't ever, ever, ever go outside?'

'No.'

'Is that allowed?'

'It must be if Grandma Daisy says so.' Eddy thought hard about what to let out of his mouth next. If he said too much he was inclined to dig himself a hole, one that Grandma Daisy wouldn't yank him out of until she was all good and ready. That meant revoking his privileges at the side window. Yes, she would. She'd told him that much already.

Grandma Daisy had been up a few times in the last day and a half and had even spoken to Reagan once. She'd put on her 'nice' voice. Her visitor's voice. Later on though, when Reagan had disappeared from her room, Grandma Daisy had come back up to have one of her 'little chats'. He wasn't to go wasting his whole day with that girl. He had some learning to do if he wanted to keep out of boarding school. The one where they beat you for no reason at all, especially the dumb kids. Almost always the dumb kids. And, even more importantly, he had better not go blabbing about how he and his grandma Daisy choose to live. That was nobody's business but theirs. When she'd asked if he understood that, he knew two things at once. One, it was an absolute waste of time to ask if he could go over and play at Reagan's house and, two, this was not one of her pretend warnings. Her nice voice was well and truly boxed away and if he didn't play by the rules…well, let's leave it at that.

She'd take my tree away and close my window for good.

'Yep, that's weird all right,' continued Reagan.

'I can st-still play from here though. Wh-what's that doll?'

11

FIRST DAYS &
MOTHER'S SMILES

The first thing Eddy noticed when Reagan raised the blind from her window the next morning was that she was dressed in a school uniform. The same one all the kids in the street wore.

'Are y-you going to s-school today?'

'Yep.' Reagan sounded as proud as proud could be. 'Do you like my uniform?' She did a quick twirl for him, making her tartan skirt dance out in a full, wide circle. 'It's my first ever school uniform. My last school just let us wear anything.'

'It's very, very n-nice, Reagan.' Eddy gave it a big smile and although Reagan's uniform did indeed look nice (anything on Reagan would look nice, of course), it also carried a sense of misgiving.

'Why thank you, Mr Eddy.' Reagan said this all funny and blinked her eyes at him. Eddy had noticed over the weekend how she did that sometimes. He'd even asked her about it once and she'd told him that was how the movie stars talked. And she was going to be a movie star one day, absolutely, no questions asked. Eddy didn't exactly know what a movie star did but he figured Reagan could do pretty much anything she put her mind to.

'So…um, that means you won't be h-home today?'

'I'll be home just after three o'clock 'cause the school's just around the corner.'

If I listen really hard maybe I'll hear her playing at lunchtime. I'll know her laugh if I hear it. I know I will.

'Y-you'll come straight home? You won't stay and play with the others?'

'No, silly willy. It's only my first day remember.'

'Oh.' Eddy did his very best to sound nonchalant and couldn't tell if it worked. Three o'clock, he knew, was when the last bell echoed through the neighbourhood. The same one that was followed by a tidal wave of hustling, bustling, yelling and screaming kids. Up until today, that was both a good and a bad thing. Good because it broke the monotony of a quiet, boring back street on a weekday and bad because, since his horrible experience with Bert and Ernie, he'd become a bit of a celebrity. Even Grandma Daisy's stern warnings from the front door hadn't stemmed the barrage of name calling and taunting that paraded by between 3.05 p.m. and 3.30 p.m. every day. It seemed that no matter what Eddy did, he was never going to be able to wash that stain away.

Now, though, three o'clock would mean something

different altogether. His one and only friend would be coming home.

Reagan was just about to say something else when her bedroom door opened wide and her mum walked in. The very first thing that struck Eddy was the way she entered the room. There was no huff and puff. There was no accusing stare that made you feel like you had done something wrong even when you hadn't. She simply walked in. No drama. No racing heartbeats.

'Come on, sweetie ... Oh, hi, Eddy. How are you today?'

'I'm g-good, Mrs Crowe.'

'Good to hear. I like your T-shirt.'

'Um, y-yes.' Eddy looked down at his chest to make sure he knew what she was talking about. 'It's blue. B is for blue. Yep ... just like R-Reagan's eyes.'

That made Mrs Crowe laugh and that was brilliant. Eddy and Reagan laughed too, even though Eddy wasn't a hundred per cent certain what was so funny. What was so great was the fact that Reagan's mum was actually happy. Happy enough to laugh right out loud. Up until then Eddy hadn't even known that grown-ups could laugh.

'Do you go to school, Eddy?' asked Mrs Crowe as she regained her composure.

'N-n-no, Mrs Crowe. My grandma Daisy, sh-she learns me stuff in books.' Eddy reached across to his desk and held his alphabet book nice and high for all to see. 'T is for Tree.'

'T, R, E, E, remember,' added Reagan for good order.

'Yep. T, R, E, E,' mirrored Eddy, loud and proud. It seemed easy when Regan showed him how.

Mrs Crowe gave him a smile. Not just with her mouth but with her eyes too. Mrs Crowe was such a nice lady. Eddy wondered what his mum was like. Could she smile like that?

'Well, Eddy,' continued this wonderful example of motherhood, 'Reagan had better be on her way now or she'll be late for her first day at her new school. And we can't have that, can we?'

'N-no, Mrs Crowe.'

'Bye, Eddy.' Reagan gave him a little wave and a carbon copy of her mother's smile. Mrs Crowe waved too and then they were both gone. Not before Eddy could return the gesture with a mighty wave of his own, though.

12

Long, Long, Long, Long, Long Days

Eddy had never cared much for time. It was just something that happened while you weren't looking. But as he learned that day – Reagan's first day at her new school – it had a way of knowing what you wanted most and then doing all it could to pull it away from you. It was sort of like Grandma Daisy on that front.

Take, for instance, the time between watching Reagan walk out of her front door and down the street and old Mrs Elsdon doing her daily round of the neighbourhood with her fluffy little dog and gnarled walking stick. That particular patch of time would usually fly by. There were some days when it felt like Mrs Elsdon literally followed the kids down the road. Today though, well, today it took an age. At first Eddy figured the old lady was calling it quits for the day and was giving it a rest. After all, he reasoned, she did walk awfully slow, and one day she was likely to stop altogether. But sure enough, just when he'd given up on her, there she was, shuffling along the pavement, her ball-of-fur dog doing its business on just about every second front garden along the way.

Yep, today was going to be a very long day.

At one stage, Grandma Daisy blew on in with a clean set of sheets for his bed. Usually he didn't care much for that because it meant she stayed a bit longer in his room than normal. But it did pull the day out of neutral for a few minutes so, while she chopped away at the sheets, he did his best to show her he was indeed reading his learning books. He even showed her the letters he understood and how they matched up with some of the pictures. If she was at all interested she didn't show it, which didn't make sense really. As far as Eddy could tell, she hadn't wanted him to go to the mean school either, so she should be happy.

When she exited the room without so much as a word, Eddy placed his book down and considered his tired, boring options. More books and some tatty old jigsaw puzzles. Eddy sighed, resigning himself to the brick wall of time, and wandered over to the side window, where, in about a million years from now, he would revel in Reagan's triumphant return from her brand-new school.

The street was quiet, the house was quiet, even the birds seemed to be holding their collective breaths today. The whole world had been put on hold. Sitting down on the foot of his bed (and reminding himself to push out the creases when he got back up), he leaned forward and rested his elbows on the window ledge. In doing so he unconsciously fiddled with the burgeoning twig under his right armpit. He hadn't forgotten that wonderful experience full of colours and sensations. That had been shortly after his ugly scene with Bert and Ernie. That's right. And it had made him feel better too. It had relaxed him and that had taken some doing after Grandma Daisy had finished with him that horrid day.

Eddy took hold of the budding twig in his left hand, closed his eyes and let those tingling, soothing vibrations massage him into a deep and colourful sleep.

And that became the pattern from then on. He'd get up nice and early to be sure to catch Reagan before she left for the day. Most mornings that meant he had a good fifteen minutes with her. Then he'd watch her, backpack-clad, as she sauntered down the street away from him, keen and ready to wave if she so much as glanced back. After that he'd have a shot at his learning books and, once Mrs Elsdon and her motley mutt had finally done her rounds (he could tell how close she was by the *click, click, click* her walking stick made on the pavement) he'd shift over to his bed, take gentle hold of his magical, mystical tree branch and let the sensations envelope him.

Over the course of a week he could be under the spell of Mr Tree for fifteen or twenty hours easy. The great thing about it was, despite the fact he would almost instantly drop into a bottomless, blissful unconsciousness, he always seemed to wake up as soon as Grandma Daisy laid her heavy feet on those creaky stairs. He knew it was strange (and he certainly wouldn't mention it to anyone – including Reagan) but sometimes he could swear it was the tree that woke him up in time. Like it was calling out to him. Warning him that Grandma Daisy was coming in for a landing.

But trees couldn't do that. Even stupid boys like Eddy knew that much.

Anyway, whether it spoke to him or not, whatever it did do to him felt really, really good. He'd wake up full of beans and refreshed, like the inside of his head had been given a great big spring clean. The kind of top to bottom that Grandma Daisy got herself into every now and then, when she'd lug brooms and buckets from one end of the house to the other and threaten Eddy that if he so much as left a speck of dust in his room after she slaved for him, she'd only cook him Brussels sprouts for a week.

All he really knew was, when he sat with Mr Tree like that, it cleared his cobwebs away.

And the one other great thing about it ... it made a long, long, long, long day seem that much shorter.

13

REAGAN TO THE RESCUE

The bell for the end of the day was ringing its vibrant tones throughout the neighbourhood and that was a sweet, sweet sound. Eddy felt the familiar tingle of expectation wiggle down his spine and planted himself tight up against the front window.

Reagan had been going to the school around the corner for almost two weeks now and Eddy had managed to create a little game around her daily homecoming. With his face lodged right up against the glass, he'd spot the telltale uniform colours before he could recognise the person inside them. So what he'd started doing over the last couple of days was count the uniforms, at least as high as his recollection of numbers would let him, until he could absolutely confirm that that blouse and skirt in the distance belonged to his bedroom window neighbour. He was quite proud of himself too. Numbers had never really been his thing. To be honest, he was worse with numbers than he was with the alphabet. But now, on a couple of occasions at least, he'd got himself well into the thirties before it all fell apart on him. That was a minor miracle from his perspective. He was so chuffed, in fact, that once he tried it in front of Grandma Daisy to see what she thought. The trouble was, it all disintegrated right when he needed it the most. Grandma Daisy had just given him one of her looks and turned tail.

But he knew. Yep, he knew he could do it.

On this particular day Eddy stuck with the tried and true pattern.

'Seventeen … eighteen … nineteen, twenty, t-t-twenty-one…'

Twenty-seven. She'll be twenty-seven today.

'Twenty-two…twenty-three. Twenty-four, t-twenty-f-five, twenty-six …and…twenty-seven! There she is!'

And there she was indeed. Eddy knew her walk by now. She had a certain swagger about her, a confidence that intrigued him. She was about as cool as the bathroom lino on a midwinter's morning.

To add to Eddy's perception of her, Reagan appeared to be the centrepiece of a happy-go-lucky threesome. She was flanked by identically dressed girls and while they were all hopping along without a care in the world, Eddy could see the real story. He'd watched way too much of people's body language from his top spot in the street to miss this message. Those other two girls, the hangers-on, were waiting on Reagan's every word. If Reagan said it was so, well then it was. If Reagan made a joke, it was hilarious.

If Reagan wore her blouse collar up high, then that was the new fashion. Eddy realised that maybe he'd been wrong before. Reagan wasn't the sort of girl who made lots of friends, she was the sort of girl that others wanted to be like. He didn't quite understand the subtle difference, he just saw it. She was special.

'Hey, Piss Pants.'

Eddy was blown out of his daydream by a group of four boys below him and he was immediately disappointed with himself. He'd been so focused on Reagan that he hadn't noticed Bert, Ernie and a couple of their wingmen swaggering along in front. He'd come to terms with the fact that they were never going to be his friends and now, whenever he spied them approaching, he would duck out of view until they'd well and truly gone past. Even then they had a habit of throwing the odd insult out, just to make sure Eddy knew where he stood in the scheme of things. 'Piss Pants' was their definite favourite though. You couldn't say much for their imagination but you could give them ten out of ten for persistence. It had reached a stage where the taunts had lost most of their impact on him. If you heard something often enough it ended up being nothing more than sounds. Things like 'Piss Pants' and 'stupid boy' could only ever run so deep, then the rest was just overflow.

But still, not now. Any time but now.

'Hey, Piss Pants,' yelled Bert insistently. 'Why don't ya give us a show?'

Eddy had no idea what to do. Should he duck even

though it was way too late? Had Reagan already seen what was going on? Would Grandma Daisy come out and make it a hundred times worse than it already was? What to do? What to do?

'Go on…we'll be your friend.' This was Ernie, right on cue, and he said these last words with a whiny, childlike voice that made the rest of the posse crack up laughing. 'Come on, Piss Pants. Flop it out and pretend to be a fountain.' That sent them into wild giggling fits and if Reagan had been oblivious to things before, there was no way she could be now. These boys were loud, so awfully loud, and she was getting closer by the second.

This called for urgent action. Knowing on one hand it was courting all sorts of trouble (from both within and without the house) but hoping whatever lay in the other hand had a shot of working, Eddy unclasped the window and pushed it as wide as it would go, which wasn't all that wide.

'P-p-p-please.' Eddy waved his hand at them as though he could swat them like flies. 'N-not n-now.'

'What's wrong, Pissy Pants? Got your knickers in a twist?'

Don't shout, Bert, please don't shout.

'Are you still wearing the same undies, Piss Pants? I think you might be 'cause I can smell them from here. All p-p-p-pissy.'

'N-no. P-p-please. Another d-day.' Eddy desperately didn't want to cry but it was coming anyway and there wasn't a damned thing he could do about it. 'P-pleeeease.' The first tear tumbled from his cheek, right out through the open window where it baked to nothingness on the hot, tiled roof below him. Right now he envied that tear.

'Go on. P-p-please, Piss Pants. Give us a show.' Ernie was nothing if not his brother's parrot.

'Yeah, you can be the clown.' Now it was the turn of one of their friends to chime in. Eddy was angry at himself now. He should never have been so stupid as to let these boys catch him out like this. He was stupid, stupid, stupid.

'You leave him alone.'

Oh no!

Reagan wasn't supposed to be here yet. She should have been at least five houses away, but in Eddy's desperation to send these mean kids off he hadn't noticed her leave her two sidekicks in the dust and sprint over to the commotion.

Other than Ernie, she was smaller than all of them but that didn't seem to put her off in the slightest. All four boys were staring at her with a combination of confusion and dawning amusement as she stood there, hands on hips, daring them not to obey her.

'I said, leave him alone.'

'Or what?' Good old Bert, he had an uncanny knack of throwing kerosene onto the fire.

'Or else, that's what.'

'You sure got a big mouth for a little girl.'

'You sure got a little brain for a big boy.'

One of Bert's unnamed friends chuckled at that one, but one stern look from the pack leader and it vanished quickly.

'What's the story with you and Pissy Pants anyway?' A light switched on behind Bert's eyes. He was revved up and ready for round two. 'Is he your kissy, pissy boyfriend?'

Reagan's walking companions had caught up by now, as had a couple of other strays looking for something better than a direct line home, and pretty much everyone but Eddy and Reagan had a snigger at that one.

'I-it's o-o-okay, Reagan,' strained Eddy, both with his voice and with his pleading eyes. 'Y-you can g-go home.'

'No, Eddy, it's not okay.' Reagan wasn't going to budge, uh-uh, no way. 'Don't you guys have ears or something. Get going!'

'That's it, isn't it? He's your pissy, kissy boyfriend.'

'No, idiot. He's not my boyfriend.'

Eddy didn't know exactly what a boyfriend was, but it did have the word 'friend' in it, so when Reagan responded the way she did his shoulders sagged deep and low. He hated Bert for doing this. For pushing Reagan to the point where she had to deny her bedroom window neighbour. In his mind he pictured the end of it all. She'd stop showing him her toys. She'd stop talking to him for hours across the breadth of his wonderful tree. She'd stop everything…just because Bert had told her the truth. That he was nothing more than a stupid little boy that would never amount to more than a pile of pissy pants.

'You and Pissy Pants sitting in a tree, K-I-S-S-I-N-G.'

Ernie had the nous to start this one and he was tickled pink to see his big brother and crew pick up the chorus.

Reagan took two or three determined steps towards the group, slinging her rucksack off her shoulder so that she grasped it down beside her.

'He's NOT my boyfriend ... but he IS my friend.'

Oh, thank you, Reagan. Thank you! Thank you! Thank you!

Reagan turned her head and smiled up at Eddy and it was a beautiful, wonderful smile.

'Now get out of here,' she ordered, returning her attention to the rotten quartet.

'K-I-S-S—'

The boys never quite got to finish the rest of their little ditty because before they knew it Reagan was on them in a frenzy. And she was quick. Quicker than Eddy would have given her credit for and most certainly quicker than Bert, Ernie and crew were prepared for.

She didn't make a sound, she just advanced on them and let that backpack of hers swing. It must've had some decent-sized things in there too because when it connected with the side of Bert's smug face Eddy could easily hear the meaty thud it made. *Thwack!* Bert hit the pavement like a brick. Everyone else in the vicinity took an immediate step backward but for one of the anonymous taunters it was a split-second too late. *Thwock!* This time the bag landed fair and square against the side of an arm and he let out a howl like a wounded dog.

Bert, who hadn't so much as twitched for a moment or two, now tried to find his bearings only to discover a pint-sized barrel of brawn standing over him, heavy backpack at the ready.

Ernie had already picked his side and Eddy watched on as the smaller brother forgot all family allegiances and sprinted feverishly toward his home up the street. All for one and forget the rest.

'Reagan Crowe, you get here this instant, young lady!'

Eddy looked across to the front yard next door and found exactly what he expected to find. Mrs Crowe was standing there, arms on hips and looking about as far from happy as you could get. Reagan was definitely in for it tonight.

Knowing that the game was up, Reagan lowered the backpack to her side and glanced up at Eddy. And, if he wasn't mistaken, she winked at him.

Before she trudged in to take her punishment and before Bert could muster the sense to get to his feet, she leaned over and whispered something to the sorry-looking boy. It was discrete enough that nobody, let alone Eddy way up there in the window, could make it out, but it must've been something awfully wicked. Bert gave her a look of shock then, scraping himself out from underneath her, he stumbled along the same path beaten earlier by his cowardly brother, all the time clutching the side of his face, which was already turning a truly ugly shade of red.

The last Eddy saw of Reagan that day was her

unrepentant figure stepping through the front door as her mother slammed it behind her.

Bert was hurt.

Reagan was in a whole pile of trouble.

But. . .

Eddy had the best friend ever. One, two, three, if you please.

14

GRANDMA DON'T

'Heaven in a handbag, Eddy!'

'S-sorry, Grandma Daisy!' Eddy had no idea what it was he'd done to earn her wrath but he'd learned over time that it was much easier to surrender up front than fight a losing battle. Not only that, but she'd managed to sneak up on him again and his words were more gut instinct than purpose.

'Just look at that tree.'

Eddy followed Grandma Daisy's dumbfounded gape to the corner of his room.

'Is th-there something wr-wrong with it?' Eddy didn't like where this was going.

'Look at it, you stupid boy.'

Eddy looked at it all over again and returned his uneducated stare back up at his grandma. He was lost. There was his tree...so what?

'You're a waste of space, Eddy, I swear.' Grandma Daisy stepped over to the side window and placed the palm of her hand on the branch. 'How in God's name did it grow so much?'

'I d-dunno, Grandma D-Daisy. It just did.'

Eddy supposed she was right in a way. He spent every day with his tree but when he thought about it, it had changed a lot over the past two or three weeks. No longer was it an adventurous outgrowth, just testing the environment within the inside world. Now it was developing into a fully fledged tributary in its own right. It was, by all definition, a real branch. Instead of winding its way a few inches past the window ledge, it had now curled to the right and was journeying along his wall, above the length of his bed. All in all, there was a good three feet of it inside the room now and it was healthy growth too. Where there had only been a handful of shiny new leaves breaking the surface like butterflies birthing from a cocoon, there was now easily thirty or forty of them, maybe more.

'I've been so busy cleaning up after you I haven't even noticed.' Grandma Daisy tried to give the branch a shake but it gave her no slack whatsoever. 'Glory be.'

'It's a g-g-good tree, Grandma Daisy. It helps m-me spell. T, R, E, E. See.'

'It's ruining my house is what it's doing.'

Please no, Grandma Daisy. Don't go there.

'Look what it's doing,' she continued. 'It's eating into the woodwork here on the window. I can't afford to get that fixed. I spend all my pittance on you.'

Eddy remained silent as he sat in his desk chair.

He wanted so much to defend his tree but anything he said would only wind her up even more. If you gave Grandma Daisy a bone she'd gnaw the thing to bits. So he watched on as she ran her hands along the length of the bough, all the way to the leafy tip, near on half the distance of his bed away. All the while she had such a look of wonder and dismay on her face that Eddy could've written the rest of her script in advance.

'There's nothing else for it,' she stated to all concerned. 'Beth Melling's husband has a chainsaw. He's just going to have to come over and chop this thing off. It gives me the creeps.'

Grandpa Nevil planted the tree.

'Wh-what?'

'I said, I'm going to get this monstrosity cut off.'

Eddy didn't tell her he wasn't talking to her. Even stupid boys weren't that dumb.

Grandpa Nevil planted the tree almost fifty years ago. When this house was built.

Eddy looked around the room. If he'd been by himself, he would've risked a 'who said that?' but not with Grandma Daisy present. Besides, his eyes told him what he already knew. There was nobody else. How could there be?

Go on, tell her.

Eddy was still considering all this weirdness when Grandma Daisy put an end to her deliberations and made for the door.

'Yes,' she agreed to nobody in particular. 'I think I'll give Beth a call right away.'

'W-wait, Grandma Daisy!'

It was too late, the words were out.

'What?' She was standing tall and broad in the door, hands on hips.

'It's just that…um…um…'

'Well, spit it out. I've got better things to do, you know.'

'I – I…um, I have a qu-question.'

I wish you wouldn't look at me like that, Grandma Daisy.

'Okay.'

'I w-was just wondering wh-who p-put the tree, T, R, E, E, there.'

Now it had been Eddy's turn to sneak up on her. She hadn't expected that one and it was written all over her face.

'What made you ask a question like that?'

'Um … I don't really know, Grandma Daisy.' At least he was being honest.

'Good Lord, that takes me back a ways.' Eddy watched with growing interest as Grandma Daisy's eyes stayed open but stopped seeing. She was looking inside – that was what Eddy took from it. She was remembering and 'remembering' begins with R.

'Was it Gr-Grandpa, Grandma Daisy?'

Her eyes came back into focus and she gave him the very briefest of looks. It had to be brief because it wasn't her style to betray her softer emotions. She pursed her lips and if Eddy didn't know any better he could swear that she swallowed back a whole bunch of stuff that desperately wanted to get out. Last of all she took a great big, deep breath and gave her head an almost imperceptible shake. And that was it. The old Grandma Daisy was back in charge.

'I think that's enough of the chit-chat.' Then she was gone, door closed and busy feet on the stairs.

Eddy didn't see her at all again that day. She didn't bring his lunch up and by the time he figured she wasn't bringing his dinner up either he was absolutely starving. Not that he was going to do anything about it, of course.

On the plus side, his tree, Mr Tree, hadn't seen so much as a blunt spoon let alone a chainsaw. And long, he hoped, it would last.

15

JAM SANDWICHES

'Eddy…Eddy, are you there?'

If he wasn't 'there' before, he was 'there' only half a second or so later.

'Hi, R-Reagan.'

'What ya doin'?'

'Just n-nothin''

'Where's your Grandma Daisy?'

'I don't know. She's hasn't f-fed m-me today.'

'What! Not all day?'

'Um…I had breakfast.'

'Well, we'll have to take care of that, won't we?' With that said she pulled a Grandma Daisy trick and strode with purpose out of the room and out of his sight. Eddy didn't know what to think. In the end he simply stood his ground at the side window and waited for whatever came next.

He didn't have to wait long though. Soon enough Reagan came bursting back into her bedroom, loaded with four of the hugest sandwiches Eddy had ever seen, two in each hand. Just the sight of them made his stomach do a triple somersault.

'Okay,' considered Reagan as she looked at the distance between her window and his. 'How are we going to do this?'

'J-just throw them.'

'No silly. Girls don't throw sandwiches, and besides, they'd just end up splattered on the ground. Now that wouldn't get your tummy full, would it?'

'N-no.'

'I've got an idea.' And with that, Reagan did just about the last thing Eddy ever expected. As if she'd done such things all her life, she placed the two piles of sandwiches on the window ledge in front of her, nicely to each side though, then, to Eddy's jaw-wide amazement, she proceeded to lift herself out of the window. Letting go with one hand and reaching out, she was able to grasp the closest tree branch to her side of the house and use it as leverage to drag her body the rest of the way out. Before Eddy knew it, she was sitting in the tree like a monkey and reaching back across for her payload of sandwiches.

'Wh-what are you doing?'

'I figured if you can't come to the sandwiches, the sandwiches can come to you.'

'Bu-but you'll f-fall.'

'No, I won't,' she said with absolute self-assurance. 'These branches are nice and big. You could have an elephant up here.'

'H-how would an e-elephant get up there?'

Reagan just shook her head at him. No need for words.

Piling all four sandwiches carefully in one hand, she made ready to make her way across to where Eddy watched on from his side window, the saliva already flowing freely in his mouth. She was about halfway across when she paused for a moment. Looking out, through the space between the houses, the warm orange light of the setting sun bathed her face. Eddy looked on and saw how the shadows made by the various twigs and branches formed jostling capillaries all over her body. Like snakes and ladders, he thought.

Hold on to her, Mr Tree. She's very, very precious.

'You should see it out here, Eddy. It's beautiful.'

'Y-you should be c-careful.'

'Don't be a scaredy-cat. Come on, why don't you come out and sit here with me? We could have our own little picnic in the tree.'

'N-no way.'

'Do you want your sandwiches?'

'Yes.'

'Then come and get them.' To prove her point, Reagan placed the sandwiches down on one of the broader branches, then sat down beside them before picking the top one up and taking an almighty bite out of it, all the while staring straight back at scaredy-cat Eddy. 'Mmmmm,' she said with a full mouth. 'This is yummy.'

'W-what about Grandma?'

'Take a risk for once, Eddy. What's she going to do? Ground you in your room?'

Eddy didn't like this. No. Not one bit.

'Please, Reagan.'

Her only response was to pat the tree over on his side of the pile of sandwiches ... of which now there were only three left. One, two, three.

Sliding his hand along the ledge, he rested his palm on his special branch and closed his eyes for a moment.

This is so crazy!

Taking a handful of quick breaths, Eddy opened his eyes again and measured the challenge ahead of him. It wasn't just the tree, of course. Other than the odd doctor's visit he couldn't even remember, he had never been outside before. Simple as that. Outside was where mean boys that called him Pissy Pants lived. Outside was where there were schools that made stupid boys bleed. Outside was big and wide and open and, most of all, it was dangerous.

Outside is also where flowers grow, and people laugh, and birds fly.

Taking one more gulp of oxygen, Eddy did what, up until a few moments ago, was unthinkable. He lifted his left foot up on to the ledge, reached forward along his branch with his right hand and, before he could release that load of oxygen, he was out of his bedroom and among the labyrinth of wrinkled bark and waving leaves.

Looking down was a bit scary but not too bad. It helped that he'd looked down from his room pretty much every single day of his life, so he was used to it in a different sort of way. That didn't stop him from holding on tight, though. He held those branches like it was a thousand-foot drop into a pit of alligators. Edging ever so slowly over to where Reagan and her sandwiches were waiting for him, he put everything out of his mind except the absolute security of his footholds and handholds. You couldn't eat a sandwich with a broken arm or a smashed up head.

He finally got there, though, and when he did he sat himself down with a great sense of accomplishment and relief. The fact that he'd eventually have to climb back was a thought he tried to push out of his mind. First and foremost, it was sandwich time. He wasn't used to just taking food, and despite his rumbling tummy he looked across to Reagan for permission.

'Go for it. There's two for you and one more for me.'

Grabbing the top one, he held it in both hands and fed as much in his mouth as he could without choking. And, oh, what an explosion of taste! So sweet and succulent, it made every taste bud in his mouth dance and sing.

'What is this?' he asked, but it came out more like *wa thith*, considering the boatload of sandwich he had in there.

'It's jam.' Reagan was giving him one of her 'you weirdo' looks. 'Don't tell me you haven't had jam before.'

'Nope.'

'Man, what is going on with you?'

'Th-this is s-so nice!' They were the only words Eddy was prepared to fit in between the first and second bites. Reagan just smiled and picked up her second sandwich. It was one of those satisfied smiles you get when you know you've done the right thing.

All four sandwiches were gone in the blink of an eye. Eddy had eaten two and a half of them, thanks to Reagan offering him the other half of her second one. Now, with appetites settled, they both just sat there and watched the sun chase itself out of the day.

'Th-thanks, Reagan. They were yummy.'

'No prob. It's nice up here, isn't it?'

'Yep.' And for Eddy it was. It was beautiful. When the sun was this low it was hard to stare at, but at the same time it was hard to look away from. With the houses across the road silhouetted against it like castle abutments you could almost imagine reaching out and touching it. But you didn't have to. It was reaching out and touching them. Its golden light seemed to tingle gently against their skin and, for Eddy at least, it played a contented melody in symphony with the energy from the tree.

For a while there didn't need to be any words. Nature spoke more than enough for the both of them.

Just as the very tip of the great, glowing orb was dipping below the horizon, Eddy looked across at his tree-bound companion. The orange fading to purple haze of sunset was still painted across her face and it only added to the impression that this was a wonderful, wonderful dream.

'What?'

'N-n-nothin'.'

'We should do this again.'

'Yep.' Even the prospect of being caught jam-handed by Grandma Daisy and climbing the gauntlet of this tree wasn't enough to extinguish that idea. Seven days a week, three hundred and sixty-five days of the year would work just fine for Eddy.

'I sure showed that boy the other day, didn't I?'

'Yep. Di-did you get into t-t-trouble?'

'A bit.'

'Um, wh-what did you s-say to him when he got up?'

Reagan smiled as she rummaged the memory out of her head.

'I told him that my dad has a gun in our house and that I know where he keeps it.'

'You didn't!' Eddy didn't know what opened wider, his mouth or his eyes.

Reagan let out a little giggle. 'Well, he ain't coming back, is he?'

'N-no, I guess n-not.' Eddy giggled too. Not too loud though. Then, in a slightly more serious tone: 'Does y-your dad have a g-gun?'

'No, you silly. But *he* doesn't know that.'

'Oh.' Eddy was glad to hear that. 'Wh-what does your d-dad do?'

'He works in an office in the city. Something to do with big companies, I think.'

'He works a lot.'

'How do you know?'

'I see his c-car leave ear-early and come home late.'

'Yeah,' responded Reagan as she considered this. 'He does work a lot, doesn't he?'

'I think I'd better g-go in now.' He didn't really want to but Grandma Daisy wasn't going to stay downstairs forever and besides, he had to say something to break Reagan's onset of melancholy. 'B-but we'll do it again r-real soon?'

'It's a date.'

Eddy and Reagan both made it back to their respective rooms just fine. How Reagan slept, Eddy didn't know, but he stayed wide awake most of the night, and that was also 'just fine'. He'd found that if he scurried down a little in his bed, he could reach Mr Tree on the wall above him and the thought of his time on the tree with Reagan and the soft sensations of his branch blossoming through his body was a combination one wanted to be awake to experience. Life just didn't get any better than this.

16

A Day to Blossom

Eddy did eventually fall asleep, of course. No twelve-year-old boy can stay awake all night long, no matter how hard he fights it. And when he did shake the morning fuzzies off, he discovered he had a surprise waiting for him.

He hadn't let his branch go all night long, but his arm wasn't sore in the slightest. And better than that, there, sitting among a patch of effervescent green leaves, was a flower. A stunning pink blossom.

Eddy sat up and wiped his eyes. Yep, it was still there. Taking his finger, ever so gently, he traced across the delicate petals and marvelled at something so precious. He remembered the beautiful sunset from the night before, the wonderful company and the delicious jam sandwiches. All of these things delivered to him, thanks to Mr Tree.

'Thank you, Mr Tree. I think you are my friend too. F is for friend. F, R, I, E, N, D.'

He made certain he was up and ready before Grandma Daisy came in. He couldn't get dressed, of course, because she hadn't been up to lay his clothes out last night. So up and ready in pyjamas it was. Eddy also hoped she would be in a better mood today. It was asking a lot, he knew, but he desperately hoped she wouldn't ruin what was turning into an awesome day.

By the time she thrust his bedroom door open, he was sitting at his desk with a learning book open (a math one to boot) and one eye on his new flowery guest. Grandma Daisy was going to spot it, no doubt about that. What he didn't know was what her reaction would be.

He didn't have to wait long to find out.

For what seemed like forever in Eddy's mind, she just stood there staring at it and chewing against the inside of her cheek, the way she sometimes did when she was thinking real hard. Then, without saying a word, she stepped over to the side window and surveyed the rest of the tree. Eddy had already done that and knew exactly what she'd find. His was the only blossom there was. Of every other branch and every other twig on this tree, his was the only one sharing this little wonder of nature.

'This all just happened since yesterday?'

'Yes, Gr-Grandma Daisy.'

She turned and surveyed him as hard as she'd done the tree and Eddy felt she could see right down to his bones.

'This is getting beyond a joke.' Reaching across

his bed (which he had taken extra care to make this morning, just to keep her happy), she plucked the blossom coldly from the branch like she was plucking the wings from a butterfly. Everything inside Eddy, his heart, his lungs, even his intestines, seemed to wrench and twist. His wonderful, beautiful blossom gone, just like that. He wanted to scream, he wanted to shout and, for the first time in his life, he wanted to get up and pound his fists against Grandma Daisy's chest ... but he couldn't and he wouldn't. If he did, that would be the end of Mr Tree altogether.

I'm so sorry, Mr Tree. I'm so, so sorry.

'I hope you're not getting overly attached to this tree, Eddy. Of all people in this world, I would think you would understand that ... with your damned mother and all.' She paused for a moment, waiting to see what reaction she'd get from the stupid boy. Eddy just sat there, stewing in the agony of his loss but determined not to fall into her trap. 'Here's your clothes.' She tossed them onto the bed. 'And remember, as soon as I get in touch with Beth Melling at number thirty-nine, this thing's coming down.'

One slammed door ... two creaky steps.

17

BANG!

The very next morning, Monday morning, Eddy and Reagan were back to the same old routine. She was delaying going downstairs and Eddy was doing his very best to help her out on that front.

She was especially late this morning but she said that was okay. Her daddy was going away on a big business trip and she was allowed to leave for school late so she could kiss him goodbye. Mummy had said so.

'Wh-where's he going?'

'To China. On a really big plane that takes hundreds of people.'

'China.' Eddy had never heard of a place called China before but it sounded really good to say it.

'Yep. And he says he gets a special seat. His seat can turn into a bed.'

'Yeah?'

'Yep.'

After a brief silence (and there were no awkward silences between Eddy and Reagan any more), Eddy said what was on his mind.

'Th-there was a fl-flower in my room y-yesterday.'

'Cool, can I see it?'

'Grandma D-daisy came and t-took it away.'

'Oh … what sort of flower was it?'

'It was p-pink. It was growing on m-my tree.'

'The one growing in your room?'

'Yep. Grandma Daisy, sh-she picked it.'

'Well then, she must've thought it was really pretty. She's probably got it in a vase downstairs.'

Eddy didn't really think so. Monday was also rubbish collection day and he had good reason to believe his blossom would be making that particular trip today. No fancy aeroplane ride to China for his flower.

'So, do you want to do jam sandwiches again soon?'

'Yep.' Eddy felt the first touch of warmth inside since Grandma Daisy's decapitation of Mr Tree yesterday. Reagan always knew just what to say to make him feel better.

And she was just about to say something else too when her attention was grabbed by something beyond Eddy's view.

'Go up to your front window … quick!'

'Wh-why?'

'Just do it … trust me.'

Eddy trusted Reagan more than anyone else in the whole wide world, so he did exactly as he was told. Not that he particularly appreciated what he saw when he got there. It was Bert – no, Nathan. Reagan had said his name was Nathan. She'd also told him Nathan's little brother's name was Dion, not Ernie.

And no hangers-on either. Not even Dion this time. Nathan must've caught the movement out of his eye (the one that wasn't still heavily bruised from his last encounter in this part of the street) because he looked up just as Eddy settled in against the window. For a second, Eddy thought that was all it was going to come to. Just a nasty stare, no 'Pissy Pants', no 'kissy, pissy girlfriend' jokes either. But in the end, it was all a little too much to ask for. As Nathan came right beneath Eddy's front window he turned his head up and mouthed a word that, to Eddy at least, made no sense. Then he put out his right hand and stuck his middle finger out, all the while keeping a very close eye on Reagan's front steps.

And then ...

BANG!

Eddy almost jumped out of his skin but that was nothing compared to what Nathan did. He hit the ground like his legs had fallen off.

BANG! BANG!

Now Nathan was crawling like a madman along the ground until he disappeared around the back of a parked car. Next thing, his head poked around behind the rear of the car and then he was off like a shot, sprinting down the street as if a T-rex was right on his tail. Arms all waving and legs struggling to keep up.

It was only then that Eddy heard Reagan's howls of

laughter. She was really going at it too. When he got over to the side window he saw that she was physically doubled over as the cramps kicked in.

'Wh-what did y-you do?'

Reagan tried to tell him but she couldn't. Every time she tried to make the noise she'd just lose it again and fall back into another fit of hilarity. In the end, she gave up altogether and decided to show him instead. Grabbing two hefty books, one in each hand, she slapped them together as hard as she could.

BANG!

Now Eddy got it … and he got the laughing bug too.

Mr Crowe may not have had a gun … but his daughter was just as dangerous.

18

WHAT A DIFFERENCE

'It's shower time, Eddy.'

Eddy heard the shower turn on down the hallway and dutifully took his pyjamas off. Grandma Daisy would be back in soon to chaperone him down to the bathroom.

Three more weekends had passed since she'd snapped his blossom off the tree but the tree was still there. Every day she'd look at it when she'd burst into the room, most days she'd shake her head too, but it was still there. That didn't stop Eddy treating every day as though it was his last day with Mr Tree though. When Reagan was at school or off shopping with her mum, or when the learning books got way too boring, or when Grandma Daisy was almost certain not to blow on in, he'd be over by his branch. It had become his oasis in a dry, barren desert.

As the days had progressed he'd discovered that the sensations he got from the tree were changing.

Not suddenly but bit by little bit. Early on it had been splashes and twirls of colours. At first, they'd been wonderful but entirely random. After a while, though, he began to make conscious connections between those swirls of shade and hue and the reality of life around him. Reagan had been a classic example. Reagan and a special type of green went hand in hand, as though they were one and the same. Grandma Daisy, on the other hand, was a patchy grey which every now and then speckled with an orange or a red. What all that actually meant went way beyond Eddy. But he didn't let it frustrate him. He was used to not understanding things and, even taking that into account, he felt a sense of surety that he would comprehend it when the time was right. In the meantime, he would sit back and enjoy the ride.

'Okay. Chop, chop.' It was time to get wet.

When Eddy shivered back into his bedroom after a particularly cold shower, he found his good clothes laid out on the bed for him. The same black shoes were parked at the foot of the bed and this time Eddy knew they were really going to hurt.

'Wh-what's happening, Grandma D-Daisy?'

'You better hope all that learning you're doing has been getting into that thick skull of yours, that's what's happening.'

Eddy knew what that meant. Mrs Stanton was paying them another visit, just like she'd said she would. And this was a big one too. If he stuffed this up it was all over, Rover. He'd be packed off to the boarding school and whipped into shape like all the other stupid boys.

Why didn't you tell me before, Grandma Daisy? I would've worked extra hard to be ready.

And of course there was Reagan. If he failed the test he may never see her again. Her *and* Mr Tree.

In the hour and half between getting all spruced up in his good clothes (he'd leave the shoes off until the very last minute) and Mrs Stanton arriving, Eddy crammed the learning books hard, real hard. And it wasn't just skimming through the pictures either. He really concentrated.

When the inevitable knock at the door finally came, it sent a nervous chill right along his spine and he got up to peer out the front window. He couldn't see Mrs Stanton because the front door was blocked by the eaves of the roof, but her car was there. He could tell because it had some writing on it. Big words. Long words.

Down below, the squeaky front door swung open and Eddy moved to the more eavesdropping-friendly location of his bedroom door.

'Hello, Mrs Stanton.'

'Good morning.'

'Come on in, dear.' Grandma Daisy was most definitely putting on her nice voice today. 'Eddy's waiting for you upstairs.'

'How's he been lately?'

'Eddy? He's been just fine. He's found himself a friend with the new little girl next door.'

'Good on him.' Mrs Stanton sounded genuinely

pleased. 'He looked so awfully lonely last time I saw him so I'm glad to hear that. Studies show that having good friends boosts intelligence, you know.'

'Yes, well … I guess we'll have to find out, won't we.'

'How's he going, schoolwise, do you think?'

'I'm not so sure, to be honest. We've been tackling the books together for a good two or three hours every day.' The door downstairs squealed close again. 'But some days are better than others. You know how it is.'

'It can be a frustrating experience but it's one of those cases where diligence pays off in the end. I would imagine though, with two or three hours under his belt a day, he must be showing some healthy improvement?'

'Like I said, it's a bit yes and no. It really depends on his mood for the day. He's such a moody child unfortunately. Very stubborn when he wants to be.'

'That's not entirely unusual. If it's a frustrating experience for you, imagine what it's like for him.' Mrs Stanton certainly had something right there but the frustration was all a one-way street from where Eddy sat. 'Shall we go up and see for ourselves?'

'Yes, yes, of course.'

Then came the first telltale creak on the stairs, but before the second one could follow suit Grandma Daisy interrupted proceedings.

'Just one more thing before we go in, Mrs Stanton.'

'Yes.'

'Eddy and me … Eddy and *I*, I should say, have been

doing everything you've asked for and more. He's not a bright kid, Mrs Stanton. You know that.' The following moment of silence was very easy for Eddy to picture in his head. Mrs Stanton would be first in line up the stairs (the creak hadn't been loud enough for it to be Grandma Daisy's footfall) and Grandma Daisy would be staring up at her, chewing the inside of her cheek and figuring what line to throw at her next. 'Look, what I'm trying to say is ... don't expect miracles. What you need to keep in perspective is that Eddy's happy here. He's got his little friend now and I think if you took him away he'd only go downhill. He needs me.'

'I'll keep that in mind and I would love to see Eddy thrive in his own home environment. Everyone wins that way. But, like I said when I was last here, if there's no obvious improvement in his cognitive capabilities I'm going to have to report that. It's what's best for Eddy at the end of the day that really matters.'

'Well, I can't see how some person in an office in the city can know what's best for Eddy better than I can.'

The next creak was most definitely Grandma Daisy's and so was the second. She must've gone right on past Mrs Stanton, an observation which was proved when Grandma Daisy opened Eddy's bedroom door. Only a split-second after Eddy made it back to the desk, mind you.

The purpose for her rush up the stairs was immediately evident as well. She had a warning for him. Not a verbal one, that would've been too risky under the circumstances, but her body language was riddled with it as she fixed him with a hard stare.

And, as if a switch inside him had flicked, the heat went on. Beads of sweat broke out on his brow and, like a summer storm blowing in, his head went from relative awareness to chaos and concern. A million thoughts tussled and tossed around inside his head but they were all fleeting. None of them seemed to touch down to a place where he could hold them, feel them and taste them. Everything he'd read these last few weeks, even these last few minutes, evaporated into the maelstrom of his panicked mind.

Grandma Daisy, please. Make her go away. I don't want to go to boarding school. Don't let them hurt me...please!

Mrs Stanton left no more room for his and Grandma Daisy's private exchange and so Grandma Daisy's eyes fell to the floor as she led the woman into Eddy's bedroom.

'Hello, Eddy.' For a lady who could send him off to a place where stupid boys were kicked and beaten, she had such a friendly way about her.

'H-h-hello, M-Mrs St-Stanton.'

'How are you feeling today?'

'A b-bit ner-nervous.'

'Well, I'm sure everything will be just fine.' She came right over to him and knelt down so their faces were at the same level. Grandma Daisy would never do that. 'I hear you've got yourself a new friend.'

'Yep. R-Reagan.' Eddy glanced across at the side window.

'Reagan. That's a lovely name. And does she go to school?'

'Yep. Almost ev-every day.'

'Does she like school?'

Eddy didn't get a chance to answer that one. Grandma Daisy heard something she didn't like and cut in between the two of them to grab one of his learning books off the desk. 'Shall we get this over and done with, Mrs Stanton? We've got places to be a bit later on...don't we, Eddy?'

'Y-yes, Grandma Daisy.'

'Okay then.' Mrs Stanton knew a hurry-up when she saw one but she didn't budge, sitting resolutely in front of Eddy. 'Eddy, do you know the alphabet all the way through?'

Jeepers, the alphabet's so long!

'Th-the whole alphabet?' Eddy glanced back at the side window, then Grandma Daisy, then back at Mrs Stanton, anywhere where a rescue from this nerve-wracking moment might reside.

'Yes, all the way from A to Z.'

With nowhere to run and nowhere to hide Eddy resigned himself to his fate and did the only thing he knew under the circumstances: start at the beginning.

'A, b...b...B, C, d...d...D, F, j-j...J.' Eddy knew it was falling apart even as it came juddering out of his mouth. What he hated most of all (apart from Grandma Daisy's furious expression) was the fact that he was sure he knew this. He did. Somewhere in his head the whole alphabet was lying in wait but it refused to get up out of the grass. Stupid thing! Stupid boy!

'It's all right, Eddy,' reassured Mrs Stanton. 'I understand you're a bit nervous so just take your time.' If Mrs

Stanton's eyes weren't as friendly as they were, Eddy would've simply melted into a ball of self-loathing and sobs. As it was, he wished with all his heart he could just crawl under the desk and close his eyes until everyone went away, never ever to return again.

'Um ...Mrs Stanton?'

'Yes, Eddy?'

'C-can I g-go over and d-do this from the b-bed?'

'Of course, if that makes you more comfortable.'

'Th-thanks. It's j-just that there's fresh air o-over there.' With permission granted, and choosing not to look across at Grandma Daisy on the way, Eddy got up from the chair and went and sat over on the foot of his bed. Mrs Stanton duly followed him over, bringing his chair and sitting in it herself after she'd set it in front of him.

'Wow, what an incredible tree you've got here, Eddy.'

'Y-yes,' beamed Eddy. 'It's m-my special t-tree. It c-comes to v-visit me.'

'I can see that. Wow.'

'Yes, we've been meaning to cut it down, haven't we, Eddy?'

'Y-yes, Grandma D-Daisy.' Eddy laid a protective hand on his branch and immediately soaked in its tingling nourishment. 'Okay,' said Eddy taking a deep breath. 'I'm r-ready now.'

'Let's start again. The alphabet from A to Z.'

'A, b-b-B, C, D, E, F, G, H, I, j-j-J, K, L, M, N, O, p-p-P, Q, R, S, t-t-T, U, V, W, X, Y, z-z-Z?'

'Good on you, Eddy.' Mrs Stanton seemed as

pleased as punch but, even better than that, Grandma Daisy had an odd combination of surprise and pleasure on her face. That alone was well and truly worth the price of admission. 'Now,' continued Mrs Stanton, 'can you count to twenty for me?'

This was too easy. All he needed to do was imagine he was counting the kids walking home from school every day.

'One, t-two, three, f-four, f-five, six, seven, eight, nine, t-ten, eleven.' Eddy paused to catch his breath and to reflect on how good he was feeling all of a sudden. He could do this. He could actually do this. 'Twelve, thirteen, fourteen, fifteen, sixteen, seventeen, eighteen, nineteen, and twenty.' Bang, just like that.

Mrs Stanton turned her head to look at Grandma Daisy and while Eddy couldn't see the expression on her face he could see Grandma Daisy's reaction. She lifted her eyebrows like she did sometimes when she wasn't expecting something, and Eddy knew deep down inside that was a good thing. That was the sort of thing that meant he might not have to go to the nasty boarding school. He might not have to leave Reagan and Mr Tree after all.

'That's really, really good, Eddy,' praised Mrs Stanton, returning her attention to him. 'You have come a long way since I saw you last.'

'I c-can sp-spell some words t-too.'

'Which ones?'

'T, R, E, E spells t-tree.'

'That's right.'

'F, R, I, E, N, d-D spells friend.'

'Good boy, Eddy. Any more?'

'J-J, A, M spells jam, and I like jam s-sandwiches.'

'I like jam sandwiches too.' Yep, Mrs Stanton was actually a really nice lady. 'How about...."pencil"?'

If Eddy had been flying high, he suddenly hit a bit of turbulence. Pencil! He'd never had to spell pencil before. How on earth was he going to spell pencil? One stupid word was going to land him in that horrible place Grandma Daisy had told him about.

Eddy closed his eyes and thought very hard and, on pure instinct alone, he strengthened his grip on Mr Tree. And something inside him opened. Not a whole lot. Not like a door opening right up wide. More like enough so that you could peek through and gauge what was on the other side. And through that little opening shot a burst of what Eddy could only describe as bright white light. Brighter than anything else he'd ever experienced before. Brighter even than the setting sun on a late summer's afternoon. It filled him deep and wide, from head to toe like a warm shower that would never, in a million years, go cold. But most of all, beyond anything else and beyond his wildest dreams, was an absolute, ten billion per cent surety that Mrs Stanton could ask him anything and he would know the answer. As sweet and as simple as that. Anything.

'Okay, then...how about...' Mrs Stanton had obviously given up and was searching for something else, maybe a little bit easier this time.

'P, E, N, C, I, L. Th-that spells pencil.'

'Desk.'

'D, E, S, K. Desk.'

Mrs Stanton did one of those looks back at Grandma Daisy again. 'Looks to me like all that study's paying off. Okay, Eddy,' she said, returning her gaze to him, 'what is two plus two?'

'T-two plus two is f-four. One, two, three, f-four.'

'Four plus four?'

'F-four plus four is eight and eight plus eight is s-sixteen.'

'What is half of twenty, Eddy?'

'Half of tw-twenty is ten.'

'Fantastic, Eddy! How many sides does a triangle have?'

'A t-triangle has three sides. Three.'

'You've turned into such a smart cookie, haven't you?' Mrs Stanton stood up and gave Eddy the sort of smile he so wished Grandma Daisy would give him one day. 'I can't believe the improvement.'

'Yes,' interjected Grandma Daisy. 'I told you we've been working hard. I think I could recite those text-books cover to cover.'

'Well, whatever it is that you've been doing, keep doing it is all I can say.' Mrs Stanton placed a warm hand on Eddy's shoulder. 'I'm proud of you, Eddy. You're a smart boy.'

Before Eddy could say thank you, Grandma Daisy was in on the act again. 'I wouldn't go as far as "smart" at this stage, Mrs Stanton, but we are getting somewhere. Certainly I think we can say outside schooling's not required now ... don't you think?'

'On the face of things, I'd have to agree with you.

I'll openly admit, Mrs Sullivan, I honestly expected I'd have to write a very different report. Eddy's done brilliantly. Mind you, he's got a hard road ahead of him.' Then, more to Eddy than to Grandma Daisy, 'But you'll manage, won't you, Eddy?'

'Yes, Mrs S-Stanton.'

'Remember, keep the study up and you can be anything you want to be.'

'Th-thank you, Mrs Stanton.'

'Good boy.'

'So, is that it?' asked Grandma Daisy.

'Yes, for now I guess it is.' Mrs Stanton stepped over to the desk and quickly checked the titles of Eddy's learning books. 'The way things are going, you'll be needing the next grade soon. You'll be getting a copy of my report so I'll make sure I include the list of curriculum books for you.'

'Do we have to pay for them? We're not made of money, you know.'

'No, Mrs Sullivan. I'll process the paperwork and the homeschool grant will cover that cost.'

'Good.'

'Okay, well thank you again, Eddy, and well done.'

Eddy just nodded and smiled. The last few minutes were too amazing to wrap up in words.

'Bye, Eddy.'

'B-bye, Mrs Stanton.'

And that was it…they left the room. They probably had more stuff to say downstairs but Eddy had lost the inclination to eavesdrop. He was still coming to terms with what had just happened to him. While whatever it was had already started to fade away, Eddy understood something amazing had just happened. He had felt an incredible energy running through him. Drawing his forefinger along the smooth bark of Mr Tree, he sat still in wonder. Mr Tree had helped him. Mr Tree had turned on a light inside his head and that light shined on things he simply hadn't been able to see before.

Way in the back of his mind Eddy figured he must've heard the distinctive squeal and squeak of the front door opening and closing but they barely registered. He had been sitting in silent contemplation for what felt like a long time before he realised that he was being watched. Grandma Daisy stood in the doorway, looking at Eddy with an expression on her face that he didn't think he'd seen before. It was somewhere between anger and confusion. Neither person said anything, and within a moment Grandma Daisy had turned and walked away, leaving the room in her mighty wake.

Eddy didn't know whether to laugh or cry.

19

BLACK CARS & RAINFORESTS

'Guess what, Eddy?'

'What?'

It was Thursday after school and whatever it was Reagan had to say, Eddy was pretty sure it had something to do with the way she was dressed up all fancy. She did look really nice though, he had to admit that. He'd never tell her that to her face, however. Her rolling eyes and his red cheeks wouldn't be worth it.

'I'm going into the city with Mum and Dad to have dinner at a restaurant.' Next came her posh, movie star voice. 'A big, expensive one.' She batted her eyelids at him and pretended to throw something invisible over her shoulder.

'Th-that sounds cool.'

'Yep, it is and I'm allowed anything I want on the menu. I hope it's not all vegetables.' Reagan screwed up her nose. The fact that she didn't like vegetables was familiar to Eddy. She'd often come up to her room after dinner only to empty a pocket load of beans and broccoli out the window. She said that at the end of the day it was good for his tree and trees couldn't taste things. It didn't worry Eddy too much but it did seem strange to him that she wouldn't eat everything on her plate, even if it didn't taste that great. Sometimes you never quite knew when the next meal would come along.

'M-maybe they'll have j-jam sandwiches.'

'Silly … they'll have steak and chocolate pudding. Lots and lots of chocolate pudding.'

'Y-yummy.'

'And do you know why we're going out for dinner tonight?'

'Nope.'

'My daddy's been given a promotion at his work and he gets a new car. A big, flash, brand-new car.' Reagan beamed like the celebrity she so wished she was. 'It's even got movies in the back seat.'

'Wow.'

'It's black and Dad says there's nothing like a new car smell.'

It was about an hour later, Reagan had already been downstairs for a while but was back up again, telling Eddy about a programme she'd watched on TV. The concept of TV was entirely foreign to Eddy but he listened anyway. Reagan could lean against that window ledge of hers and talk for eternity if Eddy had his way. It didn't matter what she said, it was more that she was there and, even better than that, that she actually *wanted* to be there.

'I was just flicking through the channels and saw something that made me think about you.'

'W-What was it?' asked Eddy, hoping he wasn't setting himself up to be the fool.

'I don't usually watch these sort of things but it was about a place in another country. A place where there're so many trees that even when you get up high in a plane, you can't see where they start and where they stop. It's like one huge green carpet covering the whole world.'

'Really?'

'Yep,' assured Reagan with a nod. 'No houses or anything. Just trees for a million miles.'

Eddy gave Mr Tree a gentle pat. 'Did you hear that, Mr Tree?'

'And you know what else?' continued Reagan.

'What?'

'They said that all those trees make a rainforest … and you know the most incredible thing?'

'What?'

'There's so many of them that they actually help the planet breathe.'

'Breathe? How?'

Reagan shrugged. 'I didn't get all of that bit. It's something trees can do. It's like they take bad stuff in and send it back out again as good stuff. The stuff that we breathe. The stuff that keeps us alive.'

Eddy didn't say anything straight away. He wouldn't have had the right words for it anyway.

That didn't stop what Reagan had told him from making sense though.

'Y-you know what?' he said at last.

'What?'

'I th-think Mr Tree helps me that way too.'

This time it was Reagan's turn to regard the tangle of branches and leaves between them.

'You really think so?'

'Yep.'

'How?'

Eddy was going to say a whole bunch of things. Things about how Mr Tree makes him feel, the vibrations and the colours, the light Mr Tree shines on the inside … and most of all how Mr Tree was the one thing that joined him to his best and only friend. Before he had time to put all this into words that would make sense, a car rolled up past his house and into the driveway in front of Reagan's place.

The shallow echo of a front door closing rippled through the air and Reagan took that as her cue. 'Gotta go, see ya later, alligator.'

'S-see ya in a while, c-cr-crocodile.' Reagan was gone even before he could finish but that didn't matter. Her joy was his joy.

Not only that, but later that night, and unbeknown to Grandma Daisy, Eddy had his first taste of chocolate pudding. And it was delicious.

THREE YEARS LATER

20

SOMETHING MISSING, SOMETHING GAINED

The seasons had come and they'd gone like somebody flipping the pages of a book. Some things had changed. For one thing, Eddy had got taller. Not as tall as Grandma Daisy though. He doubted that would ever happen.

If he got on tippy-toe, he could reach the top shelf in his closet now and that had prompted a quick spring clean by Grandma Daisy. She remained the axle upon which his days turned. Breakfast, lunch and dinner. Outside the regular meal visits, though, she was tending to leave him to his own devices more and more

The biggest change though, without a shadow of a doubt, was Mr Tree. Over the last three years his beloved companion had surged through the room with boundless energy. No longer was Eddy's branch limited to the wall above his bed. It had cast itself along the entire length of the far wall and then, for good measure, part of the way to the bedroom door along the next wall. All in all, near on halfway around the room. The bough itself had also given birth to other branches, which were themselves beginning to stretch out with their own tributaries. They spanned up and down each wall, transforming that half of the room into a virtual treehouse that was eternally green with luscious growth. It didn't matter if it was summer, autumn, winter or spring, there was a constant bed of foliage that never, not once, had so much as shed a single leaf in his room. Grandma Daisy was waiting for it though. She may not have followed through with her chainsaw bearing threats but she had a habit of letting him know she hadn't entirely forgotten the idea. If, and when, one day she found that stray leaf, she'd be on it like a shot. Even Eddy didn't think she'd necessarily cut it down now, but she'd ride him something wicked just because she could.

On that basis, not everything had changed as much as he would have preferred.

With his dose of melancholy out the way, Eddy walked over to the side window where he could see Reagan's blind was down. She never closed her window, even though she could. She just pulled her blind down when it got a little chilly. That way they could hear each other if one of them called out. Which was something that still happened an awful lot. The jam sandwich committee still met pretty much every week, sometimes twice, and by now Eddy couldn't imagine a life without her.

She did go out more often now though. But she was always going to do that. Eddy had known all along she was the sort to have a tonne of friends and she was fifteen now. Fifteen-year-old girls did stuff together and, from what Eddy could see, most of that had to do with spending money and talking gooey things about boys. He didn't mind. Not really. She always came back and she was always the happiest part of his day. She understood him better than anyone and she knew he just got her as well.

'Reagan, are you there?'

Nothing.

Eddy was about to call out again when he figured she might be sleeping in. She did that an awful lot too. On a whim, he moved instead across to the front window and landed himself at the edge that let him see down to the end of the cul-de-sac.

There was old Mrs Elsdon, shuffling slowly and carefully down a set of front steps that looked ever so hard against her frail frame. There was no leash in her hand, and no little dog tugging at the other end of it. Companion or no companion, she took the same route as she always did and Eddy watched her the entire way.

'H-hello, Mrs Elsdon,' he called out as she drew close to the house.

'Oh . . . goodness,' stammered Mrs Elsdon. 'I didn't see you up there.'

'S-sorry. I didn't m-mean to scare you.'

'That's quite all right.' Shuffling that stick of hers,

Mrs Elsdon came to a point where she could look directly up at the boy above her.

'My name's Eddy.'

Eddy felt a smile touch his cheeks, but if his was manufactured Mrs Elsdon's was downright forced. Despite the make-up she wore, there was no disguising the dark bags under her eyes.

'Hello, Eddy. It's nice to meet you at last.' Then, responding to Eddy's confused expression, she continued. 'I see you up there almost every day.'

'I s-see you too.'

'Wh-where is your dog?'

'My lovely Rosco.' Her fake smile vanished. If Mrs Elsdon had looked lonely before, she looked hollow now, and Eddy found himself struggling not to fall to the floor and hide the rest of this conversation away. With a heave so big it could make room for a broken heart, the old lady began to explain.

'Rosco passed away on Wednesday night. He gave me all the years he had and then just didn't wake up.' The silence that followed felt wrong at first, but then it softened into a place to think.

'Life has a way of doing that, I s'pose,' contemplated Mrs Elsdon. 'It just gets up and goes, leaving the rest of us behind.'

'I'm really sorry, M-Mrs Elsdon.'

'Thank you, Eddy. When Ben, my husband, died, almost ten years ago now, I got more sympathy than I could ask for. I didn't want all that sympathy back then. Why would I want a whole bunch of people telling me what I already knew. My husband, the only man I ever, truly loved, and the man I'd dedicated my entire life to, was gone.'

Poor Mrs Elsdon paused to take a deep breath, and maybe to blink away a tear.

'But after a while I understood what the sympathy was really about. It wasn't all about doom and gloom. It was a reminder; not about Ben's death, but about how many people were still out there for me, and that they were thinking of me. That they were only a phone call away in my time of need. In *any* time of need.'

Mrs Elsdon couldn't blink the next tear away.

'It's things like that that got me through. I still have rough days without Ben . . . but I can still smile.' She renewed her smile to prove her point. 'Rosco's not Ben, but I loved him too. He was all I had and he was one of the last living connections I had with Ben. We got Rosco together. Just two years before . . .'

Pulling a handkerchief from her pocket, Mrs Elsdon dabbed under each eye.

'Anyway, you are the only person who has shared my loss with me. The only person to notice poor Rosco is gone. Life's moved on, Eddy, whether I like it or not. Friends and family have moved away, or they're too busy, or they've gone to be with Ben . . . but you up there in that window today . . . well, it makes me realise people still care. So thank you.'

'I'm sorry it m-made you cry, Mrs Elsdon.'

'Eddy,' said Mrs Elsdon beneath a wrinkled smile, 'sometimes we all need a cry. How silly of me though. Crying when I've only just made your acquaintance!'

Eddy wasn't entirely sure what 'acquaintance' meant, so all he did was shrug his best shrug.

'That's some mighty tree you got there. I've watched it most days with Rosco. Is it just me or is it growing inside that other window of yours?'

'It sure is,' beamed Eddy. 'Right in and up my walls.'

'Is that so?'

'Yep. Grandma D-daisy isn't so happy but I call him Mr Tree. He's my f-friend.'

'A tree for a friend?'

'Yep. M-Mr Tree, he teaches me things.'

'Really?' Corrugated lines creased the length of Mrs Elsdon's brow. 'How does it do that?'

'I don't know f-for certain,' explained Eddy as best he could. 'He j-just makes things happen in my h-head. He makes m-me shine on the inside.'

'Well, doesn't that sound wonderful,' said Mrs Elsdon, though Eddy sensed she didn't quite understand. He sure hoped he wasn't scaring her away. After all, this could be the beginning of yet another friendship.

'Are y-you still going to w-walk every d-day?' he asked.

'I hadn't really thought about that. But you know what, I think I will. I think the fresh air will do me good.'

'Th-that's good, Mrs Elsdon. I'd like that.'

21

BAD NEWS

Eddy couldn't make out the words but it was obvious they weren't good ones by the tone of the voices over at Reagan's house. Something way out of the ordinary was going on and it gave Eddy a queasy stomach.

When Reagan finally skulked into her bedroom she had an expression on her face that Eddy didn't care for in the slightest. Usually she'd come right on up to her window and give Eddy a rundown of her day but today all she could muster was a weak smile and a face plant into her bed.

'Wh-what's wrong?'

Reagan rolled over and lay flat on her back.

'Dad's lost his job.' She said it indifferently as she stared at the ceiling but Eddy could tell she was giving this a lot of thought.

'How?'

'I dunno exactly. Mum and Dad are arguing about it now. Something about Dad's work going overseas.'

'Oh.'

Next came the first awkward silence Eddy and Reagan had had in years. Reagan was seriously stewing and Eddy didn't quite know what to do about it. He just sat there at the window and she just lay there, staring into the wild unknown.

Finally she sat up and looked at him.

'Mum says that maybe we have to sell the house and move away somewhere.'

'Oh.' Eddy was shocked. This couldn't be happening. This wasn't allowed to happen. They couldn't take Reagan away. Not *his* Reagan. It wasn't fair.

Unconsciously he placed a hand on the broad bough of Mr Tree. He needed the comfort right now.

'It's not fair, Eddy. I don't want to leave here. I'm happy.'

'S-so am I.'

More muffled voices echoed through the floor below as if to mock them, and Eddy and Reagan exchanged desperate glances. The owners of those ranting voices held the fate of their friendship in their hands.

'H-how was school today?'

'It doesn't matter any more if it's not gonna be my school for long.'

Eddy thought she was even prettier when she pouted. She wasn't in much of a mood for talking though, so he left it at that. He didn't leave his window, however. Reagan needed him more now than ever and he meant to be there the second she called out to him.

As it was, a little while later Mrs Crowe quietly entered the room and, finding Reagan still awake on her bed, she went over and sat down next to her sullen daughter.

'It's all right, sweetie.' Eddy watched as Mrs Crowe gently ran her hands through Reagan's long, black hair. 'You'll see.'

'How can it be okay?' replied Reagan as her mum looked over and acknowledged Eddy with a faltering smile.

'It just will. Somehow we'll make things work.'

'But I don't want to leave here. It's nice here.'

'It is n-nice here, M-Mrs Crowe.'

'I know it is, Eddy, and you're a very good friend for Reagan, aren't you?'

'Y-yes. And Reagan's a g-good friend f-for me too.'

Mrs Crowe sighed and looked up at something that wasn't there.

Please, Mr Tree. Can you help us? I really, really need your help.

Soon enough Mrs Crowe stood back up and Eddy sensed something more resolute about her. Reaching down and patting Reagan on the shoulder, she said something that infused Eddy with hope. Hope that he desperately prayed wasn't misplaced.

'Where there's a will, there's a way,' she said.

Soon after flashing Eddy with another smile and a wave, there were more voices downstairs. Just as before, there was no way Eddy could make out what they were saying, but these voices were definitely different. These weren't blame voices. These were ideas voices.

Reagan didn't say much for herself the rest of that evening, but Eddy was ready if she did. He was always ready for Reagan.

22

How's It Going?

'Hi Eddy. How's that amazing tree of yours?'

'It's j-just fine, Mrs Elsdon.'

Eddy was sitting up at the front window, where he'd seen Mrs Elsdon click-clacking along on her walking stick all the way from her front doorstep. Now she was standing right below him and looking up at his welcoming face.

'I've never seen anything quite like it.'

'It's m-my special tree.'

'You've got that right.'

'Are y-you going to buy a n-new dog, Mrs Elsdon?'

'No, Eddy, I don't think so. I'm not getting any younger and it wouldn't be fair on the dog if I left it behind with no one to look after it.'

'Oh.' Eddy fiddled with his fingers a bit. He had something to say but didn't know whether or how he should say it. Maybe today wasn't the right day. 'Rusco sure w-was a nice dog.'

'He was a lovely dog, Eddy.' Mrs Elsdon beamed at the hidden memories. 'He used to chew the sole out of every slipper I owned, though. I must've bought a new pair every month.'

Now it was Eddy's turn to smile.

'I made you a card,' he said, and threw down a small white envelope containing a folded piece of paper. After talking to Mrs Elsdon about her dog the day before, he had sat down at his desk with a piece of paper torn out of his notebook. Unsure of how to go about writing his sentiments, he'd taken familiar comfort in repositioning himself next to Mr Tree. He was, after all, going to need to focus on his spelling. Slowly and carefully, he wrote out the words:

DEAR MRS ELSDON
I HOPE YOU ARE NOT SAD ABOUT YOUR DOG
YOU CAN COME AND SEE ME AND MY TREE
WHENEVER YOU WANT
THANK YOU
EDDY

With meticulous care he then folded the flimsy paper in half widthways and felt very pleased with his efforts. It was only then that he realised that cards were supposed to have a nice picture on the front; Reagan had shown him her birthday cards just a few weeks ago. Some had jokes on, and some had presents and cakes with candles, but Eddy wasn't good at being funny, and cakes and candles would have been silly because it wasn't Mrs Elsdon's birthday.

At least he didn't think it was. Leant against the wall and sucking the end of his pen, Eddy placed his free hand around a familiar branch and sat in thought. As the gentle humming calmed his nerves, he began to draw a picture he didn't really understand, but he hoped Mrs Elsdon would appreciate it anyway. He began drawing her garden – he'd never seen it, but he could imagine it didn't look too different to his and Reagan's gardens. He drew trees and lots of flowers and even attempted a few birds, which looked more like flying dogs; it almost looked like the perfect little garden. Then in the middle, for no reason at all, he drew a big fat green circle.

Round and round he went with his green pen until it was all you could really look at. He stopped suddenly, lifting the nib off the paper in strange confusion. Eddy felt overcome with the thought that he'd ruined Mrs Elsdon's card. It didn't make any sense, why had he drawn a garden and then ruined it with this green blob? He took his left hand away from the branch. It had felt strangely numb without the throbs that had been pulsing through it just before.

As the card cascaded down onto the lawn where Mrs Elsdon fetched it, Eddy felt at once pleased and a bit embarrassed about what he had made.

The change in Mrs Elsdon's expression was instantaneous. It went from neutral to fifth gear and she regarded him with deep fathoms of caution.

'How do you know about ... you can't possibly know about the green stone.'

'Wh-what?'

'The green stone!'

'I j-just drew it. I don't know why. Mr Tree helped me. I'm s-sorry, Mrs Elsdon. I can be s-silly sometimes.' With that Eddy slipped out of her sight. She wasn't out of his, though, and he watched her as she tried to shake some sense into what had just happened. Failing miserably, she then ambled quietly away from the scene. A couple of times she looked back but, finding nothing resembling an answer there, she carried on, eventually disappearing into her front door.

You've gone and done it now, Eddy.

23

Problem Solved

'Eddy, Eddy … you there?'

'Wh-where else would I be?'

Reagan poked her tongue at him, so Eddy repaid her in kind.

'Guess what?'

'Y-you've got r-rabies.'

'I honestly don't know about you sometimes. No, seriously, guess what?'

'Okay … what?'

'It looks like we're not going to move.'

'You serious?'

'Sure am. Jam sandwiches?'

'S-sounds good t-to me.'

By the time Reagan was back with the sandwiches, Eddy was seated on his favourite spot of the tree. This time it was his turn to pat the branch in a hurry-up sort of way. Jam sandwiches and good news! What a day.

Scurrying across beside him, Regan handed him his two sandwiches before she eased onto her spot.

'Thanks.'

'I reckon you owe me about a thousand sandwiches by now.'

'P-put it on my tab.' Eddy's response had to be short because a huge jam sandwich had soon filled the rest. Reagan followed suit and for a while at least they savoured their little rendezvous, knowing too well that the best was yet to come.

'So, tell m-me a story,' said Eddy when his sandwich and his patience finally ran out.

'Well, it's sort of good and bad news ... but mostly good news.' Reagan had to add that last bit quickly, before Eddy's face fell all the way to the ground. 'Dad still hasn't got a job but Mum has.'

'Yeah?'

'Yep. Dad's gonna keep looking but the place where Mum worked a few years ago, they said she can have her old job back.'

'So y-your dad won't work b-but your mum will?'

'Seems so.'

'And you won't b-be moving away?'

'Nope.'

'I th-thought you s-said you had some good news.'

Reagan reached around before Eddy could adjust and thumped him hard on the arm. It hurt too but Eddy couldn't help but laugh. Reagan thumped him again, right on that same spot, and while Eddy thought it would come up in a hefty bruise he wouldn't have it any other way. Not for a million pounds.

24

Q & A

Eddy had been getting a little worried about Mrs Elsdon. She hadn't been for her daily constitutional walk for a couple of days now and he was concerned that he'd really stepped over the line. Or worse, that something had happened to her in that lonely house of hers. So, when he saw her slip out of the front door on a crisp Thursday morning he breathed a sigh of relief.

The second thing he noticed was that she didn't keep with her usual routine. Instead of turning left and circling the cul-de-sac first, she crossed the road and headed straight for his place, her walking stick beating faster than he could ever remember. She was a lady with a purpose.

Eddy considered his options but at the end of the day he stayed right where he was. He'd started this thing, now he had to see it through.

Click, clack, click, clack.

Only a couple of houses down from Eddy's, Mrs Elsdon looked up and spotted him in the window. Satisfied she'd hooked her fish she slowed down a bit and gave her aching hip a brief respite. It appeared she had some options to consider as well.

Then, stepping right up to the pavement beneath the window, she looked up and asked him the simplest of questions.

'How did you know?'

'I d-don't know, Mrs Elsdon.'

'I don't really know what to say. Do you know what you drew, Eddy?'

'A garden. And a green stone.'

'But did someone tell you about the green stone? My green stone?'

'Nope. I – I promise.'

Eddy was growing increasingly concerned that Mrs Elsdon would get Grandma Daisy involved, and he knew he didn't want that even if he didn't really know what he'd done wrong. At the time it had just felt like an idea, an urge. The old lady measured him, checking to see whether he wasn't playing games with her.

'You know, I haven't thought about the green stone in a long, long time. We called it the green stone because of all the moss on it. It sits in the shade down the end of our garden and it was covered in the stuff when we first moved into the place.' Mrs Elsdon took a moment to stretch and made a grimace as she did it. 'Do you mind if I sit, Eddy? My back's playing up at the moment.'

'There's nowhere t-to sit.'

'Oh, here on your front lawn will do just fine.'

When Mrs Elsdon had settled in, making sure her legs were tucked away all ladylike, she started back in where she'd left off.

'It took me a good while to remember how it began. It was our keystone. We used to place the spare key under there in case we lost one of ours or we'd been locked out.' She took a second or two to smile at her wealth of memories. 'I used it too, let me tell you. I was forever leaving the house without the key. Ben used to tease me about it but in the end it worked out to be a good thing. You see, Eddy, it happened so often it got to the point where Ben used to leave little notes for me under the green stone ... all wrapped in a plastic bag with the key in it. At first it was a great big joke for him. You know, he'd write things like "How's the Alzheimer's?" and silly stuff like that.

'After a while though ... many, many years we're talking about here, the notes sort of changed. They went from silly little jokes to ...' Mrs Elsdon paused to chuckle, 'to love notes, I guess you could say. Things like poems and other things, just to let me know he still loved me. *Always and forever*, he'd sign them off. Always and forever. They were beautiful, Eddy, and whenever I found one they'd make my day ... my week even. He wouldn't stow them there all the time, though. He was cheeky like that. But every once in a while I'd check and feel like I'd hit the lottery.

'When he got sick, though ... well, he couldn't do it any more, could he? So I just figured that was it.'

151

Mrs Elsdon couldn't smile any more so she stopped trying. 'He was at the hospital most of the time.' Now a tear track slipped down her face and watered the sleeve of her blouse. 'At the very end, he came home. The doctors couldn't do anything for him. So I set up a bed for him in the lounge, where he could watch TV and receive friends and family ... you know, be comfortable.

'I had no reason to check, Eddy. All these years, how was I to know? How he did it, I have no idea. He had absolutely no energy and that's the thing. He had the opportunity but no energy.

'The only thing I can think of is when I popped out for a couple of groceries or something ... he must've dragged that whole IV unit out to the backyard with him. And the whole time he didn't say a damned thing. I guess he just figured I'd find it sooner rather than later.'

Reaching into the very same handbag she'd put Eddy's card in a few days earlier, she dragged out a small plastic bag. Then, struggling a bit with her trembling fingers, she fished around inside it and came back out with a simple piece of notepaper. There was no way Eddy could see what was written on it but as Mrs Elsdon unfolded it on her lap he did spy the telltale squiggles of handwriting.

'Do you want me to read it to you, Eddy?'

'N-no, Mrs Elsdon. You don't have to.'

'It's beautiful, Eddy,' cried the gentle lady on his front lawn. 'Of all the things he ever wrote me, this is the most beautiful.'

Mrs Elsdon refolded her precious note and tucked it back away in its plastic bag. Confident it was safe and sound, she grabbed hold of her walking stick and put it to the test, as she used it to leverage her old bones back up to a standing position.

'You never did tell me how you knew ...but don't worry, I'm not going to ask again. I've been around long enough and I think I know a miracle when I see it. We'll leave it at that, shall we?'

'I guess s-so, Mrs Elsdon. I'm just glad you liked my card.'

'Thank you, Eddy. I know that's just words but I don't know how I can ever repay you for what you've done. You're a very special boy and you've made me warm again. This,' she said, holding up the plastic bag, 'this is his arms, this is his hug.'

She cast her gaze higher than Eddy and regarded the deep blue heavens above them. And she smiled a happy, contented smile.

'Would you mind if I come back and see you again? Just for a friendly chat.'

'I'd l-like that, Mrs Elsdon. W-we can be friends.'

25

THE PIECES IN BETWEEN

The next few weeks saw autumn surrender to winter. Eddy didn't care much for winter. It wasn't so much the cold thing. Well, it was in a way. Winter meant that the jam sandwich committee met on a less regular basis.

That didn't stop window-to-window rendezvous though. At Eddy's request, Reagan had got into sharing her school textbooks with him. A few of them were all gobbledegook to him, especially the ones that had letters as numbers. He could still recall the days when letters as letters were hard enough without confusing the situation even more. But there were other books that sort of 'clicked'. And that 'click', that wonderful experience of understanding something new, was bliss.

More often than not he'd be hassling Reagan about one textbook question or another but, without exception, she always put down whatever it was she was doing and tried to help him out. She was good that way. And, on a very, very, very odd occasion, the favour went back the other way. When that happened, and Eddy could indeed answer her question, he was over the moon. He did have his suspicions though. Maybe she was feeding him a couple of easy ones just to make his day. She was good that way as well.

One thing Eddy did notice was that Reagan was talking a lot more about other boys these days. It used to be just girly things or, if boys did come into the picture, about how silly they were. Now it was different. She'd rank some of the boys in her class by order of who she liked the most. Some guy called Kevin was her flavour of the day some days, then it was Michael on others. Eddy always listened intently and nodded in the right places, but this really wasn't his subject matter.

Sometimes he daydreamed about what he'd write if the two of them had their equivalent of Mr and Mrs Elsdon's green stone. Something really, really nice, he knew that, but at the same time he felt pretty certain it would never happen. She could never be interested in him in *that* way. He wasn't her sort. These Kevins and Michaels all sounded so impressive and handsome and smart. Eddy knew he couldn't compete with that.

And even if he thought he had a shot, he didn't think he would get the right words down. There was no way he could describe the way he felt about the incredible girl in the window opposite him. A stupid boy like him just couldn't do her justice.

Her wonderful friendship would have to do. It would more than do. She wasn't his only friend any more, but she was without doubt the best friend a boy like him could ever have. In those many lonely hours when Reagan was off at school, Eddy would ponder this. Without Reagan Crowe in his life, the world would be a much darker place. His heart knew that the same way his stomach knew when it was hungry.

Mrs Crowe had set about doing what she said she would. She found her 'will' and she found her 'way'.

Inside two weeks of Mr Crowe losing his job she was all dressed up and on her way to the train station for her first day back at the old job. Reagan said she worked at a lawyer's office way up on one of the top floors of a big office building. Eddy had seen pictures of tall buildings in his books and when he waved to Mrs Crowe as she wandered by early every morning, he wondered upon the marvellous views she must have from way up high. From his own front window he could see as far as the houses behind the houses across the street ... but from thirty floors up, wow ... you could probably see half the world from up there.

He'd actually asked Mrs Crowe about it once. 'Mrs Crowe, can y-you see h-half the world from your office w-window?' She'd laughed at that and told him that she wished she could. But she did qualify her answer. If she went over to one of the windows, she could see right across the suburbs and all the way to the sea.

The ocean.

Eddy hadn't even known they were anywhere near an ocean and the thought of that great big expanse of water rolling up against the shore tugged at him like the tide. What a sight it must be, to stand on the beach and look across the vastness of blue water. No houses, no bedrooms, no Grandma Daisys.

Mr Crowe was busy trying to find a new job but as the season ebbed and changed he didn't seem to have any luck. At first he'd been keen as mustard from what Eddy could tell. Back then, pretty much as soon as he'd shipped Reagan off to school, he'd be off to the train station as well, all fancied up in his suit and tie. But as time went by he sort of ran out of steam. Instead of commuting into the city every day, it'd be two or three times a week. Then it reduced to one or two days a week … and then, more recently … pretty much never. If he did leave the house these days he certainly wasn't in the business of finding a job. Not from Eddy's perspective anyway. You don't get picked for fancy jobs when all you're wearing is tracksuit bottoms and an old football top. To add to the picture, Mr Crowe also appeared to be growing a beard. Not a tidy one though. His one was all scraggy and Reagan had told him it was all scratchy too.

Mrs Elsdon worked hard on doing exactly what she said she would. Halfway through her daily bouts of exercise she'd pull up below Eddy's window and have a good old chinwag. It usually started off like any other conversation. Your 'how's it going' and 'a bit chilly isn't it' type stuff, but inevitably she always managed to swing it in the direction of Mr Elsdon, and Eddy didn't mind that one bit.

It was obvious she'd found a connection with Eddy that she couldn't find with anyone else and, while it was a different sort of satisfaction, Eddy got as much out of it as she did. The things she spoke of, the stories she told, they were all a journey of discovery for him. While the window gave him a view of his street, Mrs Elsdon's words took him places and taught him things he couldn't hope to experience from his little bedroom. If it weren't for the cold wind (Eddy knew now that it came in off the ocean) playing havoc with her old bones, she'd stand there for hours regaling him with stories of the 'good old days'. Things like how she and Mr Elsdon had met at the post office when she'd needed an extra couple of pennies for a stamp. Or how he made the best damned pancakes this side of the city…topped off with a dose of lemon and sugar.

And they were great stories, no question about it, but as she told each one Eddy saw a sense of desire rise in her eyes. An unsaid need to ask him if there was anything else he could tell her, anything at all that might take her hand and walk her back to the glorious past. Were there any more messages? Not under the green stone, of course. That one had been taken care of. But was there something more that this wonderful, special boy had access to?

It said something about Mrs Elsdon that she was so desperate to ask this question but never did. And it was for that very reason that Eddy tried as best he could for her.

In between Reagan trudging out the front door and down the street in her school uniform and Mrs Elsdon click clacking a reverse path toward him, he'd sit down and spend time with Mr Tree. Mr Tree who wasn't showing any signs of slowing down whatsoever. In those weeks where the days got shorter and the nights longer, his beloved tree had spread even further. Not content with finding purchase across the walls, it had begun to sprout new shoots across the ceiling. Given time, Eddy reckoned, his entire bedroom would be like a treehouse.

The other thing he noticed was that, while the trees outside were setting themselves for their annual hibernation, *his* tree was doing anything but. The leaves, both inside and outside his side window, were as vivaciously green as ever and it wasn't entirely unusual for people walking by to stop and have a look. They couldn't really see what was going on inside Eddy's bedroom, but the effervescent growth on the outside portion of Mr Tree stood out like the bookmark of summer caught up in the pages of winter.

And it made Eddy proud.

Correction: proud *and* confident.

These passers-by (some of them he knew and some of them he didn't) would stop in front of his house and marvel at how this tree was cheating the seasons. And there, in the window above them, would be Eddy, smiling like a father.

Some of these people would spot him up there and ask him all sorts of questions. What did he do to make the tree so wonderful? Was it always like that? At first Eddy had been a bit shy about answering them, but as time and opportunity rolled on he warmed up to the task. Most people were friendly enough and his confidence was a reflection of that. But at the same time, it wasn't unusual for him to get that time-honoured, human-nature response: the one where people recognised he looked funny, he spoke funny and he wasn't quite 'normal'. They'd just smile this pitiful smile and wander away like he wasn't there, wishing like hell they hadn't stopped in the first place. Even if they didn't come out and say it, Eddy had seen it all in his short lifetime and he knew the message written across their faces.

Mrs Stanton had called in again. Just a routine visit.

She'd tested him out again and this time the questions were harder. Things like multiplication and division; fractions and foreign places; long words and handwriting.

She ended up leaving with a glowing report for Eddy and about a dozen photos of 'the most amazing tree I have ever seen'.

At one point, straight after Eddy had aced everything she could throw at him, she'd turned to Grandma Daisy and told her that she'd missed her true calling. Based on Eddy's remarkable progress, she was obviously a natural born teacher.

Grandma Daisy had smiled at that…and she didn't

smile at much of anything. Her eyes had said something else, though. They'd said, *Keep your damned mouth shut, Eddy Sullivan*.

And Eddy, who knew he was getting smarter all the time, did exactly that.

26

NOT GOOD

'Reagan, is everything o-okay?'

'What do ya mean?'

It was one of those cold winter days when the sky told a lie. It was an unblemished blue and yet it felt as though the sun had given up on earth completely.

Reagan was leaning against her window, the steam of condensation puffing out of her mouth and the mug of hot chocolate in her hand. Eddy was doing essentially the same thing in his window, except his mug of hot chocolate was swapped for a glass of cold water.

'Well, there's b-been noises in your house.'

Reagan didn't respond except to stare defensively back at him and for a second Eddy thought she was going to start chewing the inside of her cheek the same way Grandma Daisy did. He was getting ready to leave it there when Reagan piped up.

'Dad's gone all funny.'

'N-not f-funny *ha ha*?'

'Nope.'

More silence, another sip of hot chocolate, another slurp of cold water.

'He, um.' Reagan cleared her throat, more as a delaying tactic than for any real need. 'Mum says he drinks too much.'

'D-does he?'

Reagan nodded her head. 'He gets angry when he drinks. At least he does now anyway.'

'Does he hurt you?'

'No ... but he scares me. He scares Mum too.'

'Oh.'

'Mum says if he doesn't stop it she'll leave and she'll take me too.'

'Oh.'

'I don't think she will though.' Eddy had never seen Reagan so sombre and it worried him.

'J-just be careful, okay?'

'Yep. Daddy wouldn't ever hurt me though. He's got angry before but he's never hurt me.' Reagan stared Eddy straight in the eye and he wasn't quite sure whether she did it to hammer home her point or whether she desperately needed him to agree with her.

'Th-that's good.'

But it wasn't. It wasn't good at all.

27

THROWING STONES & WITCHCRAFT

By the time Grandma Daisy made it upstairs with dinner these days, it was already dark.

Eddy and Reagan had a routine. When Eddy heard Grandma Daisy heading upstairs, he'd simply say 'playtime's up' and Reagan would slip away from her window until the mean old lady that looked after Eddy had gone again. As she explained to Eddy, it wasn't that she didn't mind talking to Grandma Daisy, but if she didn't have to, then it was easier not to. 'She says one thing with her mouth and another thing with her eyes' is the way Reagan put it and Eddy wasn't in a position to disagree.

So when his mother's mother backed herself into his bedroom, dinner tray in hand, Eddy was reading a book about aeroplanes on his bed and Reagan was listening to music on hers.

As was tradition, she placed the tray down on the desk and turned to survey the room. What it really was, Eddy had come to understand, was a chance for her to complain about something. Anything she could find, absolutely anything even slightly as it shouldn't be in her estimation, was up for a one-way discussion. And, these days, there was always one subject at the very top of her hit list. Mr Tree.

If Eddy had been some other kid, he might just have rebuked her by saying, 'If you don't like it, do something about it then', but then again Eddy wasn't that dumb. Not when it came to Grandma Daisy anyway. She wasn't someone you could bluff and get away with it.

Yep, there it was, that big sigh. But that's as far as she got.

Clack!

The sound rocketed through the bedroom, amplified by the silence created by Grandma Daisy's arrival. Both she and Eddy flinched like they'd been shot.

It was the front window. Something had hit the front window.

It wasn't broken but it must've been a close thing. Grandma Daisy stepped over to it to see what in the devil's name was going on. Eddy stayed put. Better to do what you were told before you were told to do it. He watched with quiet expectation as she leaned against the window itself, then obviously seeing something that annoyed her, she undid the latch.

'Hey!' she shouted down to the street. 'Just what do you think you're doing?'

'Sorry,' spoke a diminutive voice from somewhere out there. It was Nathan.

Grandma shot Eddy the death look and then returned her attention out the window.

'If you throw things at this house one more time, young lad, I'll call the police.' She gave the window the full once over. 'And if this window's damaged, you'll be paying for it.'

There was a mumble-mumble from out on the street and then Nathan was gone.

'What does *he* want with you?' interrogated Grandma Daisy as she closed the window.

'I d-don't know.'

'I tell you what, Eddy Sullivan, I'm sick of this.'

Eddy put the book down and reined in his arms and legs. This wasn't going to be good.

'I don't know what's got into you recently. Sometimes I don't think you really appreciate what I do for you. I didn't have to take you in, you know. I could have left you there in that horrid hospital just like your trollop of a mother did. But no, I had to have a conscience, didn't I? I had to put my whole life on hold for the handicapped kid.

'And look what I get in return.' Grandma Daisy tossed her hand in the direction of the front window. 'People throwing stones at us. What's it going to be next, Eddy? Bricks? Molotov cocktails? Are they going to barge in here and beat an old lady up?

'And don't look at me like you don't know what's going on. I'm not an idiot!' Eddy didn't know for the life of him what expression he was wearing to make her even angrier and even if he did, he didn't know how to change it. Right now, scared was all he had.

'You…this damned tree…it's not right, Eddy. And I know about Mrs Elsdon, thank you very much! I see her on the lawn. And don't even get me started about *that* girl next door. I am *not* a laughing stock, Eddy. I'm not something to be stared at and talked about by the whole town! These people come and look at you, look at *us*, like we're a circus act!' Eddy just knew she'd spoken that as loud as she did on purpose. 'I didn't ask for things to be this way, Eddy, but you don't exactly help yourself, do you? My life got put on hold when you came along, and now I can't even enjoy being in my own house without feeling under attack! I have damned well…had…enough!'

Grandma Daisy tore across the room, her whole body triggered with rage. For a moment Eddy thought she was coming for him and he brought his hands up over his face to protect himself. But when her shadow crossed him and still the blows didn't connect he peeked out and, compared to what greeted him, he dearly wished he had been the target of her wrath. Boiling in a fit of fury like he'd never witnessed before, Grandma Daisy was tearing at his precious Mr Tree. Her arms were a flurry of manic activity as she stripped the beautiful leaves from their beds and snapped any branch that got in her way. Floral flesh and blood flew everywhere and her crazed effort meant that as she wrenched each new handful away, she grunted and groaned like a madwoman.

'No … G-Grandma Daisy. Pleeeeease!' Hardly

thinking twice, Eddy pounced up and tried to grab at one of her flying arms but she was so engrossed in her spasms of destruction that he had no effect on her whatsoever. She was a bull on the loose.

'Get away from me, you evil, evil boy!' Flinging him off as though he were half the size, she continued her demolition of his beloved friend and the room was quickly becoming littered with the casualties.

Eddy couldn't believe what he was seeing. It hurt to watch. Not just his eyes…his entire body. He was viewing the execution of the very thing that had turned his life around and it ached…it ached so bad.

Reduced to tears in the corner of the room, he was a haunted witness. He didn't want to see this but at the same time he couldn't turn away. And so it was, right up until Grandma Daisy's frenetic energy waned and her anger diluted. Eventually she gave up altogether and that was probably just a reflection of the fact she'd ravaged the tree all the way down to the branches she couldn't snap.

When she was done, she turned and looked at him, her chest heaving up and down with the physical effort.

'This tree is has nothing to do with your grand-father. Do you understand me?'

Eddy remained silent.

'DO YOU UNDERSTAND ME?'

Eddy nodded his head and looked away from her, a second wave of tears beginning to sting his eyes.

He didn't see her leave. He didn't need to.

28

ARMS & LIMBS

Grandma Daisy hadn't been more than a few seconds downstairs when Eddy was shocked to feel an arm reach around his shoulders.

'Oh, Eddy,' said Reagan in disbelief. 'Are you all right?'

Eddy nodded, not able to say a word, and then changed his mind and shook his head. Reagan pulled him in close and cuddled him to her chest, a place, she knew, where Eddy could finish crying in peace.

'It's okay … it's okay.' She repeated this over and over again as she rocked him gently, feeling his tears begin to soak into her jersey. 'It's gonna be okay.'

Even tears run out in the end and when they did Reagan was still there.

'Sh-she killed Mr Tree.'

'I'm so sorry, Eddy.'

'She b-broke him all up.' Eddy felt worse than ever.

'I know, I'm sorry.' Reagan looked up and saw the

bare and mutilated remains of Eddy's prized Mr Tree. His Grandma Daisy had sure gone to town.

Eddy sat up and stared at the carnage throughout his bedroom. It was horrid. There was hardly a space left that didn't scream with the scars of Grandma Daisy's mayhem. Snapped limbs were scattered everywhere like a battlefield, and there were even twigs and leaves nestled into Eddy's untouched dinner on the desk.

It was a scene of utter desolation.

'Can I help you clean up?'

Eddy nodded … nothing else … just nodded.

Reagan slipped out from behind him and began collecting the biggest pieces of wreckage into a pile beneath the side window. For a little while Eddy just watched on in stunned silence but in the end he got up too and followed suit, being ever so gentle as he handled the remains of his dear, dear friend. Neither of them said a single word the whole time.

Soon enough the jumble of leaves, twigs and branches reached as high as the window ledge.

'I think that's about as far as we can go without a vacuum cleaner, Eddy,' said Reagan as she surveyed the sad state of a bedroom.

'Thanks, R-Reagan.' Eddy's eyes were dry to the point of stinging and it hurt to keep them open. 'Y-you'd better head b-back now or your mum will worry.'

'Okay. Will you sleep all right?'

'Yep.'

Reagan gave Eddy a furtive glance. Under Eddy's

watchful gaze, she made extra certain the single bed was free of debris and then she turned to him.

'You come and lie down here, okay?' she said. 'I'll be back in two minutes. Trust me.'

In no fit position to argue, fuss or fight, Eddy timidly did as he was asked. Placing his head on the pillow, he closed his eyes, not because he was tired but because the ravages of Mr Tree simply hurt too much to look at.

Drifting off, he assumed Reagan had crept out quietly until he felt her climb into bed next to him, her hand on his back, her voice telling him that she was here and that everything was going to be all right.

'You're a g-good friend to me, R-Reagan.'

'I'm sthpethal,' she smiled back … and believe it or not, Eddy did too.

29

FROM WITHIN TO WITHOUT

Eddy awoke some hours later. The room was still dark and he could barely make out the bare shreds of Mr Tree. He could feel Reagan's warmth at his back, and Eddy listened for a while to her slow and untroubled breathing.

As the waking moments passed in his cold and especially bare bedroom, Eddy's mind wandered a labyrinth. How lucky his estranged mother really was. That she could just get up and walk away like that. That she could just leave him like a pile of leaves on somebody else's doorstep. In a way, he envied her. In a way, he wished he could be as cold as a winter's starlit night. The sort people admire from afar but can never get near to.

And as his mind trekked life's twists and turns he did something so unconscious, so routine that at first he hadn't even realised he'd done it. He reached over and up with his right hand and placed it on the tortured bough of Mr Tree. Down here, by the bed and not too far from the side window, Mr Tree's branch was plump and strong, way too strong even for Grandma Daisy's furious holocaust. It had still been stripped bare of its beautiful suit of leaves but it remained solid at its core.

Part of the reason Eddy didn't notice it initially was because of what Grandma Daisy had done. Mr Tree was not dead – that would take much more than her frenzied hands alone – but the tree was silent and still. Nothing moved. Nothing vibrated. Everything was grey and quiet.

That was when he felt Reagan's movement. Whether she too had woken up, or moved instinctively mid-slumber, she reached her arm over and across him. At first Eddy thought she was going to cuddle into him, a potential that made his tired heart flutter. But she didn't. She took her hand and gently placed it right next to his, right there on the painful remains of Mr Tree.

Eddy closed his eyes again and for the rest of the night he willed Mr Tree to get better … a transfusion like none other. Somehow they would make things right. They just had to.

30

COLD, CLEAN &
A SPRINKLE OF SUGAR

Grandma Daisy was up early … really early. When Eddy came to, he quickly realised that Reagan was nowhere to be found, and assumed she had heard Grandma Daisy's stomps and had scarpered.

'Get in the shower, Eddy, and don't think about getting out until I say so.' Then she was gone again.

Eddy dragged himself out of bed as quick as he could but he was shattered, absolutely shattered. There was more to it than a lack of sleep, he knew that, but he also wasn't prepared to earn a second helping of Grandma Daisy's temper. So he slipped out of his clothes (no pyjama's last night) and trudged up the hallway to where the running shower was waiting for him.

At first the water was good, it rejuvenated him, but after a while it started getting cool and eventually it turned frigid. Eddy knew the tricks of the trade, though, and when it got unbearable he huddled into the far corner of the shower cubicle, his back to the icy downpour. Typically he'd only be a few shivering minutes in this position before Grandma Daisy gave him permission to get out, but today she seemed to take an eternity. He wasn't going to budge, though. Not after last night.

When she finally did come to his rescue she was as abrupt as ever. Virtually throwing the towel at him, she never so much as said another word before she sent Eddy back to his bedroom with a push of her hand between his shoulders.

Her brashness stood in stark contrast to what he found when he stepped back into his room. The pile of broken limbs and shredded leaves had disappeared entirely. The floor had been vacuumed so that, to Eddy's eyes at least, it made the carpet look brand new and, most surprising of all, sitting there on his desk was the breakfast tray. Going even one better than that, not only was breakfast waiting for him (he hadn't expected anything to eat today, to be honest), but it was a full step up from the usual cereal and water. Today he'd been treated to cornflakes with, believe it or not, a sprinkle of sugar and a full glass of orange juice. Eddy felt like royalty.

The trouble was, no matter how fine it tasted and no matter how tidy his room was, it only made the painful existence of his once-amazing tree all the more stark. Compared to what it had been only this time yesterday, it was reduced to a patchwork of sticks like the exposed ribs of an emancipated old man.

'Hi, Eddy.'

'H-hi, R-R-Reagan.' Eddy walked over to the side window and found her regarding him with sad, sad eyes.

'How's it going?'

'F-fine.'

'How's your tree?'

Eddy surveyed the damage all over again; the severed limbs showed splinters like snapped bones, the bark stripped back to show the flesh of tender wood.

'I d-don't know.' In a way, that was true, but in another way it wasn't quite the truth.

31

WHERE'S IT GONE?

On that very next Monday, as Reagan was packing herself off to school, Eddy sat with Mr Tree for a while and then, when he felt he had nothing left to give, he gathered himself up and took his spot at the front window. He wasn't feeling too hot today and if he'd had a mirror in his room he would've been struck by the deep, dark circles under his eyes. Worse than that, though, were the eyes themselves. He would've noticed how they stared back at him, faded and unfocused.

'Reagan?'

'Yep.'

'C-can I h-have a look at your English book?'

'Sure.' Reagan was halfway across Mr Tree in a flash and tossed the book the rest of the way. Eddy didn't try and catch it, catching wasn't his thing, so he let it flutter by and picked it up off the floor.

He'd seen this book a few times before. It was the

one that talked about, of all things 'Grandma', except, as Reagan kept reminding him, it was 'grammar'. She said that their teacher had told them that grammar was the glue that stuck language together…whatever that meant.

Reagan made it obvious she didn't much care for English, she did like geography though. She did a project about China for her geography class and got an 'A' for it too. Eddy had seen the big 'A' on the front page when she'd brought it home. She'd been so proud of it. Her mum and dad had taken her out to dinner that night. It'd been a pity her dad had ruined the night by getting kicked out of the restaurant for being too noisy. But still, it had been an awesome project.

The reason Eddy had taken to this particular book was because it'd been the trigger for some of those wonderfully fulfilling 'click' moments. Those flashes of understanding where all the stars seemed to line up and something that didn't make sense before suddenly revealed itself in brilliant, white light. He knew exactly where they'd been in this book and he needed to test something out.

Flicking through to the right section, the one with the picture of a man holding a big question mark, Eddy began to read. Or, more specifically and much to his dismay, he tried to read. Some of the words made sense, but they were the small ones, the easy ones. A lot of them, though, had reverted to nothing more than a bunch of letters with no apparent rhyme nor reason. It was like his old jigsaw puzzles. Some pieces fitted and some didn't and without all the pieces in place the picture escaped him.

The most dismaying thing, the thing that sent the adrenalin rushing though his body, was that only a month ago he'd read this very section and it had made sense. It had made all the sense in the world. Now, not only did he not comprehend the message in the paragraph, but he couldn't even get his head around the words.

Eddy put the book down, his head was too helter-skelter to even look at another page let alone try and decipher it.

'Reagan?'

'Yep.' She was back in her room doing something he couldn't quite see.

'S-something's wrong.'

'What?'

'M-my head's g-gone dumb.'

'Don't be silly, Eddy.'

Eddy didn't want to be silly, but he was afraid that it was starting to look like he had no say in the matter.

32

REAGAN'S BAD DAY

Eddy was going back through his learning books when the noises broke out next door. The noises had been more common lately but these particular noises sounded worse than normal. They had a bite to them that had Eddy worried, and he wasn't even in the same house.

Where's Reagan?

Mr Crowe still hadn't found a job and, as Reagan had told him, he didn't even buy the newspaper any more. Eddy wasn't quite sure what that had to do with anything but if Reagan said it mattered, then it probably did.

What Mr Crowe did do was go out for a walk every day after the rest of the household had packed off to work or school. He'd walk in the opposite direction of the school and about half an hour later he'd be back with a yellow plastic bag swinging by his side. Eddy didn't know for sure, but from the way the things in that bag clinked sometimes, he figured these were the 'grown-up' drinks that Reagan had warned him about.

Not only that but a small, eyesore collection of cigarette butts was beginning to accumulate down at the base of Mr Tree. Eddy didn't like that one bit. Cigarettes, as far as he was concerned, were bad and dangerous. They had fire in them and fire burned things, especially wood.

Mr Crowe was smoking them and then throwing them out the window downstairs. Sometimes the smoke was still coming out of them too. Grandma Daisy's demolition job in his bedroom was one thing, burning the entire tree, and probably both houses to go with it, was something else altogether. Lately it hadn't been all that unusual for Eddy to waste his morning glass of water by tipping it, or at least attempting to tip it, on the glowing embers below.

He would never say anything to Reagan about it. He didn't want to put that pressure on her but she did take things into her own hands on occasion. Not that she'd confront her dad at all. That wouldn't be a wise thing to do. Instead she'd get out there with a plastic bag (usually a yellow one) and pick them all up. She was good that way. He never needed to say a thing.

Eddy, who had been trudging through his learning books at the foot of his bed (so he could have his hand on Mr Tree), put the book down and peeked out the window. The last thing he wanted was to be caught being nosy. If Mr Crowe was as angry as he sounded, no one was safe...not even next-door neighbours.

There were a few cigarette butts assembling down there again but other than that, it appeared that the only window open in the Crowe household was Reagan's. That meant that the tirade he heard from up here must be ten times as worse in there.

Eddy nearly bumped his head on the windowpane when Reagan charged into her room and collapsed on her bed in huge lung-stretching sobs.

He'd never really seen her cry before, not all out like this, and for a moment he didn't know what to do. She'd been there for him in his time of need...but then there was Mr Crowe. What if he came up? He was still going at it somewhere down there and Mrs Crowe was joining in too. That was not a good sign.

Something crashed, something banged.

Reagan pounced off her bed, but only long enough to slam her door shut and lose herself back in the duvet.

Enough was enough.

As stealthily as he could, Eddy climbed out on to Mr Tree and snuck along the branches to where he could reach out and touch Reagan's window ledge.

'Are y-you okay?'

'No.' Reagan's back heaved up and down and Eddy could imagine the tears on her face.

'Oh.' He had to think about this. 'Wh-what happened?'

Reagan said something but Eddy had no way of telling what it was. It was muffled by her bedclothes.

'Oh.'

What to do?

'Do you w-want me to c-come in?'

Reagan just kept crying and Eddy had about decided to make her mind up for her when he got the fright of his life. Her bedroom door flew open and in came Mr Crowe as quick as Grandma Daisy on a bad day. If his attention had been any less focused on his daughter he would have spotted Eddy easily. As it was Eddy got lucky. If you can call nearly falling out of a tree lucky, that is. Instead he caught himself a painful blow where no boy ever wants to be hit and, through some miracle of willpower, held in the gut-wrenching groan. The only benefit of landing the way he did was that his head fell below the window line, out of view and out of harm's way.

'I'll teach you to talk to me like that.'

'No, Dad...please don't.'

Eddy obviously couldn't witness what went on next but unfortunately he didn't need too much imagination.

The whacks were vicious and Reagan's screams were piercing. At one point she'd pleaded with him, telling her how much she loved him ... but still he didn't stop.

Eddy sat there through it all. He hated Mr Crowe for this but, even worse, he hated himself. He hated himself for being weak. He hated himself for being scared and, most of all, he hated himself for not being Reagan's friend.

He was just a stupid boy.

33

AFTERWARDS

Eddy sat there, shivering out in the cold for a long time. Even well after Mr Crowe had gone. Eddy had heard him charge back downstairs, yell something at Mrs Crowe and anyone else in hearing distance, before storming out of the house and slamming the front door behind him.

Eddy thanked God for the small mercy that he'd chosen to walk off in the other direction. If he'd come the other way he might well have spotted him there in the tree.

Then he heard Mrs Crowe come quietly into the room above him. She was crying too. It was some small comfort to know that she was there for Reagan but his own cowardice still tormented him. He wanted to slap himself and pinch his arms until they bruised but even then his pitiful fear of being heard won through.

In the end Reagan left her bedroom with her mother

and when Eddy heard her door close behind them he also feared for a door on their friendship. And he fully deserved it too.

It wasn't until very late that evening that Reagan came back into her bedroom. Eddy had no idea what the time was but the moon was way up high and the street had been quiet for ages.

Her mother was with her for a while and although Eddy couldn't hear what she was saying, it was all said in the soothing tones he himself often yearned for. Eventually she too left, turning off Reagan's light and gently pulling the door closed behind her.

'Reagan,' whispered Eddy as loud as he dared … which wasn't all that loud. He hadn't heard Mr Crowe come back but you could never be too careful.

No answer.

'Reagan.' Just a touch louder this time.

'Leave me alone.'

That was about the very last thing Eddy ever wanted to hear and it broke his heart. His fears had come to haunt his reality. Through his complete and utter failure as a friend, he'd lost her forever.

'I'm s-sorry, Reagan. I m-miss you.' Eddy knew they weren't good last words but they were all he had and so he slunk back down into his bed and sought simple solace, a broken boy with a broken tree.

The following morning hit with a frost that lay crisp on the grass outside.

Eddy, who wasn't in the habit of sleeping much

these days, was up bright and early. He wasn't exactly parked at the side window but he was never far away from it…just in case.

Reagan was sleeping in this morning and it was a school day too.

But she had to get up sooner or later and eventually she did. When Eddy plucked up what courage he had and went over to the window he found her with her back to him, playing with her dollhouse.

She hasn't played with that thing for years.

'Are y-you all right?'

'Don't look at me.'

'Okay.' Eddy didn't know what else to say and in deference to her wishes he lowered his eyes despite her back still being to him. 'Um…c-can we still b-be friends?'

Eddy held his breath. There it was, it was out there. Part of him wished he could take it back, that he'd never asked. What if she said 'no'.

For quite some time, though, nothing at all was said. Eddy tried to keep his eyes off her (something he didn't entirely succeed with) and Reagan kept fiddling with that toy of hers.

'Yes.'

The word came out of nowhere and Eddy second-guessed himself a couple of times before he was sure he'd heard it.

She still had her back to him though.

'D-do you want t-to talk about it?' he said to the windowsill.

Reagan turned around and faced Eddy. When he

dared to glance up he saw that one eye, her left one, was completely swollen over and it screamed at Eddy in violets and blues. She also had a nasty scratch along her right cheek and Eddy just knew, deep in his heart, that it must have come from Mr Crowe's wedding ring.

'Dad hit me, Eddy.' Reagan broke down. 'He hit me.'

Without thinking, Eddy climbed out onto the tree and made the journey, for the very first time, all the way to Reagan's window. Climbing down from the foreign ledge, half blinded by a combination of adrenaline and righteous anger, he marched towards the shadow of Reagan that stood in front of him. Just as she'd held him when he needed it most, he held her, bringing her close to his chest as it muffled her sobs. There was nothing to say. The one thing she needed, and the one thing he could do, was to just be there.

That's what friends did. That's what *best* friends did.

34

PUTTING IN THE HOURS

Reagan didn't go to school for the rest of that week. Mrs Crowe didn't go to work either.

Unlike Reagan, Mrs Crowe didn't have any marks on her face but if Eddy was correct, she was walking with a limp. He reckoned she was a brave lady. Throughout the days while Reagan recovered at home, she continued to smile at him and ask him how he was. Her eyes were sad though. Sad, not just because of what had happened to her and Reagan, but because she couldn't hide it from Eddy and yet she couldn't bring herself to try and explain it to him.

Eddy wouldn't class Reagan as necessarily happy but she did improve over time. It was good having her at home. He could keep an eye on her that way and while she didn't always smile at his 'silly Eddy jokes', when she did, it was all worth it.

When she was sleeping or when she was downstairs with her mother, Eddy put in the hours with Mr

Tree. He absolutely had to. There were no guarantees anything would come of it, of course. Grandma Daisy might just have succeeded in her mission to destroy whatever it was that made Mr Tree so incredible, so magical. But, as Mrs Crowe had said once, where there's a will, there's a way.

Eddy knew that the tree was taking something from him. It had to be. He'd sit for hours on end hoping for some sign of life.

Each day was a struggle now. Like Mrs Crowe, he did his utmost best not to show it but it was getting harder and harder to hide it. Even Grandma Daisy had said he looked a bit peaky and that was saying something.

Reagan, despite fighting her own battles, had noticed it too and although she pressed him for what was wrong, he wouldn't tell her. If she knew she might try and stop him. She might even tell Grandma Daisy so she could put a stop to it and he couldn't have that.

The last thing any of them needed to know was about the blood. Over the past couple of days, after a particularly long spell of sitting with Mr Tree, his nose had started bleeding, sometimes quite profusely. The only way he'd been able to hide it from everyone was to use one of his shirts as a towel. Thank goodness Grandma Daisy hadn't noticed it missing yet but she was bound to sooner or later. It was stuffed in the back drawer of his desk and by now it was more blood than material.

But he couldn't be getting ill. He needed Mr Tree to be better. He needed that because, if Mr Tree got better, then everything would be well again.

35

WHAT ARE THEY?

Life had moved on, but not entirely.

Mr Crowe had returned and, for some reason Eddy couldn't fathom, they'd taken him back in. Reagan told Eddy that her dad had promised to be good and never hit her again. Not only that but he'd got himself a job too. Not a suit-and-tie job though. Dressed in old clothes, he'd get picked up every morning in a van and get dropped off every evening in old *and* dirty clothes.

Eddy never asked Reagan about that. It didn't seem like the right thing to do.

On this particular day, with winter now struggling in fits and starts towards spring, Eddy and Reagan were back out on Mr Tree, sharing another load of good old jam sandwiches. Her bruise was a distant memory, at least physically, and she seemed to be in a happy-go-lucky mood. Just the way Eddy liked it.

As always, Grandma Daisy was tucked away

downstairs somewhere and Eddy now knew where in fact that was. She was watching one of those television thingies. Eddy hadn't even known there'd been one in the house until Reagan had told him. She said she could see it through one of her downstairs windows and she also said that Grandma Daisy watched it for hours on end. If so, that was just fine by him.

'Do you ever want anything different than jam?'

'Nope. J-jam's my favourite.'

'Okay.' Reagan shrugged her shoulders and tucked deep into her second sandwich. 'We got honey.' She said this through a mouthful of bread.

'J-just jam. Always jam.'

'Fair enough. Guess what?'

'What?'

'Richard Duggan asked me out yesterday.'

'Oh.' That went way over Eddy's head but if he had to take a stab, he didn't like the sound of it.

'In the cafeteria, right in front of everybody. Can you believe that?'

'Nope.'

'I said "no" of course. You're supposed to say no the first time.'

'Oh.'

'That's what Molly says anyway.'

'Wh-who's R-Richard D-Duggan?'

'A guy at my school, silly.'

'Oh.' Eddy didn't like this subject any more. 'Are you going out today?'

'Yep. Mum and I are going to the shops.'

'Cool. Are y-you going to g-get that new music thing y-you wanted?'

'I have to wait till next week for that. Mum says I don't have enough money yet.'

'Oh.'

'Whew…it's getting pretty warm out here.' Reagan placed the last of her sandwich to one side, pulled her thick woollen jersey over her head and tossed it easily through her bedroom window before picking her snack back up and treating herself to the last bite.

'Wh-what are they?' asked Eddy curiously, pointing at her T-shirt.

'What?' replied Reagan looking down to where he was pointing.

'Th-those.'

'What?'

Eddy reached over to try and touch one of the things he meant.

'Eddy!' squealed Reagan, pulling away and laughing a little at the same time. 'Don't do that. You're not supposed to touch ladies there, it's rude.'

'Why?'

'That's my boobs.'

'Y-your what?'

'My boobs.'

'What's b-boobs?'

'You know, like grown-up women have.'

Eddy thought about this for a few seconds and finally it dawned on him what she meant.

'Oooh,' he said with wide-eyed wonder. 'You mean those. Like Grandma Daisy.'

Grandma Daisy did indeed have very large 'boobs' but Reagan seemed quite perturbed by that.

'If I ever get boobs like your grandma, I don't think I'll ever be able to stand up again.'

'Wobble, wobble,' said Eddy out of nowhere.

'Wobble, wobble,' echoed Reagan as she wiggled what little chest she had and they both cracked up laughing, Eddy nearly choking on the last of his sandwich.

36

EDDY!

'Eddy!'

'Eddy, can you hear me?'

'Wake up!'

'Is he all right, Mrs Sullivan?'

'How am I supposed to know, I'm not a doctor. Eddy! Wake up this instant.'

'Is he all right, Doctor Philips?'

'If I didn't know any better I'd say he's suffering acute physical exhaustion. The same thing marathon runners get hit with.'

'Eddy. Eddy, can you hear me? It's me, Reagan. They're giving you some medicine. Please be well, Eddy. I need you.'

Eddy didn't recall the hospital stay at all. Not even a snapshot. But Reagan said she'd visited with her mum every day, no exceptions. She even bought him a present with her pocket money. A watch. One that lit up in the dark. That way, she said, he would know when he shouldn't be awake. Either way, that watch was about the coolest thing Eddy had ever seen, certainly a mile better than anything else he owned.

Now he was back at home, but that didn't mean he was to be up and about either. That was doctor's orders. It was Grandma Daisy's too. She hated hospitals, she said, hated them with a passion. If he got sick again, he was going to have to go back there by himself and that was a promise.

She also wasn't hot on the idea of having to pay him two extra visits every day. Three, as normal, for his meals, and two more to give him his medicine … his yucky, yucky medicine. She'd come in like it was she that had to swallow the stuff, feed it down his throat and walk back out like there was no oxygen in the room or something. Still, figured Eddy, it was a whole lot better than having her sticking around.

In between Grandma Daisy's laboured visits, if Reagan was home, his best friend ever was by his side. She'd also purchased a joke book and so they spent quite some time together as she sat on the edge of his bed and tried to find which one would make him giggle the most. And invariably she found out.

Just like she always did.

It was during one of these bedside sessions that Reagan appeared to have taken a quiet pill. Up until that horrible experience in her bedroom with her father, this sort of thing never happened. If anything, she'd always been the life of the party. More recently though, Eddy had noticed, she could be her happy-go-lucky self one minute and then switched off the next. It worried him to see that. No, worse than that, he hated it. He hated it like Grandma Daisy hated Mr Tree.

'You are okay, aren't you, Eddy?' Everything about her, from the solemn look in her eyes to the resigned slope of her shoulders, had Eddy on notice.

'Y-yeah. Of course I am.' In all likelihood Eddy would've answered the same way if he'd had a snake attached to his eyeball.

'You one hundred and fifty per cent promise?'

'One h-hundred and fifty-one p-per cent.' Reagan didn't smile at that. She didn't so much as flinch. 'Wh-what's wrong, Reagan?'

'I just don't want anything bad to happen to you, that's all.'

That was, without doubt, the best and the worst thing Eddy had ever heard her say.

'Nothing's g-gonna happen to me. You'll s-see.' Then, for good measure, 'We're gonna b-be friends forever…remember?'

'Yeah, I know.' It was obvious Reagan's mind was caught somewhere between this conversation and two or three galaxies away. 'It's just that…'

'What?'

'Don't worry, it's nothing…nothing at all really.'

'If it's n-no big deal, then y-you can tell me.'

She flashed him a false smile. 'You're getting too smart for your own good. It's just…silly, that's all.'

'N-nothing's silly if it's w-worrying you, Reagan. And when you w-worry, so d-do I. So tell me … please.'

'You promise you won't laugh?'

'One hundred and f-fifty-two per cent.'

Reagan looked him straight in the eye, then glanced out the side window, then back at him again. 'I need you, Eddy. There, I said it.' Her cheeks took on an instant shade of pink and Eddy felt bad for her.

'I l-like being n-needed. I don't think any-anyone has ever needed m-me before.'

There was that false smile again.

'It's my dad.' Just hearing her talk about him in this sombre tone made Eddy's heart skip a beat. 'No, nothing's happened. But I don't know sometimes. He's different than he used to be. It's like he's not my dad any more and you know what?'

'What?'

'That scares me.'

'W-why?'

'Because he's my dad. And at the same time he's not.' Eddy watched as she took a deep, deep breath, setting up a barricade against the tears. 'I wish the world would just go back and be the same again. Where Dad was happy and Mum was happy … and I was happy too.' Reagan put the joke book down and Eddy had to agree, it just didn't fit in here right now. 'Don't ever go away, Eddy. Don't ever leave me, okay?'

Eddy didn't have to consider his answer. It was already lying there at the tip of his tongue.

'One b-billion per cent.'

And if he knew there was a number higher than that … well, he would've said that too.

As if on cue, the sun shuffled through its pallet of infinite shades and settled upon a hue of gold that can only be found when it spies its bed for the night. It was the sort richness that felt special. Maybe it was even made especially for moments like these.

'You wanna sit outside?' Reagan asked after a while.

Eddy still felt weak but he didn't want to disappoint her. He'd also heard Mrs Crowe say to Reagan on numerous occasions: 'The fresh air will do you good.' He'd never understood the logic of that, nor had the chance to sample its benefits properly, but he slowly climbed out of bed nonetheless and lumbered over to the window while Reagan returned with jam-based supplements.

As he looked across, it was obvious Reagan was enjoying soaking in the sun's dying rays. She sat there, facing directly into the oncoming light, eyes closed and chomping away on the sandwich du jour. This, Eddy now knew without a shadow of a doubt, was when she was at her most beautiful. With those hues playing across her delicate features like that, she could actually be that movie star she so often dreamed of being. He hadn't seen all that many girls in his compressed view of the world but as far as he could tell, there was no competition whatsoever. Reagan came in first and no one else bothered to show up.

He was still staring at her when she caught him red-handed.

'What?'

'Nothin'.' Eddy got straight back to his second sandwich, hoping that was the end of it.

'How's your grandma been?'

'Okay I g-guess.'

'She hasn't said anything about Mr Tree yet?'

'Nope. She j-just comes in and out again.'

Reagan mulled this one over for a moment before providing her considered response. 'Eddy?'

'Yep?'

'Do you think you'll ever get to leave the house?'

'I w-went to the h-hospital, remember.'

'Yeah, I know but I don't mean that, silly. I mean like *leave* leave. Where you go away, like on a holiday or something.'

'Grandma Daisy, well, she s-says we d-don't have the money t-to go away. Sh-she says the g-govimmint doesn't give her enough money.'

'But you can't live your whole life upstairs.'

'I j-just do what Grandma Daisy says. That's all.'

'Oh.'

Eddy could tell that Reagan wanted to say more but he was glad she chose not to. He didn't like his own answers either but he could only tell her the way it was. Instead they both tucked away the rest of their snack and watched the distance between the bottom edge of the descending sun get closer and closer to the top edge of the houses. It was almost hypnotic and so again Eddy was caught unawares when Reagan decided to re-engage their conversation. This time, though, down somewhat of a different track.

'Richard Duggan asked me to kiss him today.'

Eddy knew what a kiss was, he wasn't that dumb, but he had to grasp at the connotations of what a kiss actually meant. It was what people who liked each other did. At face value it seemed a pretty gross thing to do to someone you liked, but now that he was forced to reconsider it ... well, maybe it would be kind of 'nice'. And that being the case, he didn't know if he liked the idea of Richard Duggan doing that to Reagan. No, he didn't care for it one bit.

'Oh.' That, however, seemed to be the extent of Eddy's counterargument.

'We were on the playing field, down by the trees. I was with Kathy and Samantha and he and Tommy Dawson just walked right on up to me...and he asked if he could kiss me.'

'Wh-what did y-you do?'

'I said "no" of course.' Eddy sighed a massive inward sigh of relief. 'I wasn't going to kiss him in front of everybody like that. That would be weird.'

'Have y-you kissed anyone before?'

'Not like boyfriend and girlfriend, if you mean. I kissed Billy Samuels at primary school once, but we were only seven so I don't think that counts. And there's Dad, of course, but that's a dad kiss, not a boyfriend kiss.'

Eddy nodded like he understood and watched as Reagan reviewed what she'd just told him. She didn't talk all that much about her dad these days and when she did it was always as though it hurt her a little bit to do so. Today was no exception.

'I've n-never kissed anyone.'

'Really?' Then Reagan apparently reconsidered her response in light of Eddy's unique circumstances. 'Well, you're not missing much. In fact, it's overrated, if you ask me.'

Eddy nodded again, taking Reagan's word for it.

'Eddy?'

'Yep?'

'Would you like to kiss me? Just to see what it's like?'

'D-does it hurt?'

Reagan laughed one of those now familiar laughs. The sort that made Eddy smile along too, even though he knew it was at his expense.

'It doesn't hurt. Not if you do it right! So what do you say?'

'I d-don't know.'

'Go on scaredy-cat. You gotta live, don't you?'

'I g-guess so.'

'So you will?'

Trying to fit the word between massive, seismic heartbeats, Eddy looked Reagan nervously in the eye and said 'yes'. As soon as it fell out of his mouth he found himself riding a wave of adrenalin that threatened to pull him under and drown him in a concoction of delightful anticipation and pure fear. It was both wonderful and terrifying.

Unable to do anything but follow Regan's cue as best he could, he watched intently as she leaned toward him, a special glint in her eye. Leaning forward too, Eddy realised he'd never been this close to her face before. He couldn't help but notice that the nearer they came to touching the more intensely beautiful she became. If there was such thing as a perfect girl, she had to be it. She was a princess and, just maybe if they kissed, she'd be *his* princess. If that wasn't a dream come true, then nothing was.

At the very moment their lips touched, Eddy closed his eyes. He didn't want to, he desperately wanted to see himself doing this marvellous thing, but he couldn't help himself. The sensation of such delicate lips gently touching his own was incredible. How could he possibly have considered this gross before? This amazing feeling that coursed through his body had to be 'love'. It just had to be. It was so electric, so charged and so powerful he could have happily soaked it in for a year. He felt the current reach every capillary of his body and when he felt he could hold it no longer, it raced through the palm of his right hand and straight into Mr Tree.

And then it was over. *Bam*, just like that.

Eddy opened his eyes again and saw Reagan slowly pulling away from him, her face painted with the intensity of the moment.

'So what did you think?'

I think that was better than every word for 'good' in the dictionary. I think that was better than the sunset. I think that was better even than if Grandma Daisy told me I could do anything I wanted ... because then all I'd want to do is kiss you again.

Eddy didn't come out and say these things, of course. If he'd tried, the words would have tumbled and fumbled out of his mouth. So instead he took the safer route and said nothing at all. He let the captive expression on his face say it for him.

And Reagan laughed again. She laughed just like a princess.

Reagan had pretty much gone straight downstairs for her dinner and that left him with the opportunity to reminisce about his very first kiss. Had it really happened? Of course it had, but the wonderful memory of it felt so surreal, like it had happened to somebody else. He kept thinking about how she'd leaned into him. How Reagan had actually *wanted* him to kiss her. He remembered how incredibly soft her lips had been against his and how energised, how alive it had made him feel. For just a little while he was not the stupid boy that Grandma Daisy said he was. No, he was the boy that Reagan Crowe kissed. Not Richard Duggan. He was the boy who was beginning to understand what 'love' felt like. Maybe he still had a lot to learn but, from where he stood, it was a path worth treading.

But what he couldn't understand was, if love felt this fantastic, why did Grandma Daisy choose to hate? If love was so fulfilling, why did his mother choose to leave him at the hospital?

It was all so confusing and irrational, but maybe that was what made it so magical too.

37

Love in through the Window

Still riding the blissful memory of his first ever kiss, Eddy slipped back through his window on the wave of a smile. He gave the silent Mr Tree a gentle pat on his way in, more out of habit than expectation now. There was nothing. Not even a shimmer.

He pressed his hand a little harder against the calloused bark.

Still nothing…

Hold on a minute…

Yes, yes, there was something there. But it was really low.

Eddy placed his hand gently against the wounded tree itself. That familiar hum was definitely there now, tingling through the tips of his fingers and tickling up his palm.

Up? It's going back up!

Eddy held his breath. He needed to concentrate. He needed to be certain of this.

Then with timing that could only belong to Grandma Daisy, the bedroom door swung open at near on light speed. Eddy had been flying so high in the wake of that wonderful kiss he hadn't even heard the creak and groan of her footfalls on the stairs.

Instinctively he pulled his hand away. It would have to wait.

Levering himself into a sitting position, he swivelled around and placed his feet on the floor. He was going to have to be careful here. If he stood up too fast he was bound to have a dizzy spell and fall flat on his face. That would really work Grandma Daisy into a lather. So much so, she'd likely pick him up by the scruff of the neck and staple him between the sheets.

'How are you feeling?' asked Grandma Daisy in a way that made him wonder whether she was actually interested in his answer.

'F-fine, Grandma D-Daisy.'

'You're not a very good liar, Eddy Sullivan.'

'I think I'm o-okay.'

Grandma Daisy just eyed him up and down, from his toes to the top of his head and back again. She was working hard on something inside that head of hers. Real hard. That alone put Eddy right on alert.

'Did you like getting all sick like you did?'

'N-no,' said Eddy in all honesty, still coming to terms with the great gulf between his incredible experience with Reagan just moments ago and this very different moment.

'My advice,' continued Grandma Daisy, 'is take

this as a lesson. Life throws you curve balls and you just gotta deal with it.'

Eddy nodded his head. Not so much because he understood what she meant but because it was always best to pretend you understood.

'Lord knows I know that same lesson like the back of my hand,' reckoned Grandma Daisy. 'It wasn't my planning that landed you in this bedroom. Nope. Not one bit. There's other things a lady of my age should be doing. Making the best of the life I have left.'

Chewing the inside of her cheek, she went back to thinking all over again. Eddy didn't so much as twiddle a finger.

'You need to keep yourself out of stupid hospitals, you hear?'

Eddy nodded again.

'Nothin' good ever happens in those damned places.'

Grandma Daisy turned to leave but, instead of going the whole way, she turned back around to face him again. There was something written across her face that had Eddy flummoxed. Up until now he supposed he knew all the stories her face could tell, but this was different; this was new.

'We're not perfect, Eddy,' she said. 'Not you. Not me.'

When Eddy didn't respond in any way, shape or form, Grandma Daisy said what it was she really had to say.

'I'm hard on you, Eddy, 'cause life is hard, and one day you're going to have to figure it all on your own. As much as it may seem it sometimes, I don't hate you, Eddy Sullivan. You just gotta be tough in a tough old world, that's all.'

And indeed, that *was* all. Before Eddy knew which way was up and which way was down, Grandma Daisy was gone as quick as she'd arrived.

Eddy didn't know what to think, so he simply sat there and waited for the thoughts to pay him a visit instead. Among those that arrived was a recognition that Grandma Daisy, in her own way, may have just shared some feelings. If she didn't hate him, what did that mean?

Did she at all love him? How often had someone said they loved him? The answer to that one was easy. Never. Not once. He wasn't even really sure what 'love' meant. Maybe, he considered, 'love' was that feeling he got when he was with Reagan … but maybe it was something else altogether.

Maybe that's what I feel for Mr Tree. Perhaps love is like a vibration, an energy that flows, an energy that binds, an energy that overcomes. Like photosynthesis.

38

A New Beginning

Eddy had every right to believe he was in for a sleepless night that night. He simply couldn't stop that kiss from replaying over and over in his head. But somewhere amid the endless wind and rewind, his daydreams swapped places with night dreams. But if he had dreamed at all that night he had no recollection of it, such was the blissful slumber that overtook him.

When he did finally stir the next morning it was only because of the morning sun streaking into the room, playing bright orange across the inside of his eyelids. Placing his left hand over both eyes (his right hand was still resting on Mr Tree), Eddy persuaded them to open and then gradually pulled his finger canopy away.

The first thing Eddy saw, the first thing that literally invaded his senses, made him wonder whether he had died and gone to heaven.

'Reagan! Reagan! REAGAN!'

Where is she?

Reagan came flying into her bedroom, toothbrush in her hand.

'What's the problem?'

'Come h-here, quick.'

'Eddy, it's almost time for ...'

'N-no time for school. Come quick. NOW!'

Reagan must have seen something in Eddy's eyes, something that was more than a fifteen-year-old boy's games, because she tossed the toothbrush onto her bed and was out the window faster than ever before. Even that wasn't quite fast enough for Eddy. He was standing at his window, ready to drag her in as soon as she got within grasp.

'Hold on, hold on,' said Reagan, worried that his sudden bout of excitement would send her flying to the ground below. 'Move over so I can fit in.'

Ducking her head so she could squeeze through the window, Reagan planted her feet on the floor and stood tall to see what all the fuss was about.

'What? ...Oh my God, Eddy! It's beautiful!'

And indeed it was.

Reagan stared in amazement around the room, unable to fully comprehend what she saw. Every bit of Mr Tree, every square inch, was covered by an explosion of pink-and-white blossoms. Half the room seemed to glow with their soft light. Hardly an inch of the far wall was left untouched, and the room was filled with intoxicating sweetness.

Not knowing quite whether to laugh or cry, all Reagan could ask was 'How?'

'I d-don't know. It just ha-happened.'

Both Eddy and Reagan simply stood hand in hand, mesmerised, while the soft haze of falling pollen settled silently on their cheeks.

The bedroom door flew open as though in a storm but neither Eddy nor Reagan so much as glanced sideways.

'What's all the noi—' She stopped herself. Grandma Daisy stood frozen, her mouth hanging slightly open, hands poised in front of her as though ready to clutch at any explanation that might present itself.

'Isn't it b-beautiful, Grandma Daisy?'

Nothing. No response whatsoever.

'Grandma Daisy?' Eddy reached over and gently touched her arm. She looked down at her grandson, an awestruck expression on her face.

'Grandma,' said Eddy quietly, 'this is Grandpa's tree and he loves you very much.'

Grandma Daisy seemed paralyzed. She searched Eddy's face, for what exactly he didn't know, and then looked back at the brilliant garden of blossoms. She must have stood there like that for at least a minute while Eddy and Reagan watched on.

'No.' Grandma Daisy didn't say it like she usually said that word. It was more like she was trying to answer a question of herself – one she didn't know how to ask. 'No.'

'It's okay, Grandma Daisy,' said Eddy.

She stared back down at Eddy's peaceful face and, for the first time in Eddy's living memory, he watched patiently as a single tear cascaded down her cheek.

Then something about her changed, something so fundamental it changed even the way she stood. Right before Eddy's watchful eyes her stoic manner, her tightly wound muscles (even the ones below her eyes) appeared to soften, to relax and, Eddy knew, to forgive.

Another lonely tear slipped down her cheek and now some focus came back into her gaze. Not her old 'I dare you to' focus but something much gentler.

'I'm sorry, Eddy. I'm so sorry.' Grandma Daisy buckled at the knees, landing heavily on the same carpet she had once littered with the torn remnants of Mr Tree. Her tears were coming thick and fast now and Eddy knelt down beside her.

'What have I done?'

'Do we have to get rid of it?' asked Eddy quietly.

Grandma Daisy looked at him, her face doused with guilt and self-loathing. Eddy hated seeing that in her eyes. She didn't deserve to beat herself up like this, he knew that now.

'I don't understand it, Eddy,' she cried. 'I didn't understand you.'

Eddy gestured at Mr Tree. 'I d-don't understand it all either, Grandma. But it's amazing.'

His eyes drank in Mr Tree and it was impossible to deny the truth. 'Amazing' wasn't even the start of it.

'M-maybe we're not supposed to understand it all,' continued Eddy. 'I just know that Mr Tree makes good things happen. Really good things. I feel it, Grandma. I feel it light up in my head. It's so beautiful.'

Eddy felt his own tears channel down his cheek

and drip from his chin. Not sad tears, contented ones.

Grandma Daisy just kept staring back at him, her body completely limp as she surrendered to his words.

'Mr Tree's better now. Better than he's ever been. Without you I wouldn't have this.' Eddy nodded around his little bedroom. The only piece of the world he really knew. He nodded at Mr Tree, who was so much more than a piece of wood. It had become his doorway to so many new and wonderful things. He nodded at Reagan, his friend, his confidant. 'Today I am the l-luckiest person in the world.'

TWO YEARS LATER

39

A New World

Grandma Daisy was never the same Grandma Daisy after that fateful morning in Eddy's bedroom. Admittedly the change did happen over the course of time but the foundations of her personality had shifted. Even on the odd bad day, she refused to give in.

She could still express frustration, dissatisfaction and all the other emotions that come along for the ride but they were fleeting and tied to the moment as opposed to setting the stage from which she performed. And, as a consequence, the vibration in the house altered from night to day. Eddy felt it in the air around him. The fog of fear and frightened expectation had vaporised and his lungs could suck in the freshness of life again. It was a wonderful feeling.

The biggest practical change for Eddy was the previously unthinkable permission to leave his bedroom. Not just to go to the bathroom (no more cold showers either!) but to roam the house as he pleased and to even go outside. He'd taken the opportunity, too. He'd seen with his own eyes what this TV stuff was all about. The documentaries were good but he didn't care much for anything else. The very first thing he did once he got through that squeaky front door was to pay Reagan a visit. Mrs Crowe made a real big fuss about it and made him a fancy lunch. Grandma Daisy had even come over and shared the table with them. You could tell she was still a bit awkward about it but she tried hard and, best of all, she smiled. Eddy had always watched her closely but now, instead of being all about prediction and self-protection, it was about observing the gradual changes within her. It was about watching an old lady begin to realise that she never stops growing and that we're always children wandering through a magical kingdom in some form or fashion.

Eddy went to the mall with Reagan. He went into the city and craned his neck up at the impossibly tall buildings. Best of all, he went to the sea. He saw that great, immense body of water reach out and touch the land in a way that belied its underlying power. It reminded him of greater things in that respect. It reminded him of Mr Tree, his very personal conduit into a place beyond, a place he could only observe from the beach of his bedroom.

And in the end, despite all these new sights and sounds and the mystical allure of the ocean, Eddy was always drawn back to his bedroom. It was his special place. He felt the connection strongly here and it was 'home'. Neither Grandma Daisy nor Reagan could understand it. He had the whole world at his feet now and yet he chose to stay in that little bedroom of his; it didn't make sense. When they brought the subject up, which they did an awful lot, he'd simply smile and say he was happy – and they knew Eddy Sullivan wasn't in the habit of lying.

On that very afternoon of Grandma Daisy's break-through, after Reagan had forced herself off to school, she'd wandered meekly back into his bedroom with a small box in her hands. A shoebox. Then, taking Eddy by the hand, she'd sat down next to him on his little bed, placed that box on his lap and looked deep into his eyes.

'Eddy,' she'd said. 'I don't know where to begin.'

'It's all right, Grandma D-Daisy.'

'No, I don't think it is, but I intend to do whatever I can to make it all right. I just hope it's not too late.'

'It's n-never too late.'

She'd smiled at that. A sad smile, but a smile all the same.

'I've done a lot of things wrong, Eddy. More things than I can count. I took advantage of you. I did things to you that no grandma should ever do. I had the Devil in me.'

'G-grandma, it's okay…'

'I believe you. I'll never not believe you again. But I need to get this off my chest because if I don't I'm not sure I'll ever be able to forgive myself.'

'O-okay.'

Grandma Daisy shifted a trifle uneasily.

'I've hidden things from you, Eddy. At first I thought I was doing it to protect you but after a while I knew it was more to protect me than anything else. It was then that I should've stopped, but I didn't and for that I'm so sorry.

'After my daughter, your mother, got up and left you at the hospital like that, I was ashamed. I was ashamed of her and I was ashamed of you. I was too old to start all over again with babies and you were, well…different.

'It made me angry. I was still grieving the loss of Nevil, Grandpa Nevil, and here I was, lumped with what I felt was someone else's burden. I resented you, Eddy, and you suffered almost sixteen years for that. All the while you were the completely innocent one in this whole tragic situation.

'So what did I do? I locked you away in a room. I fed you, I cleaned you, I kept you alive but that was as far as I went. That's about the same as a prisoner in my reckoning. I couldn't bring myself to love you. Love had seemed to get me nowhere except heartache and pain. My husband had left me way too soon and my daughter, my one and only child, had abandoned me. I couldn't put myself out there again. I just couldn't.'

Grandma Daisy had started chewing that cheek of hers again and Eddy had reached across to hold her hand.

'I lied to so many other people about you too, Eddy. I lied to Mrs Stanton. And despite my selfishness, you still succeeded. I thought that was absolutely amazing … but the thing is, I couldn't bring myself to tell you that. That would be too close to love. But worst of all, the thing I hate myself the most for … is your mother. She did leave you that day, there's no doubt about that and what she did was about as wrong as wrong can be, but, in the end, she did see that. And when she did … well … Just open the box, Eddy. Open it and see for yourself.'

Lifting the lid and placing it to one side, he'd found the box full almost to the brim. Half of it was taken up with all sorts of envelopes, some of them tatty and dog-eared with age, but the other half was jammed with one solitary item that immediately tugged at Eddy's heart. It was a teddy bear, a small but handsome teddy bear, tucked away like a baby in a crib.

'I'm so, so sorry.' Grandma Daisy had begun to cry again and, as much as Eddy had wanted to be strong for her, he'd cried too.

Most of the envelopes had been cards. Christmas cards and birthday cards of one form or another. Eddy noted that they went right up until his ninth birthday. After then though, they appeared to have dried up altogether. When he'd asked Grandma Daisy about that she'd told him that was the last she'd heard of her too. She'd dropped off the edge of the world.

Eddy felt his mother was still out there somewhere. She wasn't dead, he knew that much. She was probably in a different country, somewhere far, far away. A pretty place, by the sea.

He would see her again one day, he knew that much too, and everything would be just fine.

He'd removed Barney Bear from the box and since then he'd held pride of place on Eddy's desk, staring back at the boy who'd taken so long to find him. Sometimes, when it was especially lonely, Eddy would bring Barney Bear over to the bed and run his hands across the artificial fur. He would think that maybe he was touching a piece of something that had last been touched by his mother, and, if that was the case, how close they were to actually holding hands.

There was one other thing in that little box that wasn't a card or a bear. It was a letter, and it had been written so long ago that the paper was beginning to discolour. Grandma Daisy had picked that one out of the bunch specifically and it was one of the few that had already been opened. She'd said that this was one he should probably read first. It was important she'd told him, and she'd sat there on the bed right next to him and waited as he worked his way through it, just in case he needed a hand with the words.

Hi Eddy,
I like your name. You won't be able to read this yourself I guess but I'm sure your grandma will. I just don't want you to think that I don't think about you. I think about you a lot.

You're also probably wondering why I'm writing a letter instead of being there to tell you in person. It's not that I don't feel love for you, Eddy. I just don't know 'how' to love. And that's not fair on you. I hate saying that and I hate knowing that, but at the same time I can't change it.

If I came back to be your mother, it might work for a day, a week, maybe even a year, but in the end it wouldn't work at all and then we'd all just be hurt again. I hope you understand. I didn't want to leave you, Eddy. I had to. For you and for me. For everyone.

I hope you like the bear and I hope you grow up to have a wonderful life.

Please tell Mum I'm sorry. I never meant for this to happen.

Thinking of you always,
Hailey XXXO

Grandma Daisy had had to explain what the 'XXXO' meant at the end of the letter and Eddy didn't quite know what to make of that. Imagine trying to put the whole emotion of a mother-to-son hug in those simple letters.

In the two years that had passed since he'd first read that letter, Eddy hadn't had cause to open it again. He wasn't angry, not in the slightest. It was just that he preferred for Barney Bear be his connection to his mother, not a confused and confusing letter written too many years ago to remember. You couldn't hug Xs and Os, but you could hug a bear.

So the shoebox in question now rested under Eddy's bed, catching what little dust Grandma Daisy allowed in the room.

40

BACK TO REALITY

Life had moved on in the old neighbourhood in the last two years. They say that over any given three-year period, a third of the people on a street will move on in one form or another. From his spot at the front window, Eddy could vouch for that.

Mrs McGinnity had moved to Europe to be closer to her grandchildren. Ted Heffernan had got a new job out of town. Dave and Polly Ashburn had upgraded to a new neighbourhood closer to the city and taken all their kids with them ... all five of them.

Mrs Elsdon was still around – Eddy had begun to think she was invincible – and she was still making her daily round of the cul-de-sac. Even though she knew Eddy's boundaries had changed, she still preferred to stand outside and engage him up there in the window. She said she liked it that way. She said it felt right that she should be looking up.

Eddy couldn't possibly count the vast subjects

they'd covered in their conversations but not once did he get bored with her company and he was absolutely certain that went both ways. It all came back to one place in the end: Ben Elsdon. That was no problem, though. Ben Elsdon sounded like a wonderful man, and that made him perfectly worth talking about. And of course there was Reagan. There was always Reagan.

In the two odd years since that first kiss on Mr Tree, it had remained Eddy's only kiss. Would he ever have the opportunity to kiss her again? That one was a bit fuzzy. Something made him want to say yes, but at the same time he couldn't class it as a certainty. He definitely wasn't going to put her on the spot. If she wanted to kiss him, she'd do it. That was Reagan. That was the way she did things. At the end of the day, he figured it was a good thing. Sometimes friends couldn't be friends any more after they kissed; something between them changed forever, sort of like taking a bite from the forbidden fruit. No, as much as that kiss had been a trip to heaven and back, if having Reagan in his life for the rest of their days meant that kisses were a thing of the past, then so be it.

She had grown up too. Whereas two years ago she was dabbling around the edges of womanhood, lately she'd dived right in. The boys at school had noticed it too, if her recent company on walks home from school were anything to go by. She seemed to have become the target of an awful lot of attention and while she didn't exactly play on it, Eddy could tell she wasn't in the mood to make it go away either.

Richard Duggan had finally got his way. He'd ended up being her first real boyfriend but, as with almost all first romances, it didn't last long. Reagan never said much about it. Something about Samantha and how that dirty little so and so could rot in hell was all he got out of her.

After that there'd been a couple of others. One of them had even come to pay Mr and Mrs Crowe a visit – a night out for dinner at the girlfriend's house. Eddy had seen him arrive. He looked nice enough, certainly not a thug. The poor guy had been so nervous Eddy could almost smell it from the front window. Mrs Crowe had been there to greet him at the front door and he'd shaken her hand like the true gentleman. That was good. Reagan deserved a gentleman. She deserved someone who would treat her well and never hurt her. She deserved someone who could sit and watch the sunset, share the world's biggest jam sandwich and have a whole conversation without having to say a single word.

No one had quite reached jam sandwiches status yet though.

The spectacular blossoms on Mr Tree had bloomed all through that first spring and then halfway into summer, well past any of its lesser cousins around the neighbourhood. But in the end, as with all things, their time came to pass and they gave way to even newer life. Such was the lushness of the bed of leaves that followed, Eddy was worried that their vibrant weight would bring some of the branches down. But he needn't have fretted. Mr Tree was strong and healthy, more so than it had ever been, and Eddy came to realise that sometimes things needed to be broken so that they could be fixed again.

41

THE SECOND NOTE

'Hey, Eddy?'

'Yep.'

'Jam sandwich time.'

'You bet.'

'Back in a sec.'

Eddy knew the routine. He climbed out to his perch on the tree and waited for Reagan to come back, the chef's special in tow.

Eddy watched her closely while she settled down beside him. His instinct had been right. There was something wrong. She had trouble looking him in the eye, and the bounce had gone out of her step. She was heavy because something was weighing her down.

'Reagan?'

'What?' she responded a little too defensively.

'What's wrong?'

Reagan didn't utter a single word. She just reached

into her back pocket and pulled out a folded piece of paper. For a while all she did was run it through her fingers, pondering all the ways, all the paths that had led her to this moment and then, finally, she handed it over to him. Still she couldn't bring herself to look at him. Her only other option was to stare blankly ahead, into a place only she could see.

Eddy took the piece of paper and opened it, reading the scrawly handwriting carefully so he didn't miss a single word.

Dearest Reagan,
I'm sorry, honey, but I have to go away for a while. I don't know how long for. I'm not well and I haven't been well for a long time now. Dads should never hit their little girls. Dads should never be angry all the time. I have to go away and think about things for a while.

Please don't hate me. I love you and that will never, ever change. Remember that. Remember that about me more than anything else.

Love and kisses,
Dad

It was short and Eddy read it twice. Then he folded it again, making sure he kept it nice and square, following the folds on ther paper.

'So what do you think?' she asked him out of nowhere.

'Does your mum know about this?'

'Yeah. She got a letter too but she won't show me hers.'

Eddy prepared himself for her inevitable meltdown but for now at least she seemed to have the floodgates locked tight.

'How did it happen?'

'What? Dad leaving?'

'No … s-sorry … I meant, how did you find the letter?'

'It was under my door when I got up this morning.' There seemed to be no emotion whatsoever in Reagan's voice and Eddy didn't like that. It didn't bode well.

'How are you feeling? Is there anything I can do?'

'No. I don't know. I don't know how I'm supposed to feel.'

Eddy scrunched over a bit and tried to put his arm around her shoulders. Immediately he knew it was the wrong thing to do and she proved his point by hunching her shoulders so he couldn't achieve his objective.

Then she looked apologetically across at him. 'What do you think's gonna happen, Eddy?'

'You mean, do I think he's going to c-come back?'

'Yeah.'

'I'm sorry, Reagan. I don't know.'

'That's okay. It's not your fault. I just thought, maybe, you know. You might have a different take on things.'

Eddy didn't know whether he had a different take on things or not. Part of him didn't want Reagan's dad anywhere near this place ever again. Not after the pain he'd caused her. But that didn't stop him from hating the other type of pain he saw in her eyes.

Which type of pain hurt the most, it was hard to tell. Which type of pain would likely last the longest … well, that was an easy one to answer.

In the end, with nowhere left to unleash her frustrations, it appeared to Eddy as though she'd just heaped it all on herself instead.

Reagan was still Reagan – she couldn't not be – but equally, she changed that day her father left the house for the very last time. Her precocious independence stood tall but it seemed to find a new outlet. Her bouts of laughter, which to Eddy's ears were joy personified, were few and far between now. Maybe it had something to do with the weight of the world resting on her chest, something to do with seeing things through a different set of eyes.

Eddy's heart broke to see it. He tried to keep things light-hearted, anything to bring her out of her funk. Invariably, however, her reaction to his desperate jokes was barely a smile and even then it only stayed on her mouth.

Their window-to-window discussions, although regular, seemed to have taken on a different flavour as well. It was a subtle thing, and when Eddy gave it some consideration, he figured it was as though it had shifted from a conversation between best-ever friends to playground buddies. Her life had moved on, for good or for bad, and Eddy was standing on the side of the road, watching her pull away.

The girl that had beaten up a bully for him, the girl that had shared jam sandwiches with him, the girl who had held him tight that night Grandma Daisy had ripped Mr Tree to pieces and the girl who still owned his only ever kiss was evolving into something that he just couldn't keep up with.

Eddy knew it was impossible for the two houses to drift apart but the distance between them seemed to grow every passing day. Sometimes he wondered, if it weren't for Mr Tree's arms binding the two buildings together, would they simply head off in different directions?

Or was it something else? Something that hurt too much to think about.

Had *he* changed in Reagan's eyes? Despite everything, all the better things happening, was Reagan now seeing him the way others used to? Was he just a dumb kid next door?

42

MRS STANTON'S CHALLENGE

Eddy had known for a full week that Mrs Stanton was coming. That was the way of things with Grandma Daisy these days. There were days past when the first he'd know of it was when her car pulled up out front. Now, though, Grandma Daisy laid on a breakfast of pancakes and orange juice, for 'energy' she reckoned. Eddy wasn't going to say no to that, so he'd dug in and given the textbooks a bit of a going over as well. Not that he was overly concerned at all. His studies had shot ahead and, if anything, Reagan tended to lean on him now. His caution was more down to old habits dying hard than anything else.

When the front door eventually squealed that recognisable squeal, he put his books aside and counted the even more familiar creaks as they climbed the stairs together.

'Hello, Eddy.' The greeting may have been directed

at Eddy but her entire attention was focused on Mr Tree. 'I swear this thing has grown again since I was last here.'

'It probably has, Mrs Stanton,' replied Grandma Daisy, smiling. 'Next thing you know, I won't be able to get in the door. Or maybe that's been Eddy's plan all along.'

'What ... and miss getting more pancakes?' Eddy smiled back.

'Pancakes, wow! Aren't you lucky?'

'Yep. If y-you can't beat 'em, join 'em.'

Mrs Stanton chuckled at that. She seemed so much more relaxed these days.

'Okay,' she said, getting proceedings back in order, 'I'm on a little bit of a different mission today.'

'Oh ... w-what's that?'

'Eddy, between you and your grandmother here, you're about the best student I've got on my books.' Eddy had time to glance over at Grandma Daisy, who winked right on back at him. 'So,' continued Mrs Stanton, 'I thought you might be up for something new.'

'Okay.' It wasn't exactly a convincing response.

'There's a whole world waiting for you out there, I think even you believe that now. You've got more brains in that head of yours than most of the kids out there who are going to school. The only thing different is that they'll come out the other end with a piece of paper that says 'pick me'. I was thinking, there's no reason why you shouldn't have that too.'

'You want Eddy to sit an exam?' Grandma Daisy

came around and placed a supporting hand on Eddy's shoulder.

Jeepers! I don't know enough to sit an exam.

'Yes, Mrs Sullivan. I'm not here to force Eddy into doing something he doesn't want to do but I honestly think he's up to it.'

'What exam are you talking about?' Grandma Daisy was getting a little defensive now but, at the same time, she was asking questions that had answers Eddy wanted to hear.

'His GCSEs.'

'So you're saying more than one exam, then?'

'Yes, I am. One for each subject that Eddy wants to take. But that's not to say he can't take just one if that's what he feels like. What do you think, Eddy?'

I'm scared out of my mind is what I think, Mrs Stanton.

'Aren't GCSEs quite tough?' Eddy was certain that's what Reagan had done last year and they certainly sounded tough.

'Technically, yes. And I'm not saying it'll be a walk in the park but I've seen what you're capable of, Eddy. I'm not in the practice of throwing my kids in over their heads. I really believe you can do this.'

'Are y-you sure, Mrs Stanton?'

'Yes. Without a doubt.'

Grandma Daisy doesn't like this. She thinks we've come too far.

'Eddy?' Grandma Daisy was looking down at him and Eddy realised that this was yet another manifestation of their changed relationship. She was going to let him make this call.

'Yes, Mrs Stanton,' he said. 'I think I can do it.'

'Good.' Mrs Stanton positively beamed at him. 'Now let me explain how it works.'

43

REAGAN'S BIG NIGHT

Both Eddy and Reagan were lodged at their respective window ledges, textbooks in hand and pens at the ready. Eddy hadn't realised how hard this study thing would be and he was getting kind of worried that he may have bitten off more than he could chew. But if he was struggling, Reagan was drowning, and he knew he had to set the example. If she saw him losing his cool, she'd throw in the towel altogether.

Since he'd told Reagan about his exams, without making it seem like a chore (Reagan didn't take to chores all that well), Eddy had endeavoured to make study a regular habit. After Reagan had settled in from a full day at school, they'd fall in beside their windows and get the ugly stuff out the way. Not on Fridays though. Definitely not on Fridays. That was a Reagan rule and hell could freeze over before that changed.

Today was a Saturday. Reagan never studied on

Saturdays either, and you could write 'never' in huge capital letters. But on this Saturday in particular, Reagan was doing exactly that and she had no choice in the matter.

Eddy had hardly ever seen Mrs Crowe angry but she was making up for lost time today. She was livid. Reagan had been grounded in her bedroom and, in Mrs Crowe's own words, if she wasn't studying every time she passed by her room, then she'd add another week to the punishment.

Talking back hadn't worked either. The updated rules were: not studying *plus* talking back meant another week of grounding. So now, outside of school, Reagan was camped in her room for two full weeks, and she was fuming.

'It's not fair,' she complained to Eddy across the windows.

'What did you do to make her so angry?'

'Nothing.'

'Y-you're in a lot of trouble for "nothing".'

Reagan stared back at him and Eddy could tell she was trying to decide whether his comment alone warranted extending her realm of loathing to him as well.

'S-sorry.'

'I stayed out late, that's all,' she finally pouted. 'I'm seventeen years old and she doesn't think I'm old enough to decide my own bedtime. How crap is that.'

If that was a question, Eddy was lost for the answer, so he just shrugged his shoulders instead.

She had been out very late last night; that was for

certain. He'd still been awake when she'd been chaperoned to her bedroom some time after midnight. Mrs Crowe had been whispering but, as Eddy had discovered, whispers could still get the message across very, very well.

'And it's not even about being out late,' continued Reagan. 'It's more that she doesn't like Ryan, is what it is. It's because he's older and he's got a car. And that's not fair.'

Eddy just shrugged again.

'Plus, there's only three years difference between us. It's not like he's thirty or something.'

He smokes cigarettes, and maybe something else too, Reagan. I can smell it on you.

'Is that w-why your mum's so angry?'

'That's the real reason. She doesn't like the idea of me growing up, I reckon. She got all pissy because Ryan let me have a couple of drinks last night. I wasn't drunk or anything, just a bit happy, that's all.'

'I think y-your mum just loves you and she was worried.'

'If she loved me, then she'd trust me. I'm not a kid any more, Eddy. I can look after myself.'

'Sorry.'

'Stop saying sorry,' she snapped back. 'It's not your fault. I'm just frustrated. I'm stuck in this stupid room for two weeks and I didn't even do anything wrong. What's worse is there's a concert that Ryan wants to go to tonight and I know if I can't go he'll take Vanessa Riley. Now she's a girl you can't trust. *Her* mum should lock *her* up and save us all a lot of trouble.'

Eddy felt choked by the fact that he'd never felt 'stuck' in a room where Reagan was just a window away, but he continued to flick through his books in silence.

Reagan's feathers were ruffled for the rest of the day. Well, most of it anyway. She went through bouts of venting, quiet moments and places in between up until about four o'clock that afternoon. That's when her mother had let her take a certain phone call. Mrs Crowe didn't look entirely pleased about it though. Not by a long shot.

When Reagan trotted back into her bedroom it was as though she'd swallowed a whole vat of happy potion. Her eyes were sparkling again and even the sun seemed brighter.

Instead of verbally bouncing her mother and this Vanessa Riley girl around the room, she appeared to have let it go completely. The old Reagan was back and Eddy reckoned that was fantastic. But Eddy wasn't dumb ... no, not any more. There was something more to this than met the eye and, while he cheerfully engaged the new Reagan in friendly banter, in the back of his mind he felt the first inklings of concern for her. Everything changed over time, that was an unavoidable part of life, but that didn't mean it wasn't hard to watch. Eddy figured, in that respect, he knew just how Mrs Crowe felt.

The one of them that had actually studied that day had fallen asleep within seconds of resting his hand on Mr Tree. When Grandma Daisy had come up to take away his dinner tray at 8.30 p.m., Eddy had been dead to the world. Even when she'd gone over to tuck the sheets up a bit higher over his shoulder, he hadn't so much as twitched.

She didn't move his right hand from his beloved tree though. There was a time when just the sight of that would have made her blood boil, but not now. Tonight all she did was smile. Not a huge joyful grin but a happy, contented smile like someone who has a journey ahead of them but has chosen to enjoy the ride instead of fretting about the destination. On the way out of the bedroom she'd paused and touched her own hand upon the branches bedded across the wall.

In the instant he woke up, Eddy didn't know what had jerked him out of his slumber. But then came the second beep of a car horn.

Continuing to lie absolutely still, he concentrated with his ears, waiting for the sounds he was certain would come.

In the end it was more than sound that betrayed her. He felt her moving across Mr Tree and slipping down the trunk, quiet but not silent. Quiet but noisy with intent.

A couple of minutes later Eddy heard the distinctive sound of a car cruising out of the neighbourhood. The sort of car a nineteen- or twenty-year-old boy could prove himself in.

Make sure you look after her, Ryan. She's the most special girl in the world.

44

RICH & FAMOUS

Reagan never got caught that night and Eddy didn't quite know how he felt about that. She'd taken a massive gamble but she was only going to see that as part of the rush. He had no doubt whatsoever she'd do it again. And again. At the same time, though, she was happy. Not exactly the sort of happy he wanted her to be but if this is what it took to bring her out of the down zone she'd been in since her dad had left, then he was prepared to take the bad with the good.

Mrs Crowe wouldn't though. If she found out, there'd be all hell to pay.

Skating the thin ice of her little secret, Reagan had even managed to escape the second week of her grounding. Mrs Crowe had obviously felt bad about the length of the punishment and by the following weekend Reagan was back in the real world. On one condition: that this Ryan boy comes and meets her. With a roll of her eyes, Reagan had agreed, and on

Sunday evening the guy in question was invited for dinner.

Eddy watched with muted interest as she pranced around her bedroom, painting herself up, asking him if the blue dress looked better than the black one and generally exuding a nervousness that was uncommon to her. Just for the record the black dress was better. In fact, the black dress was stunning, movie-star stunning. On that basis, Eddy almost told her to wear the blue dress ...but he couldn't do that, not to Reagan.

When the fancy car with the roaring engine pulled up out front, Reagan had run out of her room without so much as giving Eddy a parting wave. She was like a kid at Christmas. Eddy had darted over to the front window, feeling a sudden flush of embarrassment as this 'Ryan' caught his movement and, for a horrid moment, also caught his eye.

Ryan hesitated and looked unsure of himself for a second, then fumbled and dropped his car keys on the grass. Having picked them up, he shot Eddy one more quizzical glance before Reagan was out the door and taking his hand with the same effervescence she'd left her bedroom.

Drifting back into the dimness of his room, Eddy decided the best way to pass the time was to bury himself in the textbooks. He turned a lot of pages that night, but found that the next day he had to read them all over again.

By Wednesday afternoon an artificial normalcy had settled over proceedings. The actions were all the same but the foundation for them was something different altogether.

It was like a scene from a play where the actors knew their places but the plot seemed to have shifted to another purpose. Both Eddy and Reagan were at their window ledges, the familiar textbooks spread out in front of them, brows furrowed in concentration.

'This isn't maths,' complained Reagan. 'How can maths have letters in it?'

'It's al-algebra.'

'I don't care what they call it, it's just not maths. If "a" equals "one", just call it "one". How hard is that?'

'It's for the rest of the equation.'

'It's stupid is what it is. I mean, when am I going to need to use this stuff?'

'I d-don't know.'

'Exactly.'

'But y-you need to know it for the exam.'

If Reagan's patience was a frayed rope, then Eddy's comment seemed to have snapped the very last thread. She slammed her book closed and tossed it on to her bed with an explosion of energy that spoke of a decision made.

'I'm sick of it, Eddy. Exams, exams, exams. We have to live too, you know. Do you reckon they think about that when they make "a" equal "one"? "A" equals bullcrap as far as I'm concerned.'

'Then bullcrap also equals one.' Eddy thought the attempt at humour would help. It didn't, though.

'It's just not me,' reasoned Reagan. 'Some people

are made for this stuff and some aren't. I'm one of the aren'ts. All of this,' she said waving her arms at the books, 'is just a waste of my time. Ryan never passed his exams and he's earning all right money. Look at his car. I'm thinking that when my birthday comes around I'm gonna leave school, Eddy.'

'Oh. D-does your mum know about that?'

'Not yet.'

'What will you do?'

'I don't know. Maybe be a make-up artist or something along those lines.' Reagan's tone was defensive but her eyes dared him to challenge her.

'I thought you w-wanted to be a rich and famous movie star.'

'Maybe I still can be. Tell me where I need to know stupid maths to be a movie star?'

Eddy was getting very used to shrugging around Reagan, so he added one more to the pile.

'My point exactly. And even if it doesn't work out straight away, I'll find a job to fill in time.'

'Make-up stuff?'

'Whatever comes along. If it pays okay, then when I'm eighteen I can move in with Ryan.'

'Oh.'

45

WHAT MAKES GIRLS LIKE BOYS

'Hi, Eddy.'

'Hi, Mrs Elsdon.'

Mrs Elsdon shifted her weight over the walking stick and settled in on the footpath below.

'How's your study going?'

'It's okay. There's a lot of it, though. Sometimes I don't know how my head can hold it all in.'

'Life can be like that, Eddy,' responded old lady Elsdon with a raise of the eyebrows.

'Can I ask you a question?'

'Sure. That'll make a change from the norm.'

'What m-makes girls like boys?'

'Jeez, you don't start with the small ones, do you?'

'Sorry.'

'No, no. I was just having you on, Eddy,' chuckled Mrs Elsdon. 'It is a good one, though.'

Eddy suddenly wished he'd never asked the question at all. And even if Mrs Elsdon could answer the question, he had serious doubts he would understand it. It seemed to him that girls were such complicated creatures that even the handbook had to be gobbledegook to a boy like him. He should've just accepted his ignorance and avoided this awkward circumstance altogether. Mrs Elsdon wasn't put off, though, and after a moment to gather her thoughts, she looked back up at him and gave it a shot.

'Girls and boys are made a bit different, Eddy,' she said. 'Some would say too different and others would say not different enough. There's no rules on that front, except to say they're different. The way I see it though is it's how we were made to see the world. Girls are very mature, even when they're young. Boys, I think, tend to see the world as "today". Girls, on the other hand, tend to see it as both "yesterday" and "tomorrow".' Mrs Elsdon grimaced, not happy with her explanation thus far. 'What I mean by that is … You know your history, don't you, Eddy?'

'Yep. Some at least.'

'Back thousands of years ago, the men were the hunters and the women were the gatherers. When it came to hunting animals it's all about what happens in the moment that counts. One minute there'd be a mammoth wandering by and the next there wouldn't. You had to take things day by day. Us women though, we had to reckon with where the fruit and berries would be tomorrow and the days after that. That meant knowing where they'd been yesterday and the yesterdays before that and understanding how and when they grew for the future.'

Eddy wasn't getting this and it must have shown.

'Put it this way. When a girl looks at a boy and wonders whether he's someone she could like, she's thinking about yesterday and tomorrow. She may not know that, but she is. The yesterday is about her past experience with boys. The tomorrow is all about her security. The need to know that even if the rains don't come there'll be a place she can go to and be comforted. When it comes to boys, we're talking about somebody who can give her two sorts of things really. Those things you can see, feel and touch, like financial security, a house over her head, protection for herself and her children. And the other sort … That's the important stuff. Things like love. A good family. I guess when you look back at it, it's about wants and needs.

'What makes it so complicated I think…for boys, at least … is understanding what the girl is looking for most: yesterday or tomorrow.

'Gosh,' rounded off Mrs Elsdon, 'I'm not an expert, Eddy, and I know that sounds all over the place but it's my best shot.'

'Thanks, Mrs Elsdon,' responded Eddy honestly. 'I'm not sure I get it just yet b-but you've given me something to think about.'

'Well, don't think too hard, young man, because you've got a lot of other stuff to fit in there yet.' Mrs Elsdon tapped her head and then tapped her walking stick. 'Sorry, I'll have to make it a quick one today; looks like we've got rain on the way.'

'Okay, Mrs Elsdon. B-be careful.'

246

'I will. See you later.'

Eddy watched the old lady depart. Her left hip was getting worse by the day but she was never going to admit it. He didn't like seeing her struggle like this but he would miss her daily visits an awful lot.

'Yesterdays' and 'tomorrows'. She'd certainly given him some food for thought.

46

THE WRONG SORT OF PRESENT

'Hey! Eddy!'

'Yep?'

'I've got something for ya.'

Eddy stepped over to the side window, intrigued at this new development. Reagan hadn't been bluffing when it had come to the study. She was still playing the facade of the good student for her mother's sake but in reality she was either talking to Ryan on the new mobile phone he'd bought her or she was listening to music. The books, while laid out like they were getting used, were about as lonely as Eddy on a Friday and Saturday night.

'What is it?'

'Jam sandwiches?'

'And then you'll show me?'

'Deal.' Reagan trotted out of her room and Eddy grabbed his spot out on Mr Tree. Summer was really moving on now. The longest day had been and gone and it was a little sad to know that each new day was that bit shorter. It was like watching a good friend leave on a slow moving boat to somewhere you can never follow. It also made Eddy melancholy for another reason. Summers had always been the season of the jam sandwich committee. In the past, hardly a week went by without at least one gathering out between the houses. When Eddy thought about good times, those thoughts invariably came in strawberry flavour. This summer, though, had been a different story. This particular jam sandwich session was one of only two or three in the best part of as many months. And then even those ones hadn't been the same. She'd been preoccupied, like she was already thinking of other things and other places she needed to be. And just like Mrs Elsdon's hip, that was sad too.

Something was definitely up today, though. Reagan appeared to be in an extremely good mood, and while Eddy hated himself for second-guessing her, he was suspicious of its motive. That suspicion was further reinforced when she came bouncing back into her room and out the window. Handing him his quota of sandwiches (always two), she plonked herself down and tucked in before he could utter a word.

'So?' asked Eddy, unable to contain himself.

'So what?' responded Reagan through about three mouthfuls of bread.

'Wh-what have you got for me?'

'I said *after* the sandwiches, remember.' She gave him one of her cheeky grins, the sort he loved and hated.

Surrendering to her playful will, Eddy was just about to demolish his first sandwich in record time when she tossed something on to his lap. It almost went right between his legs too and down to the ground below but Eddy was just as quick and caught it before it could escape.

'Nithe cath,' said Reagan, mouth stuffed with the rest of her first sandwich.

Eddy looked at the small package in his hands. It fitted easily into the palm of his hand and it was gift-wrapped in dark green paper, just like a proper present.

'What is it?'

'Open it, silly, and find out.'

'It's not m-my birthday.'

'I know. It's just something to say thank you.'

This doesn't feel right.

'What for?'

'If you ask one more question, I'm gonna take it off you.'

Despite his internal misgivings, Eddy did as he was told and unwrapped the present. Beneath the fancy green paper was a small, hard box with a hinge on it.

'Go on,' encouraged Reagan. 'Open it.'

Slowly levering the lid open, Eddy sucked in his breath at the sight that greeted him. Shining back out at him was about the second prettiest thing he'd ever seen. It was a gold necklace and hanging from it, all etched with delicate engravings, was a cross.

'Do you like it?'

'R-Reagan, it's beautiful.'

'Yeah, it is, isn't it?' Reagan had a huge, satisfied smile on her face.

'Th-this must've cost lots of money.'

'You're worth it.'

Eddy desperately wanted to take the necklace out of its casing. It looked so striking in there and he was yearning so see what it felt like around his neck. But he couldn't. It was wrong. This whole thing was wrong.

'I...I can't take this Reagan.' Eddy closed the box and handed it over to her.

'What? Why?' Reagan looked from him to the box in his hand and back up at him again. She wasn't going to take it back, that much was obvious.

'H-how d-did you pay for this?'

'You're kidding me right?'

'I'm sorry. I j-just don't know where you'd get the m-money to pay for this sort of thing.'

Reagan's expression was in the process of transformation. The confusion remained but it was quickly being run down by something bigger, something angrier.

'What are you saying, Eddy? If you've got something to say, spit it out.'

Why is this happening? Why didn't you just go out with Ryan today so this never had to happen?

In an instant, Eddy felt all the confidence he'd been banking up over the past couple of years tumble down. He understood, at face value, what Reagan had done was sweet and that, under different circumstances, this would have been a day to

251

remember. But the circumstances weren't different; they were raw and unavoidable. Right now, if he could turn the world upside down and make this right, he would.

'Um, aaaah ... I j-just ... I think y-you n-need to take this b-back.'

Reagan's eyes now focused directly upon Eddy and he felt it like a knife. Then she snatched the box out of his hand in one swift motion, so that one moment it was there and the next it was gone.

'Reagan, p-please.'

'Don't "please" me. I know how it works.' Standing up so fast that her second sandwich went somersaulting to the grass below, Reagan grabbed hold of a handy branch and faced him with a look that was way too much like the old Grandma Daisy for his liking. 'You're just a little bit too good for the rest of us now, aren't you? Special little Eddy, studying for exams. What a hero.'

'Reagan ... I ...'

'Save it, Eddy. Save it for somebody who cares.' With that, Reagan had had enough. She turned away from him and made her way across to the window, everything about her expressing her uncapped emotions.

'S-stealing's wr-wrong—!'

Eddy had more to say but Reagan provided the full stop that cut his sentence short. She slammed the window closed so hard behind her that it was a minor miracle it didn't smash. It occurred to Eddy that this was the first time that window had ever been closed and he couldn't help but feel a part of him had been amputated in the process.

In the end, it was a day to remember, but for all the wrong reasons.

47

STRETCHED LIKE A RUBBER BAND

The next few weeks were a living hell for Eddy. He tried to drown himself in study but he could never quite hold his head under the water for long enough. Something she did across there would always have him catching his breath. It could be Ryan turning up outside and waving at Mrs Crowe while Reagan went charging past her and into his car. It could be seeing her shadow against the window blind, the one that was now always down. Whatever it was, there was always something, something that made her feel close yet a million miles away.

Once, as she'd been trekking off to school, she'd turned back and accidently caught his eye as he watched her from his front window. There'd been an acknowledgement in that fleeting glimpse, he could have sworn that. A sadness in her eyes that said, like him, she wished for things to be different.

Eddy chewed himself up inside. Why hadn't he

handled that differently? Why did he have to be so judgemental? She was only trying to be nice after all. But it didn't matter what he asked himself or how he wished he could replay time all over again, she'd ripped the chapter about Eddy Sullivan right out of the book of her life. And if there was one thing Eddy could count on as far as Reagan was concerned: she wasn't one to change her mind.

One day, a week or so after their parting of ways (okay, it was eight days to be exact), Grandma Daisy had obviously decided to offer what she could: an ear and a shoulder. It was around lunchtime. Eddy knew that because he'd heard the bell ring over at the school and was wondering what Reagan did for lunch these days. Did she just hang around or did Ryan come and pick her up and take her for a 'drag' in that souped-up vehicle of his. Somehow he thought it was the latter.

'How's things?' Grandma Daisy asked as she leaned over his shoulder.

'Fine thanks, Grandma Daisy.'

'Why don't you give those books a break and have a chat with me. Keep an old lady occupied.'

'Sure.'

'Do you want to come downstairs?' she asked, gesturing towards the door.

'Just up here's fine, if that's fine by you.'

'No problem. You know, Eddy, things aren't the same now. You don't have to spend all day up here.'

'I know, Grandma. I just feel comfortable up here, that's all. The world's a bit scary.'

Grandma Daisy found a spot on Eddy's bed and patted the space next to her, just like Reagan would pat his space on Mr Tree, thought Eddy, as he went over and sat beside her.

'What's on your mind, Eddy?'

'P-pardon?'

'Something's wrong and, if I'm not mistaken, it's got something to do with Reagan. Am I right?'

'I suppose.'

She paused, still a bit unpractised at these things. 'Do you want to talk about it?'

That was a good question. He did. He wanted to talk for hours and hours and hours about it, but at the same time he didn't. Talking might help him understand where it all went wrong but talking wouldn't change anything. Reagan would continue to hate him no matter what and, while what she did was wrong, it was all his fault.

'I d-don't know.'

'Well, I'll cut you a deal then. I'll talk about it and you join in, if you want to. Okay?'

'Okay.'

'Here's how I see things.' Grandma Daisy shifted so she could face Eddy a bit better before carrying on. 'You and Reagan have had a spat. A good one too, by the looks of it. She's angry and you're sad. That's the way it usually works. Now, I'm not here to be nosy, so I'm not going to ask the whys and whats, but I will say one thing. If ever I've seen two close friends, it's you two. The funny thing about being close is that when you do argue they tend to be doozies. You should've seen some of the howlers your grandpa Nevil and I had. I thought the roof was going to cave in. But you know what?'

'What?'

'We got through them all. Every one of them. It's good that you're feeling bad, and I bet she's feeling bad too.'

'Wh-why's it good to feel bad?'

'Because you're feeling something! If you weren't, then I'd be worried.'

'Why's that?'

'Because if you didn't it would mean that you'd both given up, that the friendship didn't mean anything and that it probably never did.'

'So,' echoed Eddy, 'if she's angry it means that she still likes me?'

'As strange as it sounds, Eddy, yes.'

'So one day, she and I might be friends again?'

'I think you're probably still friends. You've just got to let the rubber band relax though.'

'What?' Eddy's face must've looked a picture because Grandma Daisy laughed.

'Relationships are like rubber bands, in my opinion. When we're getting along well, they're under no pressure, but when we fight and argue, it's like they're all stretched, and that's when they can snap. What a lot of people don't seem to recognise is that a stretched rubber band is still a rubber band. If anything, it's showing exactly how strong it really is. Sometimes people just figure it's going to snap so they get out before it can sting them. But you see, Eddy, rubber bands are remarkable things, they can withstand more pressure than we give them credit for and then they'll go right back to where they started ... if you'll just give them that chance.'

'S-so right now Reagan and my rubber band is just stretched?'

'Yep, that's pretty much how I see it.'

'I hope you're right, Grandma Daisy.'

'Just give it time, Eddy, you'll see. Just give her a little time.'

So that's what Eddy did, he gave Reagan time. In reality he had little choice, but at least Grandma Daisy had given him a purpose. It didn't mean that the days without Reagan passed by like a breeze; they were hard, but he had hope.

As those long, tortured days without Reagan continued, a new and equally painful development erupted next door.

The sounds of fighting which had disappeared after Mr Crowe had run off to see the world had come back again. Only this time both voices were female, one older, one younger. It didn't happen every day but it was a good week when two or three days passed without it.

It hurt him to hear those angry sounds. On one level, it had to do with who was doing the arguing; on another, it had to do with the fact that there was arguing at all. There'd been too many years when he'd had to cower at the sound of fury and he didn't like the way it haunted him again. It was so intense sometimes that Eddy could actually feel it in the air around him.

While he couldn't actually hear the words being thrown around, especially now that Reagan's window was permanently closed, he could usually tell when it was over for the day. The Crowe arguments had a habit of rounding off with an almighty slam. In this case, there were two distinct versions. One was your plain old slam, and that meant Reagan had locked herself away in her bedroom, while the other was the slam followed by the squeal. The squeal being the rubber of Ryan's tyres burning the road outside. Eddy didn't quite know which one was the worse.

Watching Reagan screech off in that car made his heart ache. There was no use in denying it. The space in between their bedrooms had been *their* space, and seeing her silhouette behind that passenger door window only made him realise that Reagan had replaced that space with something new, something flash and something fast.

But on the flip side, knowing that she was stewing away in her bedroom, just a thin pane of glass away, was gut-wrenching. Just because she was angry at him, and just because he couldn't understand why she'd done what she'd done with the necklace, didn't mean he wasn't bursting to get through to her, to tell her that everything will be all right. That life, when it boiled down, was apparently all about rubber bands.

Instead he had to sit there and hold it all inside. That made him feel like a drinking glass. A glass can only hold so much water and right now he could feel it beginning to spill over the sides.

48

EDDY'S TURN

The examination dates were getting crazy close and that had Eddy worried. Exams were a complete unknown to him. He hadn't even been in a classroom before let alone been placed under the pressure-cooker atmosphere of an examination situation. So he was very pleased to learn that his exams would be held in the very familiar surroundings of his own bedroom. Mrs Stanton would be his observer and she'd sit in the room from start to finish.

The trouble was, it was just so hard to concentrate at the moment. Reagan was so, so close and yet so far away. Time and time again he'd read a paragraph and then at the end of it realise he had no idea what he'd just read. He needed her. She'd been his first real friend, but at the same time it was so much more than that. She'd been his umbilical cord to the big, wide world beyond his bedroom. She'd turned something that terrified him into something sane and magical.

She'd helped him find himself. That was the biggest thing. If Reagan Crowe had never happened, he'd still be that stupid boy, that Pissy Pants kid that everyone laughed at, and he loved her for that. He loved her so bad – bad enough to know how Mrs Elsdon felt without her Ben. It hurt in the day and it hurt in the night. Put simply, there was no escape.

This particular Friday night had been like any other these past couple of months. Reagan hadn't walked home, she'd run. That way she had more time to get ready for Ryan before he cruised by to pick her up when he finished work. Eddy knew that car from about four blocks away now. The rumbling engine reminded him of a modern-day dragon, coming to whisk his fair maiden away to a far-off place where even the bravest knights struggled to find her. But worse than that, this particular fair maiden actually wanted to go. She'd tried to give her knight a gift and he'd turned his back on her, he'd spurned her and now she was gone.

When Reagan had bounced out her front door and into Ryan's car, Eddy hadn't even tried to hide in the shadows of his room. It was a wasted effort. It'd been weeks since she'd checked to see if he was there. She didn't need to prove anything now, she was doing this for herself. The car had pulled away with its belting roar and Reagan was once again swallowed by the dragon.

Her curfew was 11 p.m. so, having some time up his sleeve and with nothing else left to do, Eddy hit the books. Grandma Daisy had come up at one point and tried to talk him into coming down and watching some TV with her. She'd do documentaries if that's what he wanted, but in the end he'd declined her kind offer. With a couple of weeks to go to the exams, he had to squeeze in every piece of knowledge he could. It sounded like a good excuse anyway. At best, he had half an eye on the science textbook, the rest of him was beyond the window, imagining her laughter, her sparkling eyes, that cheeky smile.

Why didn't I just take that necklace and be done with it!

It was about 10.45 p.m. when Eddy heard the familiar rumble weave through the neighbourhood. The closer it got the meaner it sounded until it came spitting and spurting right up in front of his place. Not Reagan's house; his.

The engine cut out and then nothing. Eddy kept out of clear sight this time, it was more instinct than anything else; besides, being 'nosy' was rude. That didn't prevent him from keeping a watchful eye on that car though. Parking one's car a few extra yards down the street by itself was no big deal, but there was something about it, something contrived that he didn't like.

It was so automatic that Eddy wasn't even conscious of the fact he'd done it, but he reached across with his left arm and placed his hand on Mr Tree's most adventurous of twigs. The tree had extended that far now, to the point where he could reach out and touch it while he was still standing by the front window. That meant a fair two-thirds of the room was adorned. All that was left was the space around the front window and the return journey, halfway along a wall, back to the side window.

For now, though, he had other things on his mind.

Red. Fast heartbeats. Anticipation.

Neither driver nor passenger door had so much as budged.

Another four or five minutes passed by, and still nothing. Nothing except the fact those tinted windows were beginning to steam up.

He's kissing her!

Eddy's mind clamoured. It didn't make sense. His whole body felt hot and itched with a clinging desperation to do something. Exactly what, he had no idea. He felt dizzy, like he was walking on a tightrope. As he desperately clung to Mr Tree's hand, his senses told him something was amiss, that Reagan was walking further and further away from her comfort zone. But what could he possibly do about it.

Just get out then, Reagan. Just get out!

The car doors stayed exactly where they were: locked tight.

The blood in Eddy's veins seemed to be conducting electricity and it was getting to the stage where he could no longer stand still. The energy was buzzing inside like the hum of megavolts travelling through high-tension wires. Eddy didn't hear Ryan's voice in his ears, he heard it instead in his head and he didn't like the tone one bit. Eddy couldn't think; he didn't understand.

The flight down the stairs was a blur, lost in the cascade of fears, thoughts and emotions that whirl-pooled around inside him. He pulled the front door open so fast that for once it didn't have time to squeak, instead sounding out a short, high-pitched shrill.

Crossing the front lawn in record time, Eddy didn't go for the passenger door. He catapulted around the front of the car and, without a second thought for the consequences, ripped open the driver's door with the strength that only blind fury can afford.

'Get away from me!' It wasn't in his head that time. No. This time he heard voices for real.

There, lying heavily on top of his precious Reagan, was the man in question. Reagan seemed so tiny, so helpless beneath him, and when the door flung open hard enough to dent the front panel, she peered out at Eddy with an alarming combination of surprise and fear. Her face was patchy with the heat inside the car and her obvious struggles to free herself. Her eyes carried only one very clear, very panicked message ... *Get me out of here.*

'Leave her alone!' The words came from a reservoir Eddy didn't know he had and when Ryan turned to confront whoever had the audacity to ruin his fun, he had a shock waiting for him. Before he could so much as register this strange, mental case of a kid, Eddy had his hands wrapped around the waistband of Ryan's jeans and was yanking him out of the car with undeniable force. 'I ... said ... leave ... her ... alone!' Each word seemed to add another gear and by the last one Eddy had Ryan completely out of the car.

'Hey,' yelled Ryan, as Eddy flung him aside. 'What the hell?'

Eddy didn't have time for him right now, his entire focus was on Reagan. Leaning back in the driver's door he found her quickly pulling herself together. Ryan had pretty much had her top off, but it was tugged and stretched.

'Here,' he said, reaching in toward her. 'T-take my hand.'

Instead of taking his offer though, she just stared wide-eyed and disbelieving at him. It was all too much for her and the shock of it all had her frozen to the spot.

'Reagan ...' Before Eddy could get the rest of the sentence out, he was grabbed from behind by the scruff of his collar and tossed to the unforgiving asphalt of the street. He'd be nursing a couple of nasty grazes by tomorrow morning but in the heat of the moment he didn't feel a thing.

'Look what you've done to my car, you little shit!' Ryan was standing above him, looking about ten feet tall and ready to rip the guts out of the very next thing that moved.

Eddy scrambled backwards, knowing that if he stayed within Ryan's range he was bound to wear something much worse than a scrape or two. For a second, Eddy was certain he was a goner. Looking down, he realised he'd really put a good dent in the side of the car. A car that Eddy just knew Ryan liked way more than Reagan. One, two, three steps ... Yep, Ryan was coming his way. Eddy tried to get to his feet and slipped.

Then Ryan stopped.

Get out of the car, Reagan. Run!

Eddy could see the guy was measuring his options. The stupid boy or the girl. Ryan turned his back on Eddy and strode back to the car.

Eddy didn't remember much of the next few minutes and that was probably a good thing. To have memories of those things that reduce you can be a haunting experience. He didn't remember getting to his feet. He didn't remember moving so fast that when Grandma Daisy first looked out of the front door she thought he was flying. He certainly didn't recall that moment he wrenched Ryan once more back from that rabid red car, and all memory was lost of that punch. It was tomorrow's punch on yesterday's man and it connected like a brick. In an otherwise peaceful street, the whack echoed all the way to the empty lot at the end of the cul-de-sac and back. Ryan hadn't seen it coming. His knees buckled from under him and he fell where he stood.

'Eddy, what are you doing!' If that had been Grandma Daisy or even Mrs Crowe he would've understood, but it was Reagan. She'd managed to get out of the passenger side in the end, that expression of shock still parked across her face. Things seemed to be going from the sublime to the ridiculous. Rounding the bonnet, she saw Ryan there on the road, slowly regaining consciousness and rubbing the side of his aching head. But she would go no closer, and as far as Eddy was concerned that was a good thing.

'Go inside, Reagan,' instructed Eddy, but still she just stared at him, locked in time and space. 'This man is not a good man and he hurts you. Go inside.'

Even then it was possible she wasn't going to move. That was bound to make life really awkward under the circumstances. Ryan was finding his bearings fast and he wasn't the sort to fall for the same trick twice.

'Reagan, is that you? What's going on?' It was Mrs Crowe. She was making her way across her front lawn, all wrapped up in a dressing gown.

'He – he was hurting her!' shouted Eddy. It suddenly occurred to him that he had no idea what he was doing. Standing in the middle of the street, Eddy felt confusion wash over him. *Had* Ryan been hurting her? Eddy had been acting on an overwhelming impulse but realised now that maybe this was just another thing that he didn't understand. Affording Eddy just one more worn and weary glance, Reagan raced into her mother's arms.

That was just fine by Eddy, she was safe there. Filled with a sinking feeling that she'd turned away from him forever, Eddy stood, dazed, in the middle of the road.

Ryan was sitting up now, trying hard to shake the reality of the situation back into his fuzzy head.

'I think y-you should get in your car and never, ever come back.'

'Piss off, retard.'

'Eddy, is everything okay?' Grandma Daisy was now on the front lawn, phone in one hand and, to Eddy's surprise, a cricket bat in the other.

'Yes, Grandma Daisy,' he responded in quick order. No need to have her come over here right now. 'We're just f-finishing up...aren't we?'

Ryan was gauging Eddy real close. But then Eddy saw Ryan surrender even before Ryan knew it himself. It was all in the body language. Those taut, sinewy muscles relaxed and his eyes dropped away.

Eddy took a step backwards. Not a retreat, no, definitely not a retreat. When Ryan finally got to his feet he was as wobbly as Mr Crowe used to get on a Sunday afternoon and it was plain to see he had no fight left in him.

Staggering over to his car, he collapsed into the driver's seat. It wouldn't close all the way and for a split-second Eddy felt sorry for him.

With a spit and a roar, the engine burst into life and Eddy glanced through a plume of oily, blue exhaust to see Reagan still in the warm, inviting arms of her mother. She wasn't going to watch Ryan leave; in her mind he was gone already.

Then, with the scream of rubber and a fishtail or two, that flash red car said goodbye to Willow Avenue. Eddy watched it swing wide around the corner and for a little while just listened to the timbre of the motor as it faded into the distance.

'Are you all right, Eddy?' Grandma Daisy was on the road beside him now, her hand supportively on his shoulder.

'Grandma,' he said, looking her in the eye. 'I think I almost wet my pants.'

49

MRS CROWE ANSWERS

Eddy waved out to the McKenzie family as they drove past on their way to church. He, however, was on a different mission.

Since he'd sent Ryan packing the night before, he'd been watching and waiting for some sort of reaction from Reagan. It had all been in vain, though, because once that car had ploughed down the street and out of her life, she'd turned tail too and run inside. The last he'd seen of her was her forlorn and fallen shoulders as she disappeared through her front door, followed closely behind by her mother.

If the necklace stalemate these past months had been hard, the few hours since last night had been torturous. Eddy had lain awake all night long, wondering if she was all right and what was going through her mind. It frustrated him immensely, that he couldn't reach for her. Had he done the right thing? He thought so, but as the dawn had peeked into the new day, he began to question himself. He was certain Ryan had hurt her, and it wasn't much of a stretch of the imagination to believe he hadn't finished either. And if he could do it once, he'd do it again.

He'd debriefed Grandma Daisy with the full story once they'd got back inside and she seemed to think he'd been somewhere between brave and foolish. She leaned on the side of brave for Eddy's sake, but that probably had a lot to do with the fact he wasn't the one wearing a tender head today. If Ryan had been a bit more prepared … well, it could have been a very different tale to tell.

She'd come up again to see him first thing this morning. Just to check in and make sure he was still okay. Other than a couple of grazes in need of a good soak and tired, puffy eyes, for the most part he was. Physically anyway. She hadn't accepted his 'yes' at face value and had come over and sat down at the foot of his bed. Looking across at Reagan's barricaded window, she'd asked him if he'd heard from her. That answer was easy. Then she'd asked him whether he intended to do anything about that. That answer was hard.

'What can it hurt?' she'd told him. 'All she can do is say "go away"? and what have you lost? Nothing, as far as I can see.' That idea sounded good and bad, all at the same time. 'Go on,' she'd said. 'Even if it's just for your own sake.'

In the end it wasn't exactly a hard argument for her to win. For weeks now, Eddy had been wanting to go over there, to say 'Here I am, I'm sorry and I want us to be friends', but he'd been too uncertain about the rights and wrongs. Reagan had him all nervy and, despite all the confidence Mr Tree had given him, he fell flat when it came to the ins and outs of Reagan Crowe.

After watching the McKenzies' white car cruise slowly over the black arcs of rubber left behind by Ryan's tyres, Eddy sucked in a deep breath and strode up to the Crowe's front door.

He gave it two quick knocks, each time feeling the sound of his knuckles against the wood like an electric charge throughout his whole body.

Will she slam the door in my face? I knew I shouldn't have come.

When the door swung inwards, Eddy was a knife's edge away from running, but it wasn't Reagan that greeted him, it was Mrs Crowe. She too looked tired and a bit worse for wear but at least she was dressed.

'Hi, Eddy.' It wasn't necessarily a happy greeting but it wasn't quite sad either. It represented what they'd both been through the night before.

'H-hi, Mrs Crowe. C-can I please see Reagan?'

Eddy knew the answer before she said it. It was written in her eyes.

'I'm sorry, Eddy, but Reagan's not up to seeing anyone at the moment.'

'Oh. Is she all right?'

'She will be. She's very upset right now and she's got a good knock on the side of her face too, thanks to that horrid boy.'

'Oh…Do you think she'll be ready to see me some-
time soon? I – I just want t-to say I'm sorry.'

A tender smile appeared on Mrs Crowe's face as
she regarded the special boy on her doorstep. She'd
not been blind these last five years or so. Reagan and
Eddy had been the best of buddies up until recently
and she saw in him the desperation of a boy wanting
so badly to put things back together again. But she
wasn't her daughter.

'Are you thirsty, Eddy?'

It seemed a strange question under the circumstance and Eddy sensed it was more than it appeared
to be.

'Yes.'

'Sit down there on the step then and I'll be out in a
minute with a glass of orange juice.'

Mrs Crowe disappeared inside and Eddy did as he
was told, finding that the step was already gathering
the warmth of an early autumn sun. Reagan's mum
was back in no time, a glass in each hand. Handing
Eddy his, she planted herself down beside him.

'Reagan's not quite ready to say it, so I'll say it for
her. Thank you, Eddy. I know you two aren't getting
on too well at the moment.' Eddy looked away. Did
she know about the necklace? Was she a little bit angry
at him too? 'Reagan's had to grow up a lot faster than
I'd hoped,' continued Mrs Crowe, with or without
eye contact. 'She's struggling to come to terms with a
whole bunch of things, not the least her father leaving
her. There haven't been too many constants in her life,
when you come to think about it. Me and you. That's

about it.' She paused for a moment, considering where to go next. 'She will get over this, Eddy. I can't promise you how long it'll take but I do know one thing. It has a lot to do with you.' Eddy looked back up at her, eyebrows raised. 'She's done some dumb things – we all do – but you've always been there. What I'm thinking is that it's not going to be too long before she recognises that. She needs you. She needs you because you ground her. You help her to make things make sense. I know that probably doesn't make sense but trust me, from a mother's perspective, it means a heck of a lot.

'Take that Ryan boy. I never liked him. Not from the first time Reagan told me about him. But as a mother, sometimes you have to let your kids make mistakes. It's really hard to sit back and watch but unless they learn the lessons for themselves, they won't learn them at all. That's what I like about you, Eddy. Whenever she's with you I can be certain of one thing: she isn't making a mistake.

'So my advice is to just give her a bit more time, okay? You're too special for her to make this grudge last a lifetime.'

'Okay, Mrs C-Crowe.'

It was reassuring to hear what Mrs Crowe had to say. Maybe there really was light at the end of the tunnel. But even if she was spot on, it still came down to more time when every second was driving him crazy.

'W-will you tell her I came t-to say hello?'

'I will, Eddy. Don't you worry about that.'

50

THE BIG DAY

It had been close on two weeks since his front step chat with Mrs Crowe and still Eddy hadn't had so much as an acknowledgement from Reagan. If it weren't for the other people around him registering his existence, he might well have felt he'd fallen off the face of the planet. Her bedroom window remained closed and that blind of hers was forever down. The distance across Mr Tree had gone from a handful of yards to light years and there seemed to be no possible means with which to cross it.

So Eddy had taken solace in study, burning not just both ends of the candle but right through a few pencils as well. Grandma Daisy was constantly harping for him to take more breaks but he either faked a break or refused altogether. If he filled his head with a million facts and figures, maybe there wouldn't be any room left with which to pine for Reagan. The trouble was, the mind is an awfully big thing. Awfully big indeed.

The days had been long and gruelling, punctuated by the heart-pounding sight of Reagan's travels to school and back. He wondered how her own study was going and whether her patience for algebra had improved at all. He doubted it. If Reagan didn't like something, it tended to stay unliked – not exactly a confidence-boosting thought.

Slowly but surely, Monday gave way to Friday and then it did it all over again. And this coming Friday … well, it was the big day of course. The beginning of exams. All of that learning, all of those hours were about to be put to the test and Eddy's greatest fear was that all those things floating around in his head would suddenly find some other place to be. Like they used to. Back when he was the stupid boy. It was going to be tough all right.

The one thing he needed was to be refreshed and motivated for Friday morning. That would set the foundation for everything else. So on Thursday night he'd made himself put down the pencil for the last time and had actually gone downstairs for dinner with Grandma Daisy. She'd added custard and ice cream to the back end of it too. For energy, she'd told him. You can't beat a dose of sugar and fat when a challenge came knocking.

The other thing he'd done was go to bed early. Early to bed, early to rise, makes a man healthy, wealthy and wise. In Eddy's case, though, it failed miserably. Somewhere in the early morning hours of exam day, with Mr Tree under his right palm and the moonlight spilling into the room, Eddy had made a decision, a big, exciting one. Whether Reagan was ready to hear from him or not, he was going to climb across the tree tomorrow morning, knock on her window and wish her all the best for her exams. What could it hurt? Just like Grandma Daisy had said.

In the end, though, it was all too much to hope for.

When Eddy finally entered exam day, it was most definitely not in the manner he would have preferred. Straight away he knew he'd stuffed up. The sunlight was already beaming halfway across the floor and at this time of the year that only meant one thing: he had slept in. Not just for his exams but maybe also for his plan with Reagan.

Stupid boy! I can't believe this.

Ripping his sheets back, Eddy continued to scold himself. Of any day in his entire life, this was the one not to sleep in. Mental note: he needed an alarm clock.

'Eddy, are you up?' Grandma Daisy was at the door. She never just barged in any more.

'I am now.'

'You'd best hurry if you want a shower. Mrs Stanton will be here in twenty minutes.'

'I'm coming right now!' Snatching the towel Grandma Daisy had laid on his desk the previous night, he scampered down the hallway and into the waiting shower.

Twenty minutes can seem an age and twenty minutes can disappear without a trace. For Eddy it was the latter. Mrs Stanton's imminent arrival hounded him all the way through the shortest shower he could manage and the breakfast that Grandma

Daisy wasn't going to see him go without. She could still be a very stubborn lady when she wanted to be.

Eddy was only just about to head back upstairs for a panic cram when the knock came at the door. If he hadn't taken the time to swallow right then, his heart may very well have jumped right out of his throat.

Here we go; no escape now.

Sure enough, when he opened the door, there was Mrs Stanton, spick and span, straight as an arrow and just aching to put her student through his paces.

'Morning, Eddy.'

'M-morning, Mrs Stanton.'

'So are you ready?'

'No.' And Eddy didn't think he was lying either. He was beginning to wonder how the heck he ever got talked into this.

'I'm sure you'll be just fine.'

'I h-hope so.'

After giving Eddy and Grandma Daisy the run down (for about the sixth time), it was time to head upstairs and make sure the room was foolproof and fair. All textbooks and other writing material not specifically related to the exam had to be taken right out of the room. With other home students, she said, even the posters had to come off the walls, but in Eddy's case that was a moot point. His walls were fairly bustling with that 'most amazing' of trees.

Finally the scene was set.

Mrs Stanton was checking her watch, just about to declare the exam 'commenced' when Eddy made a sudden and painful realisation.

Reagan. Oh no!

It was too late now. It had to be. School had already started and she would be sitting her exam right now. But he couldn't help himself. Springing out of his chair he raced over to the side window.

'Eddy,' exclaimed Mrs Stanton. 'What are you doing?'

'I j-just gotta open the w-window a bit.' It was a bold-faced lie, the window was always open, but it was worth it. If there was a billionth of a trillionth per cent chance he could still catch her, then he'd take it in a heartbeat. But Reagan wasn't there. The very next best thing in the world was, though.

There, taped to the window, was a blank page torn out of an exercise book. And written in black marker pen, nice and big so he didn't have to get out there to read it. It was her handwriting all right. He'd recognise that anywhere and he also reckoned they were the most wonderful three words he had ever read.

GOOD LUCK, EDDY.

51

AN EVEN BIGGER DAY

The very minute Eddy laid his pencil down at the end of the last of his five exams, the world folded back in on him. He hadn't realised how much he'd closed it out until the pressure released. The sky was brighter again, the clouds puffier. The faint breeze which tickled through the open window was refreshing and carried the scent of nature, instead of just being that pesky draught that would annoy textbook pages. Yep, he mused, it was funny how the world could be the same place and yet so different. It all came down to perspective.

The exams had been tough. Some tougher than others. And through four of the five of them he imagined Reagan going through exactly the same thing with exactly the same questions.

Right throughout that fretful week that beautiful sign had remained up on her window. For Eddy it was confirmation she'd been thinking about him and some of them at least had been good thoughts. Why else would she wish him good luck? Even the fact her blind was still down and she never once looked back when she left for school in the morning couldn't take away that good omen. It was starting to look as though Mrs Crowe had been right. Time and space were beginning to work their magic.

He would wait. He would wait forever if he had to. But he didn't have to. For Eddy, though he didn't know it at the time, it was one more sleep till Reagan.

It was just another Saturday the way Eddy saw it. Well, not quite. It was the first day in what seemed like forever that he didn't have to have his nose stuck in one book or another. His time belonged to him again and he didn't really know what to do with it. The exam results wouldn't be in for weeks yet, which was pretty unfair, and so he had to resign himself to putting such things out of his head. That was easier said than done.

He was sitting there, staring out the front window and noticing how the rubber streaks from Ryan's inauspicious escape were already fading to barely an etch, when there was a soft tap on the other window.

No, it couldn't be. It had to be one of Mr Tree's branches playing games with him.

And then it came again. *Tap, tap.*

Eddy got down off the ledge, wishing, hoping, but at the same time preparing himself for it to be nothing. One step across the carpet ... nothing – just more of Mr Tree and the wall beyond Reagan's window. Two steps ... same stuff. Three steps ... and the world was wonderful again. Magnificent, stupendous, fabulous.

'Hi, stranger,' said Reagan, standing out there on the tree, looking back at him. It was obvious she was as uncertain about this as he was.

'Hi b-back.' Eddy didn't know what to say. Why didn't they have an exam for this sort of thing?

'Watcha doin'?'

'I was waiting f-for you to knock on the d-damn window!'

She smiled. How fantastic was that! She was actually here at the window and she was actually smiling.

'Jam sandwiches?'

'I thought y-you'd never ask.'

52

THE GRAND TOUR

'Hey, Eddy?'

'What?'

'I've got an idea.'

'Yeah?'

'Let's give Mr Tree a break and go for a walk.'

'Eh?'

'A walk, you know … with the legs.' Reagan held her hand up and made a walking motion with her fingers.

'I know what a walk is.'

'Well, you had me fooled.'

A walk. That was something new. Eddy didn't think they'd ever been for a walk before. It sounded all right, he supposed.

'Okay, smarty pants, a w-walk it is.'

'Meet you outside in two minutes.' And that was it, she was gone. No further explanation, no wheres or whys, nothing.

Something's up.

Slapping on a pair of shoes (one's that fit just perfect, like they always did these days), he raced downstairs, calling out to Grandma Daisy on the way out the door.

'I'm off for a walk, Grandma Daisy, back soon.'

'Okay,' she replied from another room somewhere. 'Take your time. It's nice to see the sun out for once.'

True to her word, Reagan was out on her lawn waiting for him. First again, of course: she always had to be first.

She'd lost some weight in the last few months. Eddy didn't want to measure it in this way, but it had been since that night with Ryan really. Standing out here in her track bottoms and sweatshirt top it stood out all the more. But she seemed to be happy enough. That was what really mattered, especially after the ordeal of the last couple of years. Was she the girl she'd been at thirteen years old? No, but then again, Eddy reminded himself, he was a very different person now too. It was called 'growing up'.

'Where are we going?'

'All the way and back again.' She smiled mischievously at him and that only reinforced the big 'what's up' going off in his head.

'Did you have a bowl of weird f-for breakfast this morning?'

'Stop complaining and follow me.' Doing a 180 degree turn, Reagan started off and Eddy had to jog to catch up with her as she headed along the footpath in the direction of the dead end of the cul-de-sac.

'Well?' he enquired as he fell in beside her.

'Well, what?' She knew damn well 'what?' and while she didn't flash another one of her cheeky grins it was pushing up from within like the bubbles in a soft drink.

'Where are we going?'

'You'll find out.'

As odd as it was, Eddy had never been down this end of the street before. Sure, he'd left the house a few times now, but that had always meant going off in the other direction. The only thing down this way was more houses and the empty lot. Despite that, it turned out to be a pleasant surprise.

There, across the road, was the McKenzie place. They had twin boys who were just on two years old now and, from what Eddy had seen, they were a right handful. Then there was the Willis household. Their house stood out because they'd seen fit to paint it yellow. It reminded Eddy of the sun poking out between drab clouds of whites and greys. The lawn had recently been replanted and hadn't taken too well; something which, if you judged it by how often Mr Willis was out there, annoyed him immensely.

The Daly house had a birdbath out front and it was almost constantly a flurry of fussy feathers ... and the odd opportunist cat. For the most part, the birds came out the better of the two. Now that he was out here, it occurred to Eddy that maybe all those birds right next door had something to do with all the Willises' lawn seed going missing.

Two doors further down was Mrs Elsdon's. Always so nice and tidy. She couldn't do it herself these days of course, so she was paying one of the local kids a few pounds to mow the lawn and weed the garden every week. They were never going to leave her a note under the green stone out the back but at least she could satisfy herself that Ben would see the yard all tidy from wherever it was he was watching her. And he was watching. She was certain of that now.

Eddy marched side by side with Reagan right up to where the empty lot stood out like a broken tooth. And it was there that he discovered something he hadn't been aware of before. Right next to the fence on the other side of the lot from Heather Cooper's place, ran a well-worn path leading through a copse of willow trees and on to the next street over. He hadn't been aware of it because, being down the end on his side of the street, it was blocked from his view.

This was suddenly getting a bit more exciting.

Winding in and out of the weeping willows, they eventually came back out into the open and, for the very first time, Eddy got to see the school responsible for all those daily bells.

So this is the home of all that fun and laughter. This is where all those kids were going every day.

'Follow me this way,' instructed Reagan as she broke into a jog, crossing the street and racing through the front gate. After checking left, then right, then left again, Eddy followed suit.

He caught up with her in a playground next to one of the classrooms. She was already sitting in a swing like she owned the place and had been waiting years for him to arrive. Eddy timidly grabbed the swing next to her. He'd never ridden one of these contraptions before and it hardly seemed like enough to hold him up let alone fly back and forth on. Lowering himself gently into the strip of rubber that passed for a seat, he watched as Reagan effortlessly manipulated her weight so that she started moving by him like a pendulum.

'Come on,' she said, poking her tongue out at him.

'I'll f-fall off.'

'No, you won't.'

He did. Climbing to his feet, he could see that his giggling accomplice expected him to have another go. Under her instruction, he swung his legs out, then tucked them back in until, low and behold, he started making headway. Nowhere near as much as Reagan of course. Not on your life. But enough so the experience was a fair balance between fear and fun. In fact, after feeling a bit more certain he wasn't about to face-plant, he discovered himself smiling and actually enjoying the feel of the breeze rustling through his hair.

After a few minutes of really letting loose, Reagan pulled in the reins, letting the swing settle back to stillness and, feeling that she was wanting to say something, Eddy did the same quite easily, as he hadn't got far off the ground.

'Eddy?' she said in a thoughtful tone.

'Yep.'

'What do you think we're gonna be when we grow up?'

'God, Reagan. I think you're pretty grown up now.' Eddy could tell by her reaction his answer had meant more to her than he'd intended. In his eyes, she *was* grown up. She certainly looked like a woman, even when you took into account the baggy tracksuit, so her response was strange to him.

'Remember when I used to say I was going to be a movie star?'

'Yep. Y-you said that lots.'

'It's not going to happen, is it?' Her eyes had left the frivolity of the swing behind and now she was looking at him, almost begging for an answer that made sense.

'I think you c-can be anything you want to be, Reagan.'

'You sound like my mum.'

'Sorry.'

Then came one of those friendly moments of silence, where each of them took a trip within, just to see where it would lead them. Finally it was Reagan who broke the deadlock, and Eddy wouldn't have had it any other way.

'I'm a bit scared, Eddy.'

'Why?' That was about the last thing he'd expected to hear her say.

'It's hard to explain.' Scuffing her foot across the concrete, Reagan sent a stone skipping from one end of the playground to the other. 'It's like all my dreams are suddenly out of reach. I'm not even seventeen yet and I feel as if my life's already laid out for me. It's not fair. I watch all these people get up and go off every day to do something they hate. They go because they have to. The bills, the mortgage, the family. It's like they're dead already. They're zombies, just walking around until somebody or something does them the favour of killing them properly.' This time, choosing to pick up a stone instead, she tossed it so it clanked all the way down the slide, just like her mood. 'I don't want to be like that, Eddy. It'll drive me crazy. Look what it did to my dad. How do I do it, Eddy? How do I not be my dad?'

The expression on Reagan's face was of utter desperation. This was a tough one and she'd been chewing on it for some time by the looks of it.

'I think it's going to be okay, Reagan. It's s-simple. People have started to live *on* life instead of *in* life.'

'You've lost me,' said Reagan, trying hard to understand.

'Okay ...' Eddy looked around, spotted something that would help him illustrate the point and left Reagan in her swing as he wandered a few yards over to a nearby shrub. Coming back to take his seat on the swing next to her again, she noticed he had his hands cupped out in front of him. 'Have a look at this,' he said as he gently opened his palms. Sitting in the little bowl made by his joined hands was a butterfly. With broad wings full of gold, black and yellow, it appeared surprisingly content to be handled, stretching and arching itself but not once trying to escape.

'It's pretty, but what's that got to do with what you were saying?'

'It's a butterfly! I see these ones this time every year and found a picture in one of my science books.' Eddy walked the swing over a bit closer to Reagan's. 'Have a closer look.'

Reagan leaned in, getting as close as she dared without wanting to spook the delicate creature. 'What am I looking for exactly?'

'The w-wings. Look really, really closely. S-see the patterns? Not just the colours but how every little b-bit of the wing is made perfect to fit alongside the piece beside it. Those tiny, tiny segments all come together to make him fly. And disguise himself. And find a mate. Here,' he said, moving his hands around slowly so that Reagan could get a view from a different angle. 'And see the silvery sheen? That p-protects them from g-getting waterlogged. The little bits all make a whole.'

'*Quite* amazing, Sir Attenborough!' smirked Reagan. 'I get it, though. I mean, they're pretty when you see them on the street, but I've never got up close like this to one before. It's like each colour knows exactly where it should be. There must be hundreds of those little segments on each wing. And the colour on each one is so…stunning.'

Eddy's smiled broadened.

'That's right,' he agreed. 'They've been perfectly created. They are completely perfect and yet we walk by them every d-day without noticing them.'

'Mmm,' Reagan murmured, still confused but waiting for Eddy to finish.

'*You're* perfect, Reagan. People don't notice the beauty around them because, l-like I said, they're living *on* life. They're looking at the big things when it's always b-been about the thousands of little things.'

Eddy raised his hands and the both of them watched as the gold, black and yellow wings took to the air, no worse for the experience.

'I've read that people say "don't sweat the small stuff", but I used to live inside my bedroom so all you have is the small stuff,' continued Eddy. 'I say sweat the small stuff, the really t-teeny, tiny stuff because those are the things that really make up a life. Like JAM!'

'Jam really *did* change your life,' chuckled Reagan.

Reagan met his gaze for a minute and then looked down at her palm, the way the lines carved across her hands, the way her fingers bent and stretched. Then she lifted her head again.

'I've never thanked you about Ryan. I'm so sorry, Eddy.'

Eddy shook his head and took her hand in his. 'But you did.'

'When?'

'Every time you smile.'

53

NOT IN A MILLION YEARS

The walk back from the school playground was much slower. Eddy watched from the corner of his eye as Reagan seemed focused on everything around them, especially the willow trees. It was a good thing to see.

Greens are wonderful colours ... yes, they are indeed.

They were about opposite the McKenzies' place when Reagan checked her watch and suddenly jerked into action.

'Oh crap, Eddy, is that the time? We'd better get back.'

'Are y-you going out somewhere?'

'Yeah. Places to be, you know me.'

The pace quickened and within a couple of minutes they were coming by Reagan's place.

'Reagan ...'

'Sorry, bud. I have to love you and leave you,' she said, cutting him off. 'Mum and I've got something special on. See ya.' And with that said, she left Eddy in the dust, or, more to the point, on the front lawn.

Shrugging his shoulders, Eddy watched the house swallow her and then, figuring he couldn't stand out here forever, he headed the few yards to his own place.

'I'm home, Grandma Daisy,' he yelled as he stepped through the door.

'I'm upstairs, Eddy. Come on up.'

Climbing the creaky stairs and striding the short hallway, Eddy noticed his bedroom door was all but closed.

Pushing the door in, Eddy could never have anticipated the sight that greeted him. There, standing around Grandma Daisy's jigsaw puzzle table so they could all see his stunned reaction, appeared to be half the entire neighbourhood. There was Grandma Daisy herself of course, holding a cake knife at the ready for the massive chocolate gateau she'd baked the previous day, the same one that sat upon the little table right now. Then there was Mrs Elsdon, leaning on her walking stick and smiling like a lady who's been waiting for this for some time. Next came Mrs Stanton, Mrs Crowe and, last but not least, still climbing in through the window, his walking partner. This was, without doubt, the most people Eddy had ever seen in his room. It was positively crowded in here.

If they were seeking to surprise him, they succeeded with flying colours. Not even Mr Tree had betrayed them and that was saying something. For a heart stopping moment, all Eddy could do was stand rooted to the spot, mouth open, head spinning.

'Wh-what's going on?'

'Will you do the honours, Mrs Stanton?' said Grandma Daisy, looking across at the lady in question.

'I'd be happy to.' Stepping out from the captivated audience and up to a shell-shocked Eddy, she clasped a brown envelope in her hands. 'Eddy,' she said with crystal sincerity, 'it has been an absolute pleasure having you under my wing. I can honestly say that I've learned as much from the experience as you have, and that's saying something.

'When I rang your grandma to tell her your exam results had come in we both agreed to arrange something a little special. So here we are. Now hurry up and open this so I can have a piece of that delicious-looking cake.'

Eddy took the envelope from her hand. If someone had told him he'd got up on a different planet this morning; he might well have believed them. This was it, here in this plain brown envelope was the make or break. It was more than just a score for answering a bunch of questions right or wrong. That wasn't the half of it. This was about who he was and who he would be from this day on. A stupid boy, the weird kid that would never amount to much, or Eddy Sullivan, the boy who could. What was it going to be?

Reagan grinned at him from the corner of the room. Allowing himself one more deep lungful of oxygen,

Eddy ripped the envelope open and pulled his future out in the form of a single white page.

'Well?' asked Grandma Daisy after they'd given him a few seconds to read it. The lot of them were on tenterhooks and if they had to wait one moment longer, someone was bound to explode. And still Eddy didn't say a thing. Instead, the single tear that dripped from his cheek and on to the letter from the exam board told the story for him.

Reagan walked over and before she could put her arm around him he handed her the letter. She hadn't expected that, but now the mantel was hers.

'Eddy,' she exclaimed in short order, 'this is incredible!' Reagan's face shone like the sun. 'You not only passed, you've got a scholarship for the best sixth-form college in the county!'

It sounded good to hear her say it. *Somebody* else had to say it because if he didn't hear it come out of somebody else's mouth he still wouldn't have believed it.

'That's right, Eddy,' added Mrs Stanton. 'They'd love to have you. You knocked the socks off them. A stars, all the way through. Every one of them. You should be so, so proud of yourself because I can tell you on behalf of everyone here, we're proud of you.'

Standing tall, Mrs Stanton began clapping. For a solitary moment it was a lonely reverberation through the room, but then it gained company. As Eddy counted his blessings, one by one, everybody joined in until the bedroom rang full with their applause. Here and now, in this most wondrous of settings, with Mr Tree wrapping all the joy in emerald green leaves, Eddy felt the happiest he'd ever been. Amid it all he felt a hand touch his. It was Reagan's.

'Congratulations, Eddy,' she said quiet enough so only he could hear it. 'You deserve every bit of it.'

When the clapping finally gave way, Grandma Daisy made good with the cake knife and soon enough everybody was tucking into a luscious slice of gateau. Mrs Elsdon stepped over to where Eddy stood and handed him a gift-wrapped present.

'Y-you didn't need to do this.'

'Yes, I did,' responded Mrs Elsdon. 'I owe you.'

'Thank you v-very much.'

'Open it,' she instructed with enough enthusiasm to suggest he knew exactly what was in it.

Peeling back the gift paper, he uncovered a certificate frame, a nice wooden one.

'It's for when you get your graduation certificate,' she advised. 'You can hang it up on the wall so everyone can see how clever you are.'

Eddy imagined what it would be like to actually have something that said you weren't stupid, that even though you didn't look quite the same as other people, you still had something to offer. That would be pretty cool all right.

'This is great,' he beamed. 'I might put my l-letter in it until then.'

'Good idea,' agreed Mrs Elsdon. 'Except you haven't got a wall to hang it on.'

'I didn't th-think of that. I'll s-sort something out though.'

She was right too. Mr Tree, who only a couple of months back was only beginning to tickle the left side of the front window, had now thrust itself right on by, almost to the far side of the window frame. At no point did it obstruct the view at all; instead it wound its path above and below with an intelligence that belied its appearance. Everyone in the room who hadn't observed the years' long march of Mr Tree couldn't help but be amazed at its progress, and it was as much a topic of discussion, as was Eddy's superb efforts with the exams.

One by one, each after having their own say, Eddy's guests made their way down the stairs and off to their respective Saturday afternoons. Soon all that was left was Grandma Daisy and Reagan, all three of them picking up the remnants of the party.

'Thanks, Grandma Daisy,' said Eddy as he piled plates upon one another.

'My pleasure. How often do you get to celebrate things these days? And like Mrs Stanton said, we're proud of you and we wanted to show it.'

Placing his stack of dirty plates aside, Eddy stepped over and startled her with a big hug.

'What's this for?' she asked.

'Just because.'

Smiling, she patted her grandson on the head, the same way she never did thousands of times before. 'That's about the best reason there is.'

When the dishes were cleared, Reagan and Eddy were finally left alone up in the bedroom. Eddy sat down on his bed and looked across at Reagan, who had found her own spot on the chair.

'You knew about this all along, you s-sneak.'

'Wouldn't be a surprise if I told you, would it?' There was that cheeky grin again.

'Reagan?'

'Yep?'

'How'd you get on?'

'What do ya mean?'

'W-with the exams. How did you do?'

This was the one question Reagan hadn't wanted to hear, Eddy could see that.

'Today's about you, Eddy, not me.'

'Are you okay?'

'I'm fine,' she said, trying not to prove otherwise. 'It's nothing that I wasn't expecting.'

'What are you going to do?'

'I don't know. Mum and I had a talk about it this morning. She says it's up to me. I can either go back and redo the year, or I can start thinking about getting a job.'

Now the discussion over at the school playground was beginning to make sense for Eddy. She'd reached a big fork in the road and neither road carried a sign-post.

'M-my advice ...'

'Yeah?' Reagan may have said that with a touch too much eagerness for her own liking.

'How old w-would you say Mrs Elsdon is?'

'Somewhere in her eighties, I reckon.'

'Even in her eighties, she h-has hopes and dreams.

Some she can f-follow but most she can't. Time has got away on her. Don't make that same mistake, Reagan. T-take some time to think. Not about the decision ... but about which one takes you closer to your dreams.'

Reagan had some thinking to do, and by the expression on her face, she'd started already.

54

TIRED DAYS COMMENCE

Reagan had made her decision within a week. With her mother's wholehearted permission, she was going back to school to redo the year. Although he would never have pushed her in any given direction, Eddy was glad for it. Not simply because it meant a continuation of their happy routine, but because, deep down, he knew it was the right course. If she'd chosen to find work instead, in all likelihood she'd be choosing the path of most resistance. A path where paydays, not dreams, are measured. A path where, if she wasn't careful, her soul would be smothered and the small things merge into the background.

So the school year kicked back into gear. Reagan had taken it well too. For some it would have been tough going, having to watch everyone else slip a year ahead and having to replay a whole year of life again. Virtually every evening after dinner she'd be up in her bedroom, making sure that she not only had the homework under her belt, but that she actually comprehended the content. That was the key, Eddy told her. It wasn't just enough to fill the spaces, you had to understand why. It was a lesson in life really.

As convinced as Reagan was about her own dedication, as committed as she was to succeed this time around, it took its toll on her. It was a gradual thing and Eddy was probably best positioned to notice it. At first, he'd just figured that she was mentally exhausted from all the study and that, much the same as any muscle getting exercise, her brain would adjust and she'd come through all the better for it. But as the weeks melted into months it seemed to get worse. She was constantly tired to the point where heavy, bruised circles had found a permanent home under her eyes and where her long, hollow yawns had become so second nature that even Eddy had to remind himself to notice them. By the time Eddy first spied the changes in her 'green' he'd already arrived at a heightened level of concern for her well-being. It had reached the stage where he no longer had to force her to take breaks, or even to forget the stack of homework completely for a day or two. She had no choice despite herself and more often than not she'd be fast asleep by mid-evening. Not just normal sleep either, she'd be in so deep that only daylight could bring her out again. Considering Reagan had always been a night owl, this new development in her behaviour worried him. Him and Mrs Crowe.

One particular day, when Reagan's mum had been home on a school day, she'd called across to Eddy from her daughter's room.

'Hi, Eddy.'

'Hi, Mrs Crowe.'

'How's the studying going?'

'There's an awful l-lot of it.'

'Well, if there's anyone I know who can handle it, it's you.'

'Thanks, Mrs Crowe.'

'Eddy?'

'Yes?'

'Have you noticed anything strange about Reagan lately?' To hear this question coming from Mrs Crowe was an acknowledgement of that nagging concern and, as much as Eddy wished she had no reason to ask such a question, it was a genuine relief to hear it.

'She g-gets real tired, real quick.'

Mrs Crowe had nodded her head in thoughtful silence.

'Do you think she's okay?' she'd asked eventually.

'I don't know. She's t-trying real hard with her schoolwork. Maybe it's wearing her out.'

'Yes, maybe. Can you just keep an eye on her for me, Eddy? I've been trying to talk her into going to the doctor but she's a stubborn one.'

Tell me something I don't know.

'Sure, Mrs Crowe.'

That had been a couple of weeks ago now and since then Reagan's fatigue hadn't improved in the slightest. Eddy had been doing exactly as her mother had asked, but he wished he could do more.

'Reagan…Hey, Reagan!'

'What?'

'You fell asleep.'

'Oops.' Reagan lifted her heavy head and regarded Eddy from across the way with even heavier eyes. 'Sorry. Where were we?'

'We were stopping for the day is wh-where we were.'

'But we only just got started.' Her words said one thing but her body language betrayed the real story. She was absolutely shattered and the idea of closing the books for the day sounded mighty fine. About as fine as a soft, warm pillow, in fact.

'Yep, and you were already asleep. I'm worried about y-you.' Eddy pushed his books aside, hoping to portray how serious he was. 'Are you okay, Reagan? 'Cause your mum's worried about you too.'

'I don't know. I guess I'm just tired all the time, that's all.' Reagan shrugged her shoulders. No big deal.

'You should g-go to the doctor to have a check-up.'

'I'll be all right. I'm just studying really hard.'

'No, Reagan,' asserted Eddy. She wasn't all right. She was far from it and getting further every day. 'You're n-not all right. Will you please go to the doctor. For me?'

'I hate doctors.'

'And I hate seeing you like this. You're not my f-fun Reagan any more.'

That one stung a bit, Eddy could see it in the way she wanted to shoot back but held the reins with a massive dose of willpower. As far as he was concerned, that was a good thing. Only hearing the truth could hurt that much. He despised having to spell it out like this but right now the ends were more important than the means.

'We'll see, but I'm not making any promises ... okay?'

'Okay.' It wasn't a perfect result but it would do. It would have to do. When it came to changing Reagan's mind about something, it was all about a nibble at a time. Try and change it all in one big bite and all he'd achieve was teeth marks. 'Reagan?'

'Yep?'

'Just be careful. Can't have m-my movie star too tired for the Oscars.'

That was it. That was the smile he'd been baiting.

55

A Thousand Words

'Do you mind if I come in, Eddy?'

'Sure, Grandma Daisy.'

Eddy moved away from the front window ledge as the bedroom door swung open. In walked Grandma Daisy and immediately it was obvious there was something on her mind, something that she had a need to let go of. And more than likely it had every-thing to do with whatever it was she was holding in her hand. Eddy had heard the stair creaks almost five minutes ago, so assumed she'd been standing there in the hallway all that time. Grandma Daisy took another awkward peek at the object in her palm before regarding her grandson with an even greater sense of unease.

'What's wrong, Grandma?'

'That's hard to say, Eddy,' she said with honest conviction. 'I think it's just an old lady coming to terms with the past.'

'Pardon?'

'Here.' Grandma Daisy beckoned over to Eddy's bed. 'Come have a sit down with me.'

Eddy did as instructed, trying to maintain a sense of decorum on the outside, but on the inside he was beginning to flutter with intrigue.

'I should've done this a long time ago,' admitted Daisy Catherine Sullivan as she regarded her one and only grandchild (as far as she was aware, of course). 'I could tell you I'd forgotten about them but all that'd make me is a liar, and there's been enough lying in this household. So, I've said it to you before and I'll say it again, I'm sorry.'

Laying her old, liver-spotted hand on his young palm, she placed the contents of her apprehension and guilt at his disposal. Looking down, Eddy saw they were photos, two of them and they both had the weary hallmarks of age.

He didn't have to ask but he looked to Grandma Daisy anyway and all she could do was nod her head. It was a subtle nod, certainly subtle compared to the bolt of realisation it instilled within Eddy.

One photo showed a young lady, quite pretty, with mousy brown hair and a look in her eye that reminded him of Reagan. The way Reagan had been a couple of years back when life hadn't yet shown its capacity for being two-faced. This young lady had been looking into the sun when the photo was taken and the light bounced off her fresh, freckled face like gold sparkling at the bottom of a prospector's pan. She looked happy, Saturday evening happy.

The second photo showed three women. They were standing side by side, arms around each other's waists, the beach receiving timeless waves behind them. On the left-hand side was the same young lady from the first photo, except she was probably a year or two older in this one. It was too hard to tell for sure, given that this one was taken from a greater distance than the first photo, but it seemed to Eddy she'd lost most of those freckles. She had sunglasses on but you didn't need to see her eyes to know that times had changed. She'd ended up enjoying herself that fine day at the beach, but from start to finish, there'd been other places she'd preferred to have been.

Standing in the centre of that beachside threesome was none other than Grandma Daisy herself. Except it was a much sprightlier version of the worn and weary lady sitting here beside him. In the photo, she exuded vigour and pride, aspects that had since died back and were only lately prepared to surface for air again. The lady that had been Grandma Daisy had no reason to question tomorrows. Broken families and dead husbands were a million years away.

To the right of Grandma Daisy was another woman, this one the oldest. It took no stretch of the imagination to identify her as Grandma's mother, Eddy's great-grandmother. The resemblance settled across the eyes and the bridge of the nose. It was also there in the posture, the way they both brought their shoulders back to prove to the world they shouldn't be underestimated.

'I still remember that day vividly,' reminisced

Grandma Daisy. 'The photo was your grandpa Nevil's idea. All three generations. We had this photo up on our kitchen wall for years. Up until I took down everything that reminded me of her, that is.'

'What was she like?'

'She was my only child.' Eddy felt Grandma Daisy glance over his shoulder at the photos in his hands, at the girl she'd given birth to and raised until she was old enough to take on the world herself (even though she wasn't ready for it). 'I loved her. I guess after all these years of pretending I don't, you tend to forget that.'

'Do you still love her?'

'It depends what day you ask me. I know that sounds like a horrible thing to say about your own daughter, but it's the truth. I suppose it's not exactly a state secret, but I blamed you for how it all ended out, how our little family just disintegrated. Looking back I think I even blamed you for Nevil dying, and he was gone before you were even born.' Grandma Daisy paused and Eddy just let it stay that way until she was ready to go on. 'I loved her on the days I was prepared to be honest with myself. Trouble was, there weren't enough of them.

'You've seen the letters. She did write. At least for a while. There were times when I almost wrote back too. I'd always keep a track of the postal marks, though, so I had an idea of where she was. Back in the early days she'd headed north. I don't think she ever really knew who your father was, Eddy, and I reckon half her running had to do with that. We could've made it work. The two of us plus you. I would have been there for her.

'In the end I lost her, though. She stopped writing altogether and now I guess we're as much strangers as strangers can get.'

Eddy remained silent but looked across at his desk, where his bear still sat, pride of place. A bear that was bought by a woman he never quite knew.

'Sh-she was pretty,' he said, looking back at the photo of his mother by herself, freckles and all.

'Yes, she was,' agreed Grandma Daisy. 'She was a bright thing too, had so much promise. She was just so busy chasing life down that she forgot to realise that life finds you all by itself.'

'Do y-you miss her, Grandma Daisy?'

'That's a real good question, Eddy. I do. Yes, I do. At so many different levels too. I'm not a young lady any more. Time's creeping on me, and that gets a person to thinking. It's like the closer you get to leaving this body and being at one with your soul the easier it is to look at yourself from the outside. Some people might like what they see … but I don't. I've got a lot of catching up to do and the track's due to run out.'

'I th-think you're doing all right.'

Grandma Daisy smiled. It fell somewhere between happy and sad and Eddy figured that was about right.

'Thanks, Eddy. All thanks to you. It's funny you know, how life twists and turns the way it does. How what I curse can turn into a blessing. It's a lesson I've learned way too late, but one worth learning.'

'Grandma?'

'Yes, Eddy?'

'I don't think it's over yet.'

'What do you mean?'

'You're gonna see my mum again one d-day.' Eddy looked up into his grandmother's tired eyes. 'Right here in this house. I'm sure you will.'

56

TIME OFF

'I didn't think I saw you heading off t-to school today.'

Reagan had obviously just climbed out of bed and, from Eddy's perspective, it looked like she could quite happily climb back in for about a week.

'No,' she responded, wiping her tired eyes. 'I've had it. I can't ever remember being this exhausted before.'

'I told you, you n-need to go to the doctor.'

'I know.' Reagan reached for the ceiling in a bone yanking stretch that ended with a painful grimace. 'Man, I hurt all over. Must have slept funny or something.'

'Will you go?'

'Did you take some nag pills today?'

'No. Just worried.'

'I've just been overdoing it, I reckon.' Reagan moved over to the windowsill and virtually collapsed against it, head resting in the crook of her arm. 'All I need is a good break. A few days without schoolwork and I'll be back up and running in no time.'

'Well, make sure you rest then.'

'Jeez, Eddy, did my mum leave you a note to read from or something? You've just about got her word for word.'

'Just keen on my n-next jam sandwich, that's all.'

'So that's all I am to you then.' The twinkle was there in her eye, it was just that the smile took a little while to catch up. 'A jam sandwich delivery service.'

'The best in the business.'

'Well, I might just have to charge like the best in the business then.' There was that smile.

'You already do get p-paid.'

'How?'

'W-with the pleasure of my wonderful company.' And with that said, Eddy mirrored her with a grin of his own making. At least on the outside. As he watched her drag herself back to her feet and head out the room he placed his hand on a branch and sent all his hopes and wishes across Mr Tree's broad shoulders.

57

A Heavy Load

Reagan took the rest of that week off, and while it did seem to do her some good, it by no means transformed her into the girl she should've been and used to be. Nowhere near, to be honest, and Reagan certainly wasn't being honest. By Thursday she was playing the 'I'm fine now' trick but Eddy could see what she was doing. She was putting on a brave face just to keep him and her mother off her back.

The one good thing was the amount of sleep she got. It seemed like every couple of hours she was collapsing back onto her bed, and that was on top of a full night's sleep. If rest is what she needed, then rest is what she was getting.

On Friday, about mid-morning and with the sun promising to win the day, Reagan got dressed for the first time all week and arrived at her window with a sense of purpose.

'Hey, Eddy?'

'What?'

'How about a walk?'

Eddy looked across at her, measuring her ability to follow up on the offer. 'You sure?'

'Yep. I feel better than I have in a while. Besides,' she said, reaching her hand out to where the sun could bathe it, 'the vitamin D will do me good.'

Eddy hesitated for a moment.

'Was that a "no"?' asked Reagan.

'Sorry,' replied Eddy. 'I mean yes … but only if you're up to it.'

'I'll see you downstairs then.'

Eddy's concerns for Reagan were only deepened when he saw her standing out there on the front lawn. He hadn't really seen all of her for a little while, thanks to the window, and seeing her out here in a pair of jeans and a T-shirt made him catch his breath. As beautiful as she still undoubtedly was, there was a definite look of scrawniness about her. The sort that didn't belong on her. Her jeans, that had once painted themselves across her hips, were now hanging on for dear life around her waist and her shirt couldn't hide the gaunt ridge of her shoulders.

'Have you been eating lately?'

'Have you been annoying me lately?'

That was the end of that particular discussion.

'So where d-do you want to go then?'

'I was thinking maybe the willows. I like looking at the willows.' That was a good answer, certainly one that fell nicely on Eddy's ears. There was only one reason she wanted to go there and that was to look at the little things, the small stuff. If ever there was a time she needed reminding, it was now.

'Lead the way.' And that she did.

For a minute or so they walked in silence, soaking in the sun, their pace nice and slow. Eddy found himself caught between watching the familiar landmarks of the neighbourhood come and go and glancing across to where Reagan's jeans gathered up baggy creases in places they had no right to be. When she got over this bug or whatever it was, she was going to have some eating to do, he'd make certain of that.

'You know all this study you're doing, Eddy?' asked Reagan as they wandered along opposite the McKenzie's.

'Yeah.'

'What are you going to do with it?'

'Would it sound stupid if I s-said I don't really know?'

'You're kidding me. You're putting in all those hours and you don't even know what for?'

'I figured I'd find the reason when the time was right.' In all honesty Eddy hadn't really given it much thought at all, but when the answer fell from his mouth it had a ring of truth about it. Things happened for reasons, but that didn't mean the reason necessarily advertised itself in advance. Sometimes the action and the reason arrived some ways apart and the bits in between came down to faith.

'Okay then,' posited Reagan. 'What do you think you would *like* to do when it's all over?'

'Something that helps people. I don't know what yet…but definitely s-something that helps people.'

'I don't think you could do anything different, Eddy.'

'I'll t-take that as a compliment.' Eddy had been eyeing up someone's rose garden when it occurred to him that Reagan hadn't shot back with one of her quirky remarks. In fact, he didn't feel her presence beside him at all.

In a heart-stopping instant Eddy suddenly understood what that meant. He hadn't felt Reagan's presence beside him because she wasn't there. She was ten metres behind him, lying prone on the hard, unforgiving footpath.

'Reagan!'

Eddy sprinted back to her, his whole world caving in around him.

'Reagan, wake up!'

If she could hear him, she gave no indication. Her eyes were closed and her breathing was awfully shallow. Eddy sensed a frightening vulnerability around her and he heard a panicked voice inside his head telling him what he already knew. Reagan was slipping away. She was not just ill, she was very, very sick.

Seeing no one else up or down the street, Eddy reached under her with both arms and, with a back-breaking effort, he levered her up and into his grasp. For a girl who was all skin and bone, her dead weight both surprised and scared him. He may have had her body but her mind, her soul were slipping between

315

his fingers. He could almost feel it and every piece of him cried for it to be otherwise.

Come on, Reagan. Please.

Running as fast as her weight and his legs would allow, Eddy only had visions for making the Crowe's front door as quick as possible. He'd gone only a few yards before his arms screamed at him to put her down but he would entertain none of that. As he finally rounded into the Crowe's front lawn, his great howls for help were born from a combination of his entire body cramping in solid knots of agony and his even deeper panic. A million thoughts were racing through his head. Five years seemed to melt together in a myriad moment in the history of their unparalleled friendship. The first day she'd waved up at him. The countless jam sandwiches. Her holding him the evening Grandma Daisy had demolished Mr Tree. All the things she'd taught him in these last few years. He'd give them all away again in the blink of an eye if she could just be well again. A very real notion occurred to him, could he live without her? Was she as much his saviour as Mr Tree? Did he even want to live on if she died here today? No. Short and simple …no. She was his everything.

Slamming the front door, he suddenly realised Mrs Crowe wouldn't be there. It was a workday for her. If Hell existed, it seemed to be running the show today.

Home. Gotta get to Grandma.

Sucking in the very last reserves of energy, Eddy scuttled down the front steps of the Crowe's place and back across the lawn. If there'd been a boundary fence between the two properties he would've been in real trouble, but as it was he was able to let his momentum take him the rest of the way.

'Grandma. Grandma, quick!'

Grandma Daisy arrived at the front door just before Eddy, and the expression on her face only reinforced the fear pulsing through her grandson.

'Eddy, what happened?'

'Call an ambulance, Grandma. She's gonna die!'

They swapped a terrified glance before Grandma Daisy turned and moved faster than she had in years. Since the day she had seen her own husband collapse before her very eyes, in fact.

Sinking to his knees under Reagan's weight, Eddy cradled her limp body to his chest, watching, searching her precious face for signs of life and receiving no consolation. She looked so calm and peaceful, so at odds with his own world right now.

'It's going to be okay,' he said quietly as he stroked her cheek. 'I promise you it's going to be okay.'

In reality, he didn't know if this was going to be the first real lie of his entire life.

58

HOLDING ONE'S BREATH

The next couple of days were a blur for Eddy. Every conceivable emotion seemed to be riding high in his throat, just waiting for a call to action with a hair trigger.

Since riding in the ambulance all the way to the hospital (and in the process ignoring the subtle expressions of the paramedics regarding this 'handicapped' kid wanting to hitch along), Eddy hadn't once been back home. And pity anyone who tried to change that. Grandma Daisy had been surprisingly understanding. When Eddy had made it abundantly clear he wasn't budging from the hospital ward, she'd put up a muted protest but in the end she'd gone home and packed a bag for him. Eddy thought he knew why too. With Grandpa Nevil, it had been a very different story. His passing had been sudden. So quick, in fact, he'd probably been holding hands with the angels before he'd even hit the floor. If it hadn't been that way, though, if he'd put up a fight and lingered, she would have stayed too, until the big man upstairs had had His say, one way or the other.

Inside half an hour of Reagan being whisked down the corridor on the gurney, Mrs Crowe had stormed into the hospital. Eddy had been there in the waiting room at the time, but such was her emotional wreckage, she hadn't noticed him huddled in a corner as she interrogated the nurse. He figured it was probably best to leave it that way. She was a mother who desperately needed to be with her child ... he could understand that. He'd watched closely as her whole body tensed on the tightrope of sanity, having to stand there and wait while the hospital staff worked out where Reagan had been taken. He'd seen how she'd ground her hands together so hard that her wedding ring was going to leave a red mark on the neighbouring fingers for a week. And he'd wondered to himself, would his mother have agonised like this for him? He hoped so.

He'd waited in that cold, hard room for four hours. Grandma Daisy had ended up being there for most of it. She'd even offered to buy him a chocolate bar but he just wasn't hungry. He'd lost all memory of what it felt like to be hungry. Every thought, every memory had been eclipsed by the recollection of Reagan lying helpless on that pavement. One moment chatting about the future (his future) and the next ... nothing.

The green he had associated with Reagan since the day they had met had now faded to a murky grey.

He probably waited there even longer than he had to. Ignorance was hope. No news was good news. He was afraid that if he asked somebody how she was, that somebody, that doctor, that nurse would suddenly own a new expression, one that had become time worn in their profession but never easy to mask. And then they'd tell him something he never wanted to hear. They'd chew the inside of their cheek and wish they'd taken that other shift instead, the one without poor retarded boys who'd just lost the best friend you could ever imagine.

It'd been Grandma Daisy who'd lost patience and checked at the information desk. Seeing her talk to that lady, watching their lips move but having no idea what they were saying, made him want to scream. For a moment there, he'd wished he'd never met Reagan so none of this would matter, but then he scolded himself. Of course it mattered. It had to.

The news was indeed bad but not his worst nightmare. Reagan was doing rough, she was going to be in hospital for a while too, by the sounds of it ... but she was alive.

The day that had started so warm and so promising ended in a room with hard corners and hospital beds. By the time Eddy was allowed into Reagan's room, the only light outside was from the security lamps down in the car park. It had already been the longest day of his life but seeing her lying there, barely a ruffle in the sheets, he'd known that sleep would have to stay away. The fancy doctors and nurses had even fancier words and gadgets but they didn't have what he had. They didn't love her like he did and they never would. She was going to need that right now. Every bit of it.

59

WHY!

By Sunday afternoon everything outside the straight line from Eddy's line of sight to Reagan's hospital bed was numb. There were faces and names (Mrs Crowe was always there, you could take that for granted at least); there were sounds with meaning and sounds without; there were even conversations; but none of it got any deeper than it had to.

None of it got anywhere near to making it all go away.

That Reagan was stable was all they were prepared to say. They were doing 'tests' like she was some weird experiment or something. Every now and then they'd pull Mrs Crowe aside and have a doctor-to-frightened-mum chat. Eddy didn't get any insight to those. Mrs Crowe's face told him all he needed to know, and if she wasn't prepared to share the rest then she was probably only looking after his well-being in the process.

The important thing was that Reagan was still here.

'Eddy?'

Eddy hadn't even realised he'd drifted off until Mrs Crowe gently shook him awake. He looked up at her face and was struck by how haggard she'd become and how fast it had happened. Rubbing his eyes, he sat up.

'The doctor says she seems to be settling. He also thinks now's a good time for us to go and get freshened up a bit. You feel like a shower? I know I do.'

'You mean go home?'

'Yeah. Reagan needs her rest right now. She'll be ready to talk to us a bit later if she's feeling up to it.'

'Actually *talk* to us?'

Mrs Crowe nodded her head. 'That's what they say.'

If there was better news than that going around, Eddy certainly wanted to hear it.

Leaving Reagan behind in the hospital had felt like a betrayal of their friendship but Mrs Crowe had made it bearable. If she thought it was okay to head off for a little while, then that had to be a good sign. No mother would leave her child if she so much as had a sniff of something going wrong. And a shower would be good. It would be mighty good. Enough to set him up for another couple of days at least.

Eddy was sitting in the passenger seat of the Crowes' car, Mrs Crowe concentrating on the road ahead of her and him worrying about everything else.

'W-will Reagan be okay, Mrs Crowe?'

The mother of his best friend said nothing for a while and Eddy had about figured she hadn't heard him when she finally registered his question. It was a short answer, but even short blades can sting.

'The doctor thinks she's got cancer. A special type. Some kind of leukaemia.' And that was it. She didn't look at Eddy, instead choosing to grip the steering wheel like it was a miracle cure that couldn't get away.

But will she be all right? You didn't answer that question.

The city blocks gave way to suburbs and malls, to places where people lived and loved in little subsets of society. Where other people's pain was nothing more than fiction. Eddy observed the pedestrians in all their blissful ignorance, going about their daily chores as though they were the centre of the universe.

Did he envy them that? He didn't rightly know.

When Mrs Crowe piped up again, with only a few minutes to go before they pulled into Willow Close, Eddy almost jumped. He'd assumed they were destined to stew silently in their own sense of pity all the way home.

'I don't think the doctors are all that hopeful. They're not ready to come right out and say it that way, but you can tell. You can see it in their eyes.' Mrs Crowe looked pale and she still wasn't prepared to face him. She was playing statue there behind the wheel. Statues were cold, hard and unfeeling and that's just how she needed to be. Anything less than that would see her world come tumbling down around her.

'C-can they help her?'

'They're going to do their best is all I keep getting from them. They said it's pretty advanced.'

'Oh.'

Ignorance was indeed bliss. Why couldn't she have said something else? Something like, 'They'll give her a pill and she'll be fine in a week.' Something that would make this just a bad dream from which they could wake up and laugh at over a jam sandwich or two.

'They're going to try chemo as soon as she regains enough strength. Chemo and a whole bunch of drugs.' Finally Mrs Crowe was prepared to risk a glance over at him and he wished straight away she hadn't. She was a haunted woman. It wasn't just in her hallowed expression. It emanated from everything about her. She was haunted and alone. 'It's not going to be good, Eddy. It's going to hurt her.' And with that, the statue cracked and the tears flowed down both cheeks.

Grandma Daisy was waiting for him at the front door when they pulled up. Eddy felt real bad about getting out of the car but he didn't know what else to do.

'Please let m-me know when you're going back in?' he asked, leaning in to grab his bag.

'I will.' Eddy was just about to close the car door when she had one more thing to say. 'Thank you, Eddy. Reagan needs all the help she can get right now.'

Forcing a guilt-ridden smile, Eddy closed the car door and walked up to where Grandma Daisy stood. He heard the car move off and felt it pull into the driveway next door. It was half a peripheral vision thing and half recognition of his absolute failure to help Reagan. How long had he seen her going downhill? Weeks? Months? And yet he did nothing. What sort of a friend was that? Abandoning her when she most needed him, that made him worse than his own mother.

'How is she, Eddy?' asked Grandma delicately as he stepped through the doorway past her.

'She's g-got cancer. Bad cancer.' That was blunt. He shouldn't have said it that way; after all, none of this was Grandma Daisy's fault. That lay fair and square on a different set of shoulders. But he couldn't help it.

So he left her alone in stunned silence before he could make it even worse. Climbing the stairs, he stomped into his room, threw his bag on the floor and just stood there in the middle of nowhere. In seventeen long years Eddy Sullivan couldn't remember once being this angry. Okay, he'd been frustrated, annoyed, exasperated at times, but that was canned stuff, the sort that stayed below the surface. This thing boiling inside him was completely different. He was the bottle and someone had shaken him badly. From deep within he felt it rise, and while somewhere in the back of his mind he was loathe to release it, there was another part of him that called it forth, that craved the explosion that was sure to come.

'Why?'

As much as he had to fight the urge, it wasn't an angry 'why'. It was soft and subtle; the same way one desperate and confused lover would ask another once the infidelity had surfaced.

'I just n-need to know why.'

Eddy looked all about him, at this marvellous tree, the one that had started as a fledgling little twig poking in through the window. Now it was strong and proud, soaring through his room so that it all but touched back at the side window again. Another foot or so and it'd be there, the full circle, the whole embrace. It was a mighty thing to behold, all robed up in its luscious coat of green leaves.

Together with Reagan, it had turned his life on its tail, and all for the better ... up until now. Looking back across those years it occurred to Eddy that Mr Tree and Reagan had actually worked in symphony with each other. They'd been a partnership, driving him forward in ways that he simply couldn't have imagined five years ago. But that only made all this so much harder to understand. There was an intelligence behind those striking branches, he just knew it. It was an intelligence that had connected with him in so many different ways. The colours, the visions, the voices. That hadn't all simply spurned from within; no, Mr Tree had been feeding him these all along, through those extraordinary vibrations.

The tingling sensations were strong when he laid his hand upon the sturdy limb at his bedroom window. Eddy thought about how people could grow together like plants in a garden, so that they share the same root system. So that when one thrives, so does the other. So that when one withers and dies, so does the other. That was how it was here. That was the way of Eddy Sullivan and Mr Tree.

So how could Mr Tree let this happen? How could it possibly play dead when death itself was truly on the cards? Had it already forgotten the way Eddy himself had placed his own body on the line after Grandma Daisy had ripped its branches and shredded its leaves?

'Why?'

This time a bit louder, a bit more forceful.

Did it not want Reagan to live? Was that it? Can a tree be jealous? Can it pull you into such a deep embrace that there's no room for anyone else?

'Why!'

That bubbling, that boiling was rising closer now and Eddy felt his jaw tense up and his teeth grind.

'WHY!'

Moving without thinking, Eddy charged up to the branches above his bed, the branches closest to the heart of this treacherous malformation of nature, and with a rage that consumed him, he beat his fists against it with all of his might. The lava had arrived and it burned with a heat that threatened to consume everything in its path.

'Why!…Why!…Why!'

The words were hard now, not just because he was crying but because he realised he had to find his own answers. He and Reagan had been deserted. There was no Mr Tree. There never had been. It was all just a fickle combination of coincidence and foolhardy faith. This tree, this 'thing' …maybe it was amazing like his neighbours always told him, but they didn't know what he knew. It was a liar. It was a coward … and more than anything else it was nothing more than a lump of deformed wood.

'I hate you! I hate you, Mr Tree!'

He pounded those branches so hard that his hands were bleeding, but he wouldn't have stopped even if he'd noticed.

'Don't you dare let her die. I love her!'

Somewhere in the recesses of his mind, Eddy knew Grandma Daisy was standing out in the hallway.

Knowing that the whole world was watching, that anything and everything under the wide blue sky was impotent, and immune to his pain, Eddy finally collapsed onto the bed sheets. The bed sheets that Grandma Daisy had freshly washed and lovingly folded back into place.

In the exhausted moments before he fell into a deep, dreamless sleep, Eddy came to realise he would awaken to a whole new world tomorrow. And it would never be the same again.

60

PRAYERS

Reagan came home a week later, but for Eddy it wasn't the experience it should have been. The doctors said she had a real battle on her hands and, Mrs Crowe had been right, they felt the cancer had the high ground. It wasn't impossible though, they added; nothing's impossible.

When Reagan was lifted out of the car (she could walk, but it took everything she had), she was but a shadow of the girl he knew. There was a hollowness about her that scared Eddy. It was as if death was a journey for her and she'd already wandered past a few of the milestones.

He did his best to smile and sound happy. They all did. And they all failed miserably.

The drugs didn't help. As far as Eddy could tell, they only made things worse. Reagan would go through bouts of vomiting so powerful that Eddy himself could feel his insides cramp up. The dark circles he'd noticed under her eyes all those weeks ago had transformed to fully laden, accompanied baggage, but that still wasn't the worst of it. What sat above those puffy sacks was the saddest thing of all. Those wonderful, life-enhancing eyes of hers had dimmed and diminished. They weren't just the windows into a sick and suffering girl, they were the signals of a quiet surrender. Almost eighteen years in and none to go. It was just so hard to see.

Eddy knew she cried a lot. She'd hardly ever do it in front of him but that didn't take it away. He knew in those silent, lonely moments when the lights were all out, she'd pull her pillow up close and ask God for help. And when he didn't answer, the tears would come. She'd let it come on as quietly as the cancer itself had and, much as his grandma had done when he'd laid into Mr Tree, Eddy could only stand on the outside and look in. She didn't want pity, even if you dished it on a plate for her. She was too proud for that.

And, in Eddy's eyes, that made her all the more precious, all the more beautiful. The little girl who'd got out of the car that day and had waved back at him was dying. Eddy knew it, Mrs Crowe knew it, Grandma Daisy knew it, and, most painfully of all, Reagan knew it.

Reagan *had* to live. Reagan still had something to give and he craved with every cell of his being to work out just how that was supposed to happen.

61

BEDTIME STORIES

Eddy had taken to sitting with Reagan, just like she had sat at his bedside when he had been sick.

'Are you comfortable?'

'Yes, for the fifth time, Eddy.'

Reagan was lying in her bed, reclined up against a few pillows that hardly seemed to flex under her weight. Beside her, on the duchess, was a collection of pill bottles the likes of which had never been seen in one place before and Eddy was amazed at how a single person could fit them all in. It just didn't seem right, and it most certainly wasn't fair.

'Do you w-want a drink of water?'

'No, thanks.'

Reagan shifted against the pillows a touch, releasing a grimace of pain in the process.

'They think they'll start the chemo next week,' she continued. 'Mum knows more than I do. I guess I just get to go along for the ride.'

'Your mum's going to let me know when so I can be there too.'

'Cool.' It wasn't the bright acknowledgement it was probably meant to be. Instead it came out diffused of all emotion. It appeared to Eddy that Reagan was getting wiped of all emotion these days, and to him that was another step along her journey toward death.

They both sat and pondered their respective roles in this new development before Reagan decided to break the ugliness of the silence between them. 'It makes your hair fall out.'

'I heard that.' In fact, Eddy had read it. He hadn't told Grandma Daisy or Mrs Stanton yet, but he hadn't done any proper study for a while now. He was still doing a heck of a lot of reading though. Anything about cancer he could get his hands on, actually.

'Mum reckons I can wear a wig. We'll go out and pick one. What do ya think?' she said with a good attempt at a smile and a model's swagger. 'Blonde or redhead?'

'Blondes make better movie stars.'

Her smile stayed but her eyes wandered and Eddy immediately hated himself for saying that. How dumb was that? Reminding her of her dreams for a future she could never have.

'Eddy?'

'Yep.'

Reagan reached over with her hand and took his.

'What are you going to do?'

'Wh-what do you mean?'

'After I'm gone. You're the most special boy in the

world, Eddy, and I think the biggest thing I'll miss is watching the incredible life of Eddy Sullivan.'

'Reagan, please d-don't talk like that. You're going nowhere.'

'Just do me a favour then. Tell me a story. Tell me the life and times of Eddy Sullivan.' Then, with a longing look. 'Please.'

Eddy suddenly felt uncomfortable. In all honesty, he didn't want to consider a life without her, not yet, not when she was still sitting here, talking to him. There had to be hope somewhere, he just had to dig for it.

'Reagan, do I have to?'

'Yes.'

Eddy resigned himself to her determination. It wasn't going to be easy though. A future without Reagan wasn't really a future at all. But he'd give it a shot…for her.

'I haven't really thought about it. Things have been happening so fast. I g-guess I've just been taking one day at a time.'

'Well then,' interjected Reagan. 'Here's your chance to figure it out then.'

'The study's all good and everything but at the same time it's frustrating.'

'How so?'

'I don't know. It's sort of h-hard to explain. It's like all the stuff in those books … it's missed the point. It's like everything we learn is only scratching the s-surface. Does that make sense?'

'More and more every day.'

Eddy nodded, appreciating that she probably knew exactly where he was coming from.

'So what are you going to do about it?'

'I think I want to teach, Reagan. Yeah, I w-would love that. I would love t-to be able to show people there is so much more to this existence than m-meets the eye. To make them open their eyes.'

Reagan's smile was real this time. The pain was still there – it always would be – but for a moment at least, it took second place.

'And you know wh-what?'

'What?'

'When people get it, when they *understand* it, they'll never b-be able to forget it. I know it sounds like a crazy thing to say ... but that sort of thing could change the whole world.'

'I believe you, Eddy. I truly do.'

'It would make people h-happy. Really happy. Not just surface happy, here today and gone tomorrow. Deep happy. Soul happy. That's what I want t-to teach.'

'Eddy?'

'Yeah?'

'I can think of no better person in the universe to do that than you.' Reagan gave his hand a squeeze and Eddy fell in love with her all over again.

62

THE SLIDE DOWN

About a week and half after she'd fished his future out of him, Eddy accompanied Reagan and Mrs Crowe back to the hospital. This time they had an appointment. It was chemo time.

Reagan was nervous as anything, but on that front she was only marginally ahead of the rest of them. Where she stood head and shoulders above them was in the pain stakes. It appeared to Eddy that the cure was worse than the disease. They'd instructed her to up the meds leading in to the chemo and that took a massive toll on her. It seemed to be ripping her from the inside out. Watching on as she threw her head back to swallow yet one more pill, he was both crushed with sorrow and amazed at her courage. Each new pill was another package of side effects and horrid reactions and yet she continued to take them.

Yet while she was brave on the outside, inside she was still a frightened little girl. When they'd taken her into the radiology suite, she'd looked back at Eddy with an expression that had killed a piece of him. A pile of pills a day was one thing, this was something more sinister altogether. But what stabbed him worst was that he could do nothing to stop her being wheeled away from him. She had to go, even though she so desperately didn't want to.

And in the end, it had been every bit as bad as he'd hoped it wouldn't be. She stayed that full next week and a half in the hospital, most of it spent recovering from the vein-deep bouts of radiation that, despite their best efforts of targeted application and pain management, wracked her to the bone.

Seeing her there, amid the four corners of her recovery room, Eddy felt an immutable urge for circles. Life was all about circles, not squares. Squares had ends, hard, sharp ends that refused to budge. Circles, on the other hand, never ended, they just kept renewing themselves. Hospitals would be much better places for healing, he concluded, if they were designed as circles. No architectural reason, just a sense.

Reagan wasn't up for talking most of that time. He couldn't blame her. She had more tubes poking in and out of her than an engine, and Eddy figured maybe that was how the doctors saw her. An engine. Something to be tinkered and tweaked. *Does this work? Does that work? What if I tighten this or loosen that?*

Damn it, she was a girl, a human being, a creation too great to fully comprehend. There had to be a less intrusive way. If she was going to die, let her die in peace.

When the doctors and nurses weren't measuring one thing or another, Eddy would read to her. Happy stories. Stories with pages of hope and blessed ever-afters. A lot of the time, he wasn't even sure she heard him, but that didn't deter him. It gave him something to do, something that, even in the tiniest of ways, might just make her painful existence a touch easier.

When she was consumed by a sudden and vicious bout of vomiting, he'd be there too, the first to grab the bucket and hold back her hair. The same hair that would soon begin to thin and fall out.

And at no time whatsoever, despite seeing her at her lowest of lows, did he ever stop seeing her as anything but beautiful.

Those times when she was fast asleep, when he knew she couldn't hear him, nor could anybody see them, he'd put the book down and watch her. Her appearance may have changed but she was so much more than that. The girl who'd made him countless jam sandwiches was still in there, and he'd tell her that. He'd talk to her in those solitary moments. Not much more than a whisper, but loud enough so that if she was awake deep down inside, she'd be able to hear him still. So that his words would touch her soul and find a haven that could never be wiped away. She'd stamped herself on his soul and he just wanted to do the same for her.

63

TIME RUNNING OUT

Two days later, Reagan came back home. She was worn and battle wearied, but she was happy to be out of the hospital. The staff there were friendly, she said, but not the same as home.

The frightening thing was that, with every passing day, another part of her faded into nothingness. Not just her physical weight. It was her spirit, her hopes and her determination as well. That precociousness that had been her calling card was but a shadow of its former self, and even when it did show up, it was forced for the sake of Eddy. He didn't know if this was the chemo or the cancer. It was impossible to tell the difference and he just wanted it to stop.

'Eddy.'

'What are y-you doing out of bed?'

Seeing her standing there at her window, he noticed that not even the sunset could paint away the paleness. Her disease had even beaten the sun.

'I need you to do me a favour.'

'What?'

'Climb over here and help me out the window.'

'I can't d-do that!'

'Why?'

'You know why.'

Reagan had been expecting his refusal. She'd rehearsed.

'Eddy, listen to me, okay?' she continued before he could respond one way or the other. Some things still hadn't changed. 'Let's just say it was you who was sick. I mean really sick. Counting down the days sick. Here's this stunning sunset, and right here in front of us is the best place on earth tonight to watch it. What would you do?'

'I'd go b-back to bed.' That was about the second lie Eddy had ever told to Reagan.

As a result, Reagan gave him 'the stare', the one that said, *Don't make the same mistake twice, buddy, because I know where you live.*

'Come on, Reagan,' he pleaded. 'Your mum will k-kill me.'

'She's having a nap. She doesn't need to know. Not for long, I promise.'

Eddy must've given the impression he was still firmly on the 'no' track because, once more, she got in first. 'Please, Eddy. I really need this.'

'This is crazy. You know that.'

'About as crazy as it gets,' she agreed in that maddening fashion of hers.

Wishing she'd never asked the question, Eddy

climbed out his window and across Mr Tree until he could reach over and grab Reagan's forearm.

'Don't you dare let me fall,' she said, as she mustered the strength and the courage to move.

'Hey, this was your idea.' Eddy reached even further, as far as his anchor hand would let him. Letting her fall was not an option.

As she levered herself out the window, with the support and careful guidance of Eddy, her face struggled to belie the pain. It rose in her cheeks with a hot flush and he could tell she was doing everything in her willpower to stop from groaning.

We should not be doing this.

'Stop complaining,' said Reagan out of nowhere. 'You got the easy part.'

Eventually he got her out the window and on to the tree limb. Then, shuffling along to their jam sandwich committee spot, he gently lowered her until she was sitting on the broadest part of the branch. Satisfied that she was as safe as she was going to be under the circumstances, he planted himself beside her, not quite sure what was coming next.

Reagan seemed to be true to her word, and for a while she just sat in silence, watching the power source of the solar system complete its daily rounds. Eddy was caught halfway between the orange sunset and sneak peeks across at her, wondering if she was okay and trying to guess at what was going on in that mind of hers.

'It's beautiful, isn't it?' she finally said.

'It is,' he answered, still caught somewhere between the sun and Reagan.

'I like the sun.'

'Why's that?'

'Even when it dies it's beautiful. And then it gets up and lives again every day.' They were poignant words, and Eddy hated them for that. He didn't want to hear her talking about death. It was close enough without her having to invite it in.

'Somehow it's going to be all right, Reagan. I know it is.'

Now Reagan looked across at him.

'Do you know that, Eddy? Do you really?'

Eddy had to look away. With one silly comment, he'd failed her all over again. Mercifully Reagan went back to appreciating what was indeed a gorgeous sunset. Great swathes of purples were beginning to transform from among the oranges, like an artist layering the background for a wonderful masterpiece, and Eddy supposed in a way that was absolutely correct.

The quietness was absorbing, a black hole into which every noise a neighbourhood should make was swallowed, so that he and Reagan sat in utter stillness. So much so that even the silence had its own physicality, and Eddy felt it bounce around between them, wanting to be released but too blind to escape. In the end he could stand it no longer.

'I'll always be here, Reagan,' he said softly. 'No matter what happens, I will always be here for you.'

'I know, Eddy.' Reagan let the sunset go and looked

back at Eddy with sad, sorry eyes. 'Can you hold me?'

Shuffling over so that his hip touched hers, Eddy gently placed an arm around her shoulders and leaned in close. He tried not to notice how the hard bony knobs of her sickness-ravaged frame poked through against his hand. Not now. He had to embrace her for who she was: the girl whose soul had reached out and touched him when he'd most needed it. He wasn't going to deny her that. Not here, not with this wonder of nature before them. Not here, not in the place where there had been so many joyful times. So Eddy held her close, as close as he dared, and loved her with all his heart.

'I'm scared, Eddy.'

'I know.'

'Never leave me, please. Never let me go.'

'Not in a million years.'

'You promise?'

'I promise.'

64

A ROCK IN THE RIVER

Reagan stayed home for another week before she was due back in. Eddy didn't know what was worse. Having her home so he could watch her fade away in fractions or have her packed off to hospital where she was dragged through the oncology unit like a product on a conveyor belt. Okay, so they were trying their best at the hospital, but it wasn't working. He could see that, so surely they could too.

Mrs Crowe wasn't saying too much. That didn't bode well. She appeared to Eddy as though she was bearing a mother's responsibilities with the grim determination of a soldier in the trenches. She certainly knew more than she was letting on. Eddy figured that in her eyes ignorance was hope and if she kept the worst of the news from Reagan then maybe, just maybe, such blind ignorance could fool the cancer. Call it clutching at straws, but right now any straw, even the smallest of small, could be enough to keep the world turning.

Eddy stayed with her as often as possible in the hospital. No matter how hard he tried, he never seemed to be able to get comfortable in that place. It was haunting, as though there were too many living souls caught between those walls, fighting against the current, refusing to face the ocean in front of them. Even some, he sensed, that saw the ocean, beautiful and blue, couldn't quite get there.

He wondered where Reagan might fit in that picture. Was she wishing for an end to this now? Was the pain becoming too much for her to bear? Or was she holding on for him? Waiting for him to come to her rescue. Waiting for him to stop the fall.

As each torturous day passed, he would spend his nights with Mr Tree, sitting and thinking. The nights were best; they always had been. It was as though their connection was strongest when the world was quiet. In those hushed moments, so much of the bigger picture seemed to reveal itself. The stars in the night sky were brighter, the air seemed thinner and, if you listened hard enough, you could hear the earth spinning on its axis. It all made Eddy wonder if, when people slept soundly in their beds, the answers to all the biggest questions showed themselves. Just for a precious moment, peeking between the clouds. And if you knew what you were looking for, if you felt their presence, could someone so insignificant as Eddy look up and see them? Would the answers all become clear? He'd had a taste of it, but now that he wanted to know more, he found he couldn't. For him at least, the feast of knowledge had a limited menu, and the most important answer of them all right now wasn't even on the page.

If you won't let her fall, Mr Tree, what do you call this? Look at her. She's falling like a rock.

For the two weeks that Reagan spent back at the hospital, Eddy only came home twice. It was on the second such occasion that he found himself back up at that front window of his, so lost in contemplation that he didn't even notice Mrs Elsdon limp on up to the front lawn below him.

'Hi, Eddy.'

'Oh hi, Mrs Elsdon.'

'How's Reagan doing?'

'Not so good.'

'I'm sorry to hear that.'

'She's back at the hospital, having m-more chemo.'

'Do you think it's working?'

'I don't really know. Mrs Crowe says it's supposed to make her sick, but if you ask me, I think it's worse than the cancer.'

'How are *you* bearing up, Eddy?' That was a good question, and one he couldn't recall being asked up until now. Everything was about Reagan, and it had to be that way. She was the one suffering.

'I'm okay, I guess.' Now that he was put on the spot, Eddy gave himself the emotional once over. How was he doing? His best friend was lying in some cold room having radiation forced through her body and he should have seen it coming.

Damn it. He *had* seen it coming. And even now, with the disease having lain its spawn, there was still the expectation he had something to offer, that he should be saving the day. No, he wasn't okay; he wasn't okay at all.

Mrs Elsdon wasn't blind, though. Old, yes; blind, no.

'It's hard, isn't it, to watch someone you love fade in front of your eyes?'

Eddy just nodded. The right answer simply couldn't be put into words.

'Ben had always been such a strong man. He had one of those lucky metabolisms where he could eat all day and not gain an ounce of fat. I used to like that about him and it used to make me jealous at the same time. I so much as look at ice cream and I put on weight. But he was so wiry. Even when he read the paper you could see the muscles working away in his forearms.

'I always figured people like that lived long, healthy lives. No reason for it I suppose, just that they don't seem to be carrying around any unnecessary baggage. So I'd set myself up for a long life of married bliss. A diamond anniversary was a given. If anything I was going to have to be the one to live up to the mark.

'When he started going downhill, I couldn't believe it. That wasn't what was supposed to happen. That sort of thing happened to other people, not us. You know something, I didn't even cry for two weeks after he went to the doctor that first time. I refused to accept it. Not my Ben. Never my Ben.'

Mrs Elsdon did her customary shift of position on that walking stick of hers before continuing on. It was such an unconscious act for her now but Eddy saw in it the proof that this lady had become very used to pain. To the point where it showed more on the outside than it did on the inside.

'It was only when he'd changed so much that I was forced to admit it. The doctors had all their big words. They could categorise it. They could talk about it. They could even pretend to treat it, but for me it wasn't real until Ben aged ten years in about one. The man who was going to live forever was dying in front of my eyes.'

Mrs Elsdon shifted back to her original position again. Today was a particularly bad day.

'I felt so guilty that I would go on living. Isn't that the strangest of things? I was going to see more of what would make history and I hated myself for that. In the end, it was a combination of that guilt and the love built up over three and a half decades that made me the best damned nursemaid you can imagine. I looked after that man in his worst hours. Near the end that meant close on twenty-four a day, seven days a week. And I wouldn't change a thing.

'I guess what I'm trying to say in a roundabout way is that you can't stop it from hurting. It'll always hurt. There's no magic bullet for that problem. But the greatest thing you do can do right now is hide it for her sake. Be strong for her. I know you already are, what I'm saying is keep it up. Keep it up like a running race and only when you reach the finish line can you afford to collapse.'

'I'm t-trying. It's just so hard.'

'I know, Eddy. I know. But you'll see, if she makes it through this you'll know you stuck beside her and ... well, if things work out differently, you'll know you acted with dignity, integrity and uncommon love. That's the point. If I'd gone into my shell, had got myself stuck in a pile of pity and denial, I'd be in a much worse place right now. I'd either be in some asylum or I would've topped myself off, I reckon. All because I couldn't have lived with knowing I'd let my Ben down when he needed me most.

'Bottom line: it'll hurt, Eddy, but it won't hurt like it could if you do the right thing now, while you still can. Be strong, be brave and let tomorrow take care of itself.

'Well, that's about enough talking for an old lady on a chilly day. Just keep your chin up, okay?'

'Okay, Mrs Elsdon,' replied Eddy, his head swimming with her advice. 'And thank you. I really appreciate what y-you said just now.'

'My pleasure, young man. Life is full of lessons; you just need to know where to look for them.' With that, she did a wide U-turn and headed back the way she'd come. Back, Eddy knew, to a piping hot bowl of tomato soup and two slices of well-buttered toast.

Thank you, Mrs Elsdon.

Eddy understood what this kind old lady had been trying to say. Pain visits twice but it was up to him

349

how to manage it. He could wallow and miss some wonderful memories today, or he could be there for her. Tomorrow's pain would be a lonely pain and he'd have the rest of his life to come to terms with it.

Pain was a rock in the river and he just had to get around it.

Time to get back to the hospital.

65

CHASING AMBULANCES

Eddy never left the hospital through the rest of Reagan's latest bout of treatment until she was ready to come home herself. And by then, she was more than ready. If he wasn't too fond of the hard edges and straight faces, she had grown to abhor them. It may have been the place carrying her greatest hope of a medical cure but there was a part of her, a part that expanded a bit more every day, that surrendered to the agony and just wanted to make it go away. Sometimes even death seemed inviting.

Eddy could see that balance of willpower failing within her as well. He didn't need Mr Tree for that, not that the tree would necessarily have helped anyway. It still refused to release its riddle. It was still letting her fall despite itself.

Just like when she was at the hospital, he read her to sleep every night. Then, after climbing back across to his room after she'd drifted off to a quiet place, he'd lie in his own bed and listen. If she woke up in the night, as she often did, he wanted to be there for her. He knew exactly what pills she needed when, and she was in no fit position to get them herself. Mrs Crowe didn't mind. She always got up too. She'd moved her bed to the spare room next to Reagan's so she could be closer as well. Mrs Crowe was a really nice lady and Eddy couldn't for the life of him understand why Mr Crowe had left her. If his mum was half the mum she was, he'd be as happy as happy can be. In fact, she and Eddy had made quite the team these last few weeks and they had the routines down pat. She took care of the 'womanly' things and he took care of the pills, the bed and stuff like that. It never felt like enough though. People died every day in comfortable beds.

So after being used to broken, interrupted nights, Eddy was surprised one night to be awoken by something other than the expected rustle and groan from Reagan. There were lights circling through the room. Not streetlights either. These lights were white and blue, coasting through one cycle after another, and he knew immediately they could only belong to one thing, the lights above an emergency service vehicle.

Yanking the sheets back and praying that it all had to do with some completely separate and innocuous event down the street somewhere, he peered out the window only to realise his greatest nightmare.

It was an ambulance and it was parked right outside the Crowe residence. As his mind caught up with his feet, he spotted movement at the rear of the vehicle. A paramedic had just closed the back doors and Eddy watched under the spell of burgeoning adrenalin as the uniformed man jogged around and jumped into the passenger seat. Things were happening fast, awfully fast, and it hit Eddy like a slap to the face.

Pyjamas or not, Eddy was out of his bedroom and down the stairs before the ambulance driver had lodged his foot on the accelerator. His heart was going ten million miles an hour and his feet seemed to be going in reverse.

'Reagan!'

The front door didn't even squeak this time. It didn't have time to purchase with the floor, so hard was it ripped open.

'Reagan! Wait.'

It was all too late. As he laid his first bare foot on the dampness of the front lawn, the ambulance moved past him, those same blue, white, blue lights now dancing right throughout the neighbourhood like aliens coming in to land.

From somewhere behind him Eddy heard the muffled sound of Grandma Daisy's voice coming to terms with the middle of the night.

'Reagan!'

Arcing to the left, not losing an inch of manic pace and almost tumbling head over heels as the lawn slipped beneath him, Eddy made the footpath and then the road. Fists and knees pumping, he was not going to let her down. He had promised her. He would be there...always.

He hardly felt the stabbing pain of stones under his feet. There wasn't enough energy to spare for pain right now. He needed every bit of it to catch those back doors cruising further and further away from him. Past Bill Wilson's place he went. Past Beth Melling's place.

'Reagan.'

A light went on in an upstairs window somewhere but to Eddy it meant nothing. Let them look. Let them see the freak kid running down the street at midnight in his green pyjamas. They didn't know. They were the lucky ones.

When Eddy arrived at the intersection of Willow Close and Crimson Avenue his lungs were gone. They screamed and begged for air, unable to keep up with the frantic demand that even adrenalin couldn't fix.

Looking right, in the direction the ambulance had turned, he was devastated by the sight of a flash of the brake lights as they turned the next corner up, heading for the main road and on to the hospital. It was gone. He had failed ... just like he always did.

Collapsing to the tarmac, Eddy looked lost and forlorn at that spot where he'd last seen those lights, as if by doing so he could connect with the driver and force a brief U-turn. It wasn't to come though. He knew that. He also knew it was selfish to wish for such a thing. Reagan was in danger and she needed help fast.

Folding his face in his hands, he sat there in the middle of the intersection and sobbed hard, soulful sobs. Sobs that hurt all the more after his lungs' gut-wrenching service.

How long he would have stayed there was anyone's guess. From his perspective he was lost in a desert with no oasis for a thousand miles in any direction. There were no cars, no houses, no roads; this was a place that people left and never came back.

It was only the feeling of a warm hand on his shoulder that brought him back to earth. Looking up through agonised eyes, Eddy saw Mr McKenzie. He was wrapped in a dressing gown, Mrs McKenzie's by the looks of it. Under different circumstances it would have been hilarious. Tonight, though, it barely registered.

'Come with me, Eddy,' he said. 'I'll take you in.'

'T-to the h-hospital?'

Rory McKenzie nodded.

Taking his offer of a hand up, Eddy noticed Grandma Daisy wasn't far behind. She was doing her best grandma jog up the footpath, her hair going every which way and a look of concern strapped across her face.

'Eddy,' she said, finally catching up to them. 'What's going on?'

'An ambulance just left,' replied Rory McKenzie on his behalf. 'I think they've just taken Reagan away.'

Grandma Daisy took one look at Eddy and knew it was true.

'Oh, Eddy.' It wasn't so much a pitiful response as one full of pity. Her grandson was facing an education in life, one that he would never forget, one that would leave a scar.

'If it's all right with you,' continued Mr McKenzie, 'I'm going to take him into the hospital.'

'Are you sure, Rory? It's so late.'

'No problem. It's the least I can do.'

Eddy listened to all this from afar. Their conversation might have well been on the moon because all he could think of was Reagan lying in that ambulance. Things had to be serious. An ambulance didn't just turn up in the middle for the night for a routine check-up. And he wasn't there ... that's all he really knew for certain: he wasn't there.

When Rory McKenzie herded him up the street towards his little white car, Eddy went along with numb obedience. What else was there left to do?

By the time they pulled into the parking lot at the hospital, a good deal of Eddy's senses had returned. Like a stubbed toe, the numbness was wearing off and he was starting to wish he could go back to being numb again, to where confusion reigned and consequences didn't.

After thanking Mr McKenzie profusely for his act of kindness, he raced into the emergency department, his heart in his mouth, his pyjamas flapping around him. He was so afraid of what he might find. Had his last goodbye been the one last night? No, that wasn't allowed. Life couldn't be that vicious ... could it? She wasn't ready to go. She shouldn't be going at all.

What if she'd died in the ambulance on the way

here? What if she'd called for him as she found that white light calling for her? What if Mr Tree had indeed let her fall?

Pouncing up to the after-hours desk, he at first said the words so fast they couldn't understand him. Instead the man behind the bench regarded him with a mixture of annoyance and self-consciousness. Here was a retarded kid about to make a bad shift even worse.

'Are you lost or something, kid?'

With a humungous effort of willpower, Eddy forced himself to take a big breath and ask again.

'Reagan C-Crowe. I'm looking for Reagan Crowe.'

The seconds seemed to cross the universe and back again while the attendant checked his register, his fingers climbing up and down a list Eddy couldn't quite see.

Come on, come on!

'Okay,' he said finally. 'She's the one just come in. I'm sorry but you'll have to wait until I can get someone to come and see you.'

'No.'

'Pardon?' This guy obviously wasn't used to hearing 'no', especially from kids.

'I've g-got t-to see her.'

'Look, kid …' Considering his options, and seeing how desperate this boy was, the attendant took a new track. 'Are you her brother or something?'

'No.'

'Then I'm sorry but—' He never got the rest of the sentence out. Eddy wasn't going to let him. Instead,

357

with wide-eyed shock, he watched as this determined kid took things into his own hands and charged through the swinging doors beside the counter. 'Hey, you can't do that!'

It's funny how one's worst nightmares can be so vivid in advance and yet, when they turn up, they end up taking a different, more macabre form altogether.

Eddy ended up finding Reagan in quick time. If anyone had a pretty good idea of how to find things in this place, he did. It was his second home, after all. It wasn't easy from one perspective, though, and it took some fast talking by Mrs Crowe to stop him from being manhandled out of the hospital like a common criminal.

Eddy didn't care about security staff, though. If they'd won the day he would've found some other way in, even if it meant climbing through a window or something.

The docs had wasted no time in whisking Reagan upstairs and Eddy's first glimpse of her was through the window separating her room from the corridor. Her eyes were closed and she was utterly motionless as the white-coated staff fussed and flurried around her like she'd pulled in for a pit stop. He'd come this far and it was so hard to wait when he was so close but couldn't reach out and touch her. He so desperately wanted to go in and hold her hand. That's all, just hold her hand and let her know that he was here, that he hadn't failed her in the end.

Mrs Crowe stood stoically beside him, watching,

waiting, praying. Her baby was in a bad way and if Reagan ever left her, then everyone had left her and she would truly come to know the meaning of alone.

A forever and a half later, one of the older doctors came out and pulled Mrs Crowe aside. Eddy didn't care for the body language one bit. This man wasn't supposed to have that look in his eye, the one that said, *This just doesn't get any easier*. He wasn't supposed to hold his clipboard between himself and Mrs Crowe like it was some form of emotional defence that would bounce back all the suffering and pain he was about to deliver. And, most of all, he wasn't supposed to make Mrs Crowe cry.

66

Two Talks

'Eddy?'

'Yes?' Eddy didn't want to have this conversation. It was like driving past a car accident, you didn't want to look but you had to. Night had turned to day somewhere out in the real world, but time didn't really matter any more. Not when Reagan was just lying there as though she were in a queue for Heaven.

He was on one side of the bed, holding that hand he'd been so frantic for earlier on, and Mrs Crowe was planted on the other side. It made sense really, to have the two people who loved her the most be here like this.

'The doctors say she'll wake up soon. They kept her in a coma for a while so they could stabilise her, but soon she'll wake up by herself.'

'Okay.'

Okay, but what?

'Eddy?'

'Yes?'

'The doctor said they can't do much for her now.' Eddy followed the tear tracking down Mrs Crowe's tired face as she looked back at him across her beautiful daughter's sleeping body. The daughter who should never have to die before she herself did. Seventeen was no fair age to die, it was a fair age to live, to dream and to hope.

'Okay.' It wasn't the right word for the occasion, that was obvious, but it had to be because Eddy's throat couldn't fit anything else through. It was locked tight with emotion and this was a tough enough fight as it was.

'They asked if I thought she should stay here or whether she should come home and be with us there.' It was both a statement and a question, and Eddy sincerely appreciated that. They'd been through this together and, by God, they'd see it through together.

'Can she c-come home?' Now he couldn't hold it back any longer and as Mrs Crowe's tears found a hard landing on the cold linoleum floor, so did his.

'We'll make her comfortable, won't we?' said Mrs Crowe through her pain.

Eddy nodded. What he wanted to say most of all however was *I will not let her fall. I refuse to let her fall.*

By two o'clock that afternoon Reagan was awake, if awake was what you could call it. It was like there was a dimmer dial turning this way and that inside her, one moment making her reasonably lucid, the next semi-conscious.

When she was up to speaking, it was so hard to know what to say. If ever there was a time to say something profound, something to make an impossible situation seem better, this was it; except he seemed to be incapable of anything other than limp chatter. 'How are you feeling?' That was a classic. 'Are you sure you're comfortable?' It just kept getting better. Anything to avoid the excruciatingly obvious.

It was only when Mrs Crowe had to leave for a while to process the discharge papers that they had some time to themselves...and Eddy was determined not to let this go to waste. Nothing could go to waste now. Every opportunity was precious.

Reagan must've known that too.

'Eddy?'

'I'm here,' he said, leaning in and squeezing her hand ever so gently.

'It doesn't hurt so bad now.' She tried to smile and almost got there too. Whether she knew it was because the doctors had pumped her with painkillers, Eddy didn't quite know, but at least she wasn't suffering.

'That's good. We're going to bring you home soon. Back to your place.'

'I'd like that.' That was it and there it was. She understood what was going on just as much as he did. She was coming home to die. The knowledge was there in her eyes. It was an acceptance of her fate that Eddy hadn't witnessed up until now. She had fought hard, but her enemy had been great. It wasn't fair but then again, what was? 'You won't leave me, Eddy?' This time she squeezed his hand back.

'I haven't left you since I was twelve years old. I'm not about to start now.' It was his turn for that pained smile.

'Thank you, Eddy.'

'What for?'

'For everything. You made me the leading lady in the best movie of all.'

'Yeah?'

'My life.'

I love you, Reagan Crowe.

'I love you too, Eddy Sullivan.'

67

JUST ONE MORE TIME

Reagan came home the following day the same way she'd left it: in an ambulance. The day was wet and miserable, which seemed perfectly in tune with the underlying mood.

Mrs Crowe had been lent a hospital gurney bed by a charitable trust for terminal patients and so she'd had this set up in Reagan's bedroom. The bedroom hadn't been Mrs Crowe's intention, however. Her idea had been to have Reagan downstairs, but her daughter would have nothing of it. Her bedroom was her bedroom and that's where her bed was ... simple as that. Some things never changed.

Eddy remained her shadow throughout, making sure the bed was set at the right angle and making sure she stayed without pain. The irony of it all being that all she had now was a couple of lonely bottles of medication versus what had once been a whole battalion. It was a case of *be careful what you wish for*.

'Do you think it's pretty?' asked Reagan during

one of her better periods. Mrs Crowe was sitting in the room too, but Eddy felt the question was directed more at him.

'What do you mean?'

'On the other side. Heaven.'

Mrs Crowe looked up, the sting of her daughter's words written plainly across her face, but she remained silent.

'Remember the butterfly?' said Eddy at last. 'The one at the school that day?'

'Yes.'

'Remember how when you looked up really close you could see how perfect it really was?'

'Yes.'

'That's what it's like in Heaven, except you don't have to look close because it's always there, right in front of your eyes. Everything's just perfect.'

Reagan closed her eyes and smiled. 'I like that, Eddy,' she said.

Mrs Crowe promised to leave the side window open that night when it came to Eddy's bedtime. She also promised to call him across if Reagan so much as blinked. Eddy made her cross her heart, but he stopped at 'hope to die'.

The original plan was for him to stay on over there. Mrs Crowe didn't mind one bit. But he had something he needed to do, something he absolutely had to do ... just one more time. To make him feel closer to her, Eddy had asked if he could move Reagan over to the window. It was a warm night, and as he wheeled her bed across the room he noticed that the tree had grown on this side too. In fact, one of the branches was actually tucked up against the window ledge now, so that it wouldn't be long before Reagan too had a little leafy visitor. Sensing that Eddy had something he'd like to say to Reagan in private, Mrs Crowe left the two best friends alone in the dimly lit room. One friend was desperate, the other broken and fading fast.

Eddy took a deep breath and leaned in close. 'All of us, everybody,' he whispered, hoping Reagan could hear him from a place so deep. 'We're like icebergs. When we struggle through each day, we only ever get to understand the piece that sticks out of the water, but there's so much more to us than that. We just need to look under the surface to know the truth. Not truth like people out there talk about truth, I mean the real truth, the sort that answers the questions we don't even know how to ask.

'We all have the ability to touch every life we meet in the most incredible ways. You did it for me. You did it every day since the first day we met. We can do it because under the surface we're all connected with something amazing. Below the surface we're all white light. We've just got to believe it, because believing is seeing.'

Eddy took his hand and softly stroked the length of Reagan's arm, the arm that had once held a necklace out to him, a necklace stolen, but full of good intentions.

'It doesn't stop here. It doesn't stop at the skin.

When I'm gone, remember that. I'll never be far away. I'll never let you fall.'

The tears cascaded now. In this place, in this time, this would be the last he would ever be able to touch the girl who was his everything. She was his night and his day, his up and his down. She was the stuff that filled the places he couldn't reach. She was his angel on earth and she was his every joy under the sky. There was never a sunset that compared to her, this girl on the bed beside him. No hue could ever come close to her. No oranges, no purples of the setting sun. She was untouchable. And this was the toughest thing, to leave her and know that she would have all those years; years where he could be oh so close and yet not be able to hold her hand.

'I love you.'

Leaning forward, Eddy placed a faint kiss on her lips. It was the second and last ever kiss in Eddy Sullivan's short life. And they had both been perfect. As he lifted his face back away from her, one more tear landed on her forehead. It tracked the curve of her nose and down the side of her face to where it melted into the pillow.

Eddy had never done anything so hard as climb back out of that window. It was a beginning and an end. He couldn't count how many times they'd scrambled across these branches, how many hours they'd spent just talking and laughing, just spending time together, growing together. How they'd hugged each other through the bad times and the good. How many jam sandwiches they had shared, knowing it had nothing to do with being hungry. How, some-where over the span of five short years, the two of them had become one.

Reaching back in, Eddy took her left hand tenderly in his and brought it delicately out to where he could place it on Mr Tree's closest limb. For a moment he held it there, between his own hand and the hand of the tree that had brought them together. From here he could still see her face, silhouetted by the night lamp.

68

THE GREATEST GIFT

Stepping back into his bedroom, he decided to leave the light off. Having the only light coming into the room being that from Reagan's lamp seemed right. There was a certain symbolism in it that he couldn't quite capture in words.

And there was another reason for wanting the darkness too. In the dark, you could believe even the wildest of notions. In the dark, the impossible became possible. It was just him and his tree.

Lying down on his bed, he reached out without looking and placed his right hand on Mr Tree, on that big, broad branch which had first come to visit five remarkable years ago. In his own anger and resentment Eddy realised he hadn't done this for a while. If Mr Tree was going to let Reagan fall, he'd wanted no part of it, whatever the other precious gifts it had offered. In his eyes, they'd become false offerings. Now though, with the end so close and so clear, he had begun to sense something. He'd forgotten something. Yes, that's what it felt like. In his grind to become accepted as a boy, as a son, as a grandson, in his desire to live a normal life, he'd forgotten the most important thing – there was no normal life. If anything, he'd blinded himself. He'd misplaced the extraordinary, the amazing, the heavenly with something less, and if ever there was a perfect time to remember it again, this was it.

The world was indeed filled with magic and wonder if you were only able to *see* it. And Eddy saw it now.

I'm here.

He felt the familiar vibrations and at once he was calm, connected to the tree through invisible roots.

Just before he closed his eyes, he witnessed a precious sight that gave him comfort. Up there, above him, a single leaf stretched out, unfurling with the splendour of new life. As he watched, he realised that this leaf too had a purpose. It was on the furthest twig, the furthest extremity of Mr Tree's circuit around his bedroom, and as it gently unfolded it reached out and touched the same branch from which it had been born. The circle was complete and the cocoon was spun. Eddy would go to sleep tonight, a broken boy in the eyes of this world, bar some, and he would wake up a butterfly. His life for hers.

AFTERWARDS

69

THE REMEMBER ME THINGS

When Grandma Daisy went into the kitchen to get a coffee, she found to her surprise a full breakfast already laid out for her. There, in the middle of the table, was a perfect stack of pancakes with a bottle of maple syrup just begging to be tipped over it. Next to that was a big glass of orange juice, freshly squeezed, just the way she liked it. Just the way she and Eddy used to have it on special occasions.

And resting on top of that stack of mouth-watering pancakes was a folded piece of paper. Her curiosity well and truly sparked, she stepped over, picked the paper off the stack and reached for her reading glasses with a smile. He was such a good boy, doing something like this for her. Especially after all those years she'd been so horrid to him. If ever there was a lesson in the power of forgiveness, Eddy showed the way.

Unfolding the piece of paper, she read the single

sentence in a heartbeat. And a heartbeat was about right too, because that's right where it touched.

I'll be there to hold your other hand, Grandma.

At about the same time Grandma Daisy was coming to terms with a certain note she'd found downstairs, Reagan woke up to a brand new day. There was something different, so very different that at first she couldn't identify it.

She actually wondered if she'd died. The idea that they'd receive her in a familiar place made sense. It would certainly ease the shock. She even wondered how Eddy would take her passing on. Would she be able to look down on him and watch his life unfold. She hoped so.

But everything seemed so real, so 'as it should be'. The only thing that was missing was ... the pain. Yes, the pain was gone. Completely gone.

Something wonderful had happened overnight. Double-checking reality by feeling the sheets beneath her fingers, she breathed in a deep, long lungful of fresh air. It was then that she realised her other arm was cold.

What the ...? How did the bed get over here?

Pulling her hand back in from where it had been resting on one of the tree branches, she was just about to call out, to let the world know she was back, when she heard something crinkle at her side. She came close to ignoring it completely. Picking it up, she suddenly realised what it was. It was a wrapped lunch. Yes, it was. Pulling back one of the folded flaps, she found two huge sandwiches in there, both of them dripping full with strawberry jam – her favourite.

It was only then that she noticed the familiar, scrawling handwriting on the top of the paper. Three simple words.

'I owed you.'

Eddy's funeral was a sad affair. No one had expected this, least of all the close-knit community of Willow Close. And they all understood the reason for that closeness – a special little boy. A boy who was too good for this world. A boy who had changed them all in such a way they could never be the same again.

Among the gathered that day were two boys. Of course Grandma Daisy hadn't thought to invite them, but when they'd shown up on her doorstep that day, all dressed up in their finest, she couldn't turn them away. Eddy would've wanted it this way.

Nathan and Dion kept to themselves; barely a word was said between them, let alone to anyone else. A life lesson was setting in on them, the likes of which they would never forget.

Grandma Daisy insisted on having the wake back at the house. Everyone offered to take on the workload of setting up the food and drink, but, while she accepted the kind offerings of a plate here and there, she was determined this was her duty. It was just something she had to do, no rhyme nor reason, just a need.

But there was another purpose for it. One she wouldn't tell them until they all found out for themselves. Another miracle in Willow Avenue.

When the service was over and done, when the tears were put on hold for Eddy's sake, and when the memories unfolded in a room full of gentle smiles and jam sandwiches, Grandma Daisy tapped a spoon against her glass.

'Excuse me, everybody,' she said as people turned to face her. 'There's something I need to show you all. I could try and explain it to you but I just couldn't do it justice.' Holding back the tears with a swallow of her throat, Grandma Daisy continued. 'We all know just how special our Eddy was.' Grandma Daisy noticed how almost everybody in the room glanced across at Reagan, the person whose funeral, all money suggested, would have been today. Their miracle girl. 'Well, he's left us something to remember him by, something wonderful. Follow me.'

With that, Grandma Daisy turned and walked up the stairs. The entire lounge full of people filed up behind her, silent and curious, not knowing what to expect. They followed her along the hallway, down to the end, where a closed door marked the place where Eddy Sullivan had lived most of his life. A room where, for over half of his life, he was only allowed to leave to go to the bathroom. A room from where he watched the world pass him by. But that was wrong, most of them in that hallway knew that now. Eddy Sullivan hadn't been trying to catch up with the world. No, it was the other way around: the world was trying to catch up with him.

With one easy swoop, Grandma Daisy turned the handle and pushed the door wide open. And behind that door was the most amazing sight you could ever hope to see. Mr Tree was decorated in such a glorious coat of blossoms that the whole bedroom seemed to shine. The full circle they went, across every wall and the length of the ceiling so that walking into the room was like walking into nature's cathedral.

The people filed in until they filled the room. Not a word was said. Grandma Daisy had been right: this was too great for words. But in the end it was Reagan who managed to sum it up best.

'It's perfect.'

Reagan was the first one to notice the stone. A big, green one resting against the base of Mr Tree. It definitely hadn't been there before.

What she didn't know was that Mrs Elsdon had lugged that thing all the way from her backyard to this very spot. It had taken a mighty effort, especially for an old lady with a failing hip, but she'd been resolute throughout. This was where it belonged now.

She continued her daily stroll through the neighbourhood and, more often than not, still stopped in front of a certain house and a certain front window. It was hard to look up there and not see him any more. As hard as not having Ben.

So she started something that continues to this day. She began placing notes under that green stone. Notes of prayer, of love, of well wishes and hopes. Before too long, others caught on too. It was the strangest thing. No matter how many notes were stuck under that rock they never seemed to overflow. It was like the tree took them in. It took them to a place where the light was white and the answers were clear.

It became known as 'Eddy's Tree' or sometimes even the 'Wishing Tree', and there was hardly a day went by without somebody standing in front of it. A lot of the time it was Reagan. It was the place where she spoke to him, where she never forgot him.

She didn't know it yet, but she was going to have the most remarkable of lives. Some would say she already had, but she was only just getting on for the ride.

And, dotted within that wonderful existence, would come three precious children to a wonderful, caring husband. The sort of man Eddy would have approved of. The first child would be a boy…and his name would be Eddy.

One fine day, six months after Eddy had offered up his life, there came a knock at Grandma Daisy's door. She hadn't been expecting anyone so she answered it without expectation.

There, standing proudly on her front doorstep, was a lady and two children. The lady, obviously the mother, had a gentle hand resting on each child's shoulder, as though showing them off for Grandma's benefit.

Behind this collection of souls stood another person,

a man. He looked nervous, not for himself but for his dear wife.

'Hi, Mum,' said the lady in a soft tone, a longing, a yearning in her eyes.

Grandma Daisy had to hold on to the door. If not she would have fallen in a heap to the floor.

'Hailey! Oh dear Lord! Is this your beautiful family?' Grandma Daisy did not hate her daughter for disappearing all these years. She did not hate her for abandoning a boy seventeen long years ago. She had forgiven her and she had learned how to forgive from the best. 'Why? How?'

Hailey Sullivan held a note out to her mother, a lady she hadn't seen in almost two decades. 'I'm sorry it took so long,' she said. 'I got this a few months back in the post and I guess I needed this long to make things right.'

Grandma Daisy took the note and her heart fluttered. She knew the handwriting immediately. It belonged to a boy she knew. A boy they both knew. And it was a note, short but exquisitely sweet.

I'm not a stupid boy any more.
I'm a beautiful boy now, Mum.